"My dance, I believe?"

"Are you sure you've danced with every other female in town, from the oldest to the youngest?" Sarah asked archly.

He raised a brow, and in that moment she knew she'd made a mistake.

"Ah, so you were watching," he said, grinning.

"I most certainly was not," Sarah insisted. "I never sat down myself, except when the musicians took a break. I only just realized that you hadn't made good your threat to claim a dance."

"'Threat?'" he echoed. "I believe I only requested a dance, as proof of your goodwill. And I was waiting for a waltz, Miss Matthews."

"Oh? Why?" she asked. Was this girl asking the daring questions really her?

Again, the raised brow. "If you have to ask that, Miss Sarah Matthews, then it's no wonder the South lost the war."

Books by Laurie Kingery

Love Inspired Historical

Hill Country Christmas
The Outlaw's Lady
*Mail Order Cowboy
*The Doctor Takes a Wife

*Brides of Simpson Creek

LAURIE KINGERY

makes her home in central Ohio, where she is a "Texan-in-exile." Formerly writing as Laurie Grant for the Harlequin Historical line and other publishers, she is the author of eighteen previous books and the 1994 winner of a Readers' Choice Award in the Short Historical category. She has also been nominated for Best First Medieval and Career Achievement in Western Historical Romance by *RT Book Reviews*. When not writing her historicals, she loves to travel, read, participate on Facebook and Shoutlife and write her blog on www.lauriekingery.com.

LAURIE KINGERY

The DOCTOR TAKES A WIFE

Steeple
Hill®

Published by Steeple Hill Books™

STEEPLE HILL BOOKS

Steeple
Hill®

Recycling programs
for this product may
not exist in your area.

ISBN-13: 978-0-373-82853-1

THE DOCTOR TAKES A WIFE

Copyright © 2011 by Laurie A. Kingery

www.SteepleHill.com

Printed in U.S.A.

But God has not given us a spirit of fear,
but of power and of love and of a sound mind.
—II *Timothy* 1:7

To the wonderful people of San Saba County, Texas, and in memory of the real settlement of Simpson Creek, and as always, to Tom

Chapter One

"You look very lovely today, Miss Matthews," said the voice in an accent that was as far from the usual drawl Sarah heard around her as Maine was from Texas. She stiffened, schooling herself to assume a polite expression as she looked up into the blue eyes of Dr. Nolan Walker.

A lady, she reminded herself sternly, did not make a scene in public, and most certainly not while standing in the receiving line at the wedding of her sister. Even if the speaker was a Yankee outsider who had no business being here.

"Thank you, sir," she replied in a carefully neutral voice, and did not quite meet his gaze. "May I present Lord Edward Brookfield, Viscount Greyshaw, the groom's eldest brother, come all the way from England?" She watched out of the corner of her eye as the Yankee doctor shook hands with the English nobleman next to her.

The men exchanged greetings.

"And may I also present—" she began, intent on passing the Yankee on down the line away from her.

Nolan interrupted her. "Miss Matthews, I was wondering if we might sit together while enjoying the refreshments?" He nodded toward the punch bowl and the magnificent quadruple-tiered wedding cake that Sarah considered the crowning achievement of her baking career. "I...I'd really like to get to know you better." He had dropped the "g" on "wondering," while "together" and "better" came out "togethah" and "bettah," and yet his accent was wholly unlike a Southern drawl.

The utter effrontery of the man! Hadn't she already made it clear back in October, when he'd come to town to meet her that she Was Not Interested in being courted by a Yankee and a liar? He'd written her a handful of letters telling all about himself, except for the one fact that made him Unacceptable—that he was Yankee. She'd only found out when he'd come to meet her on Founders' Day—right before the Comanche attack.

"I'm afraid that's impossible," she said crisply. "I'll be busy helping to serve the cake and the punch. Now—"

"Perhaps a dance, then? I understand there'll be dancing later."

She glared at him. "Out of the question," she snapped. "Now, *if I may be permitted to continue,* you're acquainted with Miss Caroline Wallace, aren't you, the bride's best friend?" She gestured to the bridesmaid standing next to her.

She didn't miss the surprised look Lord Greyshaw gave her, nor the sympathetic one he bestowed on the Yankee. Perhaps there would be a chance later, after the wedding, to explain to Nick's eldest brother why a properly brought up young lady of the South did not encourage familiarity with pushy northern interlopers?

Mercifully, the doctor now allowed himself to be handed on down the line. The next person to approach was Mrs. Detwiler, an elderly widow, resplendent today in deep purple bombazine. Sarah hoped the woman had not heard what had passed between her and the Yankee doctor, for Mrs. Detwiler was sure to have an opinion on it, likely one contrary to Sarah's.

But luck was with Sarah—the older lady had indeed missed hearing the Yankee's words and Sarah's tart replies.

"You girls all looked lovely up at the altar," she proclaimed. "Was it dear Milly's idea to have her attendants decked out in different fall hues? She certainly picked colors that looked good on each of you."

Sarah smiled and glanced down at the gold *Gros de Naples* fabric she wore, knowing it complimented her blond coloring just as the mossy green cloth complimented Caroline Wallace's brunette hair and as the rust color played up Prissy Gilmore's strawberry-blond tresses. "Yes, and she sewed them all, too, as well as her bridal dress," Sarah said, gazing at Milly who was at this moment sharing a happy smile with Nicholas Brookfield, her English groom.

"My, her fingers must have been busy!"

Mrs. Detwiler didn't know the half of it, Sarah thought. Milly had not only had all that sewing to do, but had also determinedly learned how to cook under Sarah's tutelage. While she wasn't yet the confident cook and baker that her sister was, Sarah thought it wasn't likely Nick and the rest of the men would starve with Milly minding the ranch kitchen once Sarah moved in to town. Now that Milly was a bride, Sarah had wanted her sister to be free to manage her house, and she had wanted to try her own wings, too. So when Prissy had begged Sarah to teach her cooking and the other housewifely arts, Sarah found a way to kill one bird with two stones and had agreed to move in with her.

"I declare, it's the wedding of the decade for Simpson Creek," Mrs. Detwiler gushed.

Sarah nodded. At the very least, it was the first wedding since the war ended, as well as the first which had resulted from Milly's founding of the Society for the Promotion of Marriage—or, as it was more commonly known, the Spinsters' Club. Milly deserved to be the very first bride, and the happiest, Sarah thought, growing misty-eyed with love and pride.

"Now it's *your* turn," the old woman announced, cupping Sarah's cheek affectionately.

Sarah cringed inwardly, hoping no one else had heard. "Oh, I don't think so, ma'am. Several others in the club have made matches and are engaged to marry, and I don't have a beau at the moment. But I'm in no hurry," she added in the most carefree tone she could manage. She wouldn't want Mrs. Detwiler to guess that her words had made Sarah remember Jesse, her fiancé who hadn't returned from the war.

"Pshaw," the older woman retorted. "A pretty girl like you? You should have beaux by the dozen. Why don't you see if you can catch the bouquet when your sister throws it, hmm?"

"I—I'll see what I can do," Sarah mumbled, feeling the crimson blush creeping up her neck and into her cheeks. "Um…may I present Viscount Greyshaw, the groom's eldest brother?"

Mrs. Detwiler allowed herself to be distracted, and gazed up at the Englishman. "I've never met a real lord before," she burbled. "Am I 'sposed to curtsy?"

Edward Brookfield smiled graciously. "We could just shake hands if you like."

Everywhere she went during the post-wedding festivities, Sarah felt Dr. Walker's gaze upon her—when she helped Milly cut and serve the bridal cake, while she ladled out cups of punch, during her chats with other guests, such as Nicholas's visiting English brothers, the viscount and the vicar.

"So you're going to move into the cottage with Prissy when we come back?" Milly was asking. She and her groom were spending their wedding night in the hotel, then leaving in the morning for a week's honeymoon in Austin.

"Yes, Prissy's very excited about it," she said, seeing her friend laughing and talking across the room with some of the others from the Spinsters' Club. "Well, we'll see how it works out. You'll take me back if I don't like it, won't you?"

"Of course," Milly and Nick said at once, then Milly added, "The ranch will always be your home, too—but I think this will be good for you. Sarah, you *will* write down all your recipes as you promised before you go, won't you? You know them all by heart, but it's not so simple for me."

"You'll do fine," Sarah assured her. "And don't you worry about a thing while you're gone, you two," she said. "I'll keep Josh and the rest of the hands well fed and looked after, I promise you."

"I'd never doubt it," Milly said. "Sarah, who do you keep glaring at?" she said, following the direction of her sister's gaze.

"That…that Yankee!" Sarah sputtered. "He keeps staring at me. He's got nerve, coming here just as if he belonged!"

"We *did* invite the entire town," Milly pointed out mildly, looking surprised and somewhat disappointed at her sister's outburst.

Sarah couldn't blame Milly for her reaction. Sarah *had* always been the meek one, the quiet one. She'd never exhibited such a dislike of anyone, so her open dislike of the doctor was bound to attract her sister's attention.

"And he *is* the new town doctor," Milly added.

Sarah sighed. If Dr. Harkey hadn't been one of the few casualties during the Comanche raid on Founder's Day, when everyone was gathered in town to celebrate, Nolan Walker might have ridden right back out of town after she refused to talk to him. But now it looked as if he was going to stay forever.

"He does rather look like a hungry lion who's spotted a lonely gazelle," Nick said with a grin, after glancing at the man. He turned back to Sarah. "Would you like me to go have a word with him?" he asked, assuming a fierce expression and clenching fists. "You're my sister now, and I won't have blackguards bothering you."

Sarah tried not to laugh at his mock-menacing

features and failed. "No, thank you. I'll take care of it," she muttered, rising to her feet.

"Sarah—be nice, please," Milly said in a warning tone. "Just for today, at least."

"I won't challenge him to a duel, I promise," Sarah said, and stalked across the floor full of milling guests.

She saw him watching her advance, as he leaned negligently against the wall in his black frock coat and trousers, sipping a cup of punch.

"I won't have you staring at me," she announced. "Stop it immediately!"

A slow smile spread over Nolan Walker's angular, high-cheekboned face, making him even more handsome than he had been a moment ago, blast the man. "But you're the most beautiful woman in the room, Miss Matthews. You even outshine the bride. So why wouldn't any normal man want to look at you?"

She blinked in astonishment at his audacity, hating the flush that crept up her neck again. "In the South, we're taught staring is ungentlemanly and rude. So I'd like you to desist—please." She resented having to add that polite word.

"Tell me, Miss Matthews, just why *do* you dislike me so much? You hated me on sight."

Not on sight, she thought. *On hearing.* She'd been more than pleased with her first sight of him, happy and relieved that he had proven to be every bit as appealing in person as he had seemed in his letters. Then he'd spoken, dashing her hopes with the evidence of his deception. He was worse than just a Yankee—he was a Yankee who had almost tricked her into caring for him. And yet his outlandish accent was curling around her heart in such a dismaying way.

"I don't *hate* you," she argued. "It's wrong to hate. But it ought to be very obvious why you're not welcome here."

A spark flared in those blue eyes. "I'm not? Your sister invited me here today. The other single ladies speak to me. Townspeople with ailments and injuries have shown no hesitation to come to my office. The South is a hospitable region, I've always been told, and so I'm finding it here. Only you, Miss Matthews, have been openly hostile to me. Why? Or are you too cowardly to tell me?"

Sarah felt her fists clenching at her sides. She took a quick look around her, to make sure no one else was watching them, but the other conversations buzzed on, unabated. Even Milly's face was turned away from them, however Sarah suspected that to be a deliberate act on Milly's part rather than lack of curiosity.

Sarah drew herself up. "This is neither the time nor the place," Sarah said, falling back on her dignity.

"So you will tell me, some other time?" he challenged, his blue eyes dueling with hers, and finally, making her look away first.

"If it's so important to you."

"Oh, it is, I assure you, Miss Matthews, or we would not be having this conversation. But I have a suggestion to make to you."

"And that is—?" she asked, wary. He was leading her into a trap.

"Why don't we make a truce, just for today, at this special occasion? Your sister's been giving us these worried little glances the whole time we've been talking."

Sarah jerked her head around, only to see that Milly was in deep conversation with Nick's middle brother, Richard. Was Dr. Walker lying about Milly, in an effort to make Sarah feel guilty?

"Why don't we agree to be civil, even pleasant, to one another today?" Dr. Walker went on. "We can go back to being best enemies tomorrow, if you like."

"'Best enemies?'" she repeated, and sternly smothered an impulse to laugh. "What an absurd man you are, Dr. Walker! Very well, just for today I'll pretend I don't wish you'd ride out of town and never come back."

She'd thought her last words would make him flinch, but he only grinned. "If you mean it, you have to agree to dance with me, Miss Matthews. Just one dance."

Chapter Two

She opened her mouth to reply—to refuse, Nolan was sure—but she was interrupted by Prissy Gilmore, who dashed up to Sarah and tugged at her arm.

"Sarah, come on! Your sister's going to throw her bouquet!"

Sarah looked back at him, as if she still might toss off a refusal before joining the gathering group of women and girls in the far corner of the church social hall, but he spoke before she could.

"You won't catch it," he told her, as if it was an accomplished fact.

His words stopped her, made her go rigid—just as he expected.

"Oh? And why is that, Dr. Walker?" she inquired, giving each word chilly emphasis.

He gestured at the women. "Look at them. Lots of tall ladies there. Besides, you don't want it badly enough."

As he'd hoped, she responded to his words as if they had been a dare. Raising her chin, she demanded, "Is that so? Well, we'll see about *that*." She whirled around and caught up with Prissy.

He grinned when the mayor's daughter, unnoticed by Sarah, smiled conspiratorially at him over her shoulder.

"Prissy" was short for Priscilla, he knew, but what an inaccurate nickname. There was nothing the least bit prim and proper about the cheerful, outgoing girl. She'd been so kind to him after Sarah had taken to him in such dislike the day he came to town, and had helped him save face by letting him escort her to the picnic. He guessed with a little effort on his part, she would have been willing for him to court her instead. But it had been just his luck that the moment he had spotted the willowy golden Sarah, he'd lost his heart.

He wished it wasn't so. It made no sense. He'd never been one to chase disdainful women just to see if he could change their minds about him, merely because it was a challenge. But he'd begun falling in love with Sarah Matthews when he'd read her letters, and once he'd laid eyes on Sarah, Prissy Gilmore could be nothing more than a friend to him—and he was glad to have her friendship, for he sensed that she'd be willing to do whatever she could to help him win Sarah.

He wasn't sure anything would work, though. He faced the fact that he might eventually have to give up and admit Sarah would never do more than despise him. And then he'd have a choice to make—stay in town and watch her choose someone else in time, or leave Simpson Creek and go back home to Maine. He had no one there any longer who mattered to him, though.

Did she hate him because he was a Yankee? Was that all there was to it, a rebel Southerner's reflexive dislike because he'd been part of the Union army?

Nolan had been charmed by her first letter, introducing herself as a representative of the ladies who'd advertised for bachelors for the small Texas town. He knew he ought to have told her which side he'd fought on in one of the letters he'd written from his friend Jeff's home in Brazos County. But he'd been aware of enough anti-Yankee sentiment in Texas to think he'd have a much better chance of acceptance if Sarah got to know *him* first through his letters. They were getting along very well as long as they communicated by letter, but as soon as he'd uttered his first syllables in her hearing, she'd backed away in disgust.

He sighed, watching as the guests fell silent, and the bride turned her back to the clump of unmarried ladies of all ages and heights. Sarah had made her way to the front. He thought he saw her dart a glance in his direction, but then the bride made a few feints at throwing her flowers, and Sarah Matthews became all business, staring at the silk bouquet with the intensity of a sheepdog spotting a straying ewe.

Milly flung the bouquet, and Sarah leaped for it, catching it despite the efforts of a taller girl behind her trying to lean forward and snatch the prize while it was still airborne. The bride ran over and embraced her sister, followed by the groom, while everyone cheered and gathered around them. Sarah was soon hidden from his sight—but not before he saw her shoot him a triumphant look.

It was a start, he thought. Even if she'd sought his

gaze only to mock him, it was better than the icy way she had ignored him ever since he'd arrived in town. Now she had caught the bouquet, though, and tradition decreed that meant she would be the next to be married.

"And now we'll have the throwing of the garter," Prissy announced, cupping her hands to project her voice over the hum of conversation. "Would all the unmarried men please gather at this end of the room?"

Nolan walked toward the gathering throng made up of grinning young boys, a couple of graybeards and men whom he knew were courting various members of the Spinsters' Club. As he approached, he spotted the new Mrs. Brookfield and her husband leave the social hall, but by the time he had positioned himself behind a short youth not old enough to grow a beard, they had returned. Smiling, Nicholas Brookfield waved a circlet of blue, lace-trimmed ribbon over his head.

"Catch it, Pete!" called one of the bridesmaids, the one who had been standing next to the English lord in the receiving line. "I want us to get married next!"

A dark-haired fellow on the left side of the group called back, "I'll try, sweetheart!" and everyone laughed.

Nolan surveyed the crowd. Was Sarah watching? She was, and pretending not to care, he noticed with amusement.

The Englishman turned his back to them, just as his bride had done to the ladies. "Good luck, gentlemen!" he cried. "Who'll be the next lucky groom?"

Nolan dared a wink at Sarah, but before he could see

her reaction, Nick Brookfield tossed the garter. It flew through the air, and Nolan launched himself upward as the tiny missile flew straight and true as if the groom had been aiming it precisely at him.

And perhaps he had. Brookfield met his gaze and grinned as Nolan waved the bit of ribbon and lace above everyone's heads as they applauded and clapped him on the back.

"Thanks," Nolan murmured, handing the garter back to Brookfield, who returned it to his blushing bride before turning back to him.

"Don't mention it, old fellow. And don't give up. Sarah's a good woman—I think you'll find she'll be worth a bit of persistence on your part."

Nolan's eyes sought and found Sarah, who was watching him with an unreadable expression on her face. Then she turned away, pretending a great interest in something her sister was saying to her.

It means nothing, Sarah told herself. She wasn't a believer in omens, so there was no significance to Nolan Walker catching the garter as she had the bouquet. It was all just part of the traditional tomfoolery at weddings. Catching the bouquet or garter guaranteed nothing. Anyone could see that Caroline Wallace and Pete Collier would be the next bride and groom, despite not winning those prizes.

At the opposite end of the room, the fiddlers were tuning up for the dancing. She supposed she *would* have to dance with the cursed Yankee, if only to spare herself the scene that might follow if she refused.

The first dance, of course, was the bride and groom's dance, and the musicians struck up a waltz. Sarah forgot all about the Yankee while watching Nicholas Brook-field, her new brother-in-law, whirl her sister ever so gracefully across the floor as if they had been dancing together all their lives.

They were so perfect for each other, she thought, seeing the loving way Nick gazed down at her sister, and she up at him as if no one else existed in the uni-verse. She felt the sting of tears in her eyes. She remem-bered how he had only had eyes for Milly from the first day he had arrived. *Lord, please grant them a long and happy life together, and lots of children.*

She felt a twinge of aching sadness, too. Milly's happiness also meant changes for Sarah's life. It would never again be Milly and Sarah, two sisters alone against the world. Milly now had a husband to tell her deepest hopes and secrets to. *Please, Lord, if You see fit, find me a husband, too, a good man who also loves You. I know that if it's Your will for me to marry, You'll send a man who's neither a liar nor a Yankee!*

Almost against her will, her eyes searched the hall for Nolan Walker, but she didn't see him. Had he left? *Good*, she thought fiercely. She could relax and enjoy herself if she knew he wasn't here to plague her any more.

Then someone tapped her on the shoulder. She started, giving an involuntary cry that came out soundng remarkably like a mouse's squeak, thinking Dr. Walker had managed to circle his way around to her without her noticing his approach and was now claiming his dance. But it was only Edward, Viscount Greyshaw.

"Oh, I *do* beg your pardon, Miss Sarah," he said,

looking as startled by her reaction as she felt. "I—I didn't mean to take you unaware. It's time for us to join in, I believe," he said, nodding toward the pair still waltzing in the middle of the hall.

"O-of course," she said, giving a weak laugh. "I didn't mean to jump. I'm afraid I was so intent on watching my sister and your brother dance, I didn't see you coming."

"They *do* make a handsome couple, don't they?"

Fitting her gloved hand to his, she joined him on the floor, thankful that she had lately practiced with Nick and could give a competent accounting of herself. It would not do to tread on a lord's feet.

In a few moments, Caroline Wallace and her counterpart among the groomsmen, Richard Brookfield, joined them in their waltzing, and then Prissy and old Josh, the foreman of their ranch. They certainly made an odd couple, the old cowboy and the young, vivacious Prissy, and Sarah knew that old Josh would have rather faced a horde of Comanches again than be dancing in a fancy frock coat. But Nick had become like a son to him, so he'd been honored when Nick and Milly had asked him to be in the wedding. Sarah saw him laughing at something Prissy had just said, and figured Prissy's lively chatter was keeping Josh's self-consciousness at bay.

A Virginia reel followed next. Lord Edward remained with her, remarking, "You know, we call this one 'Roger de Coverley' at home." He was a good dancer, and so was his younger brother, Richard, who claimed her for the Schottische which followed. He drew back when a square dance was called after that, though, unfamiliar with the American dance. Josh came to Sarah's side and asked her to partner him.

Sarah had seen Dr. Walker in the crowd during the waltz, and when the band struck up the reel, she saw him ask Jane Jeffries, one of the Spinsters who had been widowed by the war, to dance. To Sarah's surprise, Jane accepted, a smile lighting her usually somber face. *Didn't she know that Dr. Walker had served in the same army responsible for her husband's death?*

Nolan sat out the Schottische, taking a chair next to Maude Harkey, another of the Spinsters. Maude wasn't dancing tonight, for she still wore deep mourning for the death of her father, Dr. Harkey. How did Maude feel, speaking to the man who had taken her father's place as town physician? Yet she seemed pleased that Dr. Walker had sat down with her.

How kind of him to keep Maude company since she can't dance tonight, a voice within Sarah whispered, but Sarah firmly squelched it. *He probably just feels guilty that he's the town doctor only because her father died.*

Sarah was even more surprised to see him up again when the square dancing began, partnering Faith Bennett. *Well, aren't you the ladies' man?* The spiteful thought distracted her and caused her to stumble in the "Allemande left" the caller announced.

Pay attention to your steps, Sarah. Did you expect him to gaze longingly at you until he finally gathers his courage to claim his dance? Of course she wasn't jealous, she told herself. One wasn't jealous over someone one didn't want. His behavior just proved he was a liar and a deceiver—a typical Yankee, in short!

Chapter Three

The lead fiddler announced the last dance of the night, a waltz. After this, Milly and Nick would go to the hotel for the night, and the guests would all disperse to their homes.

By this time, Sarah's nerves were raw, expecting at the beginning of every dance that Dr. Walker would come to claim her, but so far he hadn't. She had not lacked for partners, for someone else always asked her, but dancing with others did not mean she avoided him. Every dance but the waltz meant being passed to other dancers for at least a few seconds. Still, Dr. Walker had seemed intent on charming every woman in town except her.

Once, he had even managed to get Mrs. Detwiler up on the floor, and the older lady had clearly enjoyed it, though she was red faced and out of breath by the end of it. Sarah saw him fetching her punch while she sat and fanned herself. Sarah wouldn't have minded spending some time in a chair herself, being fetched a cool drink, for her feet were aching from all the dancing and her hair had long since fallen from its elegant knot.

Now, though, she felt a kinship with the gazelle Nick had mentioned earlier as she saw Dr. Walker crossing the floor toward her.

"My dance, I believe?"

"Are you sure you've danced with every other female in town, from the oldest to the youngest?" Sarah asked archly.

He raised a brow, and in that moment she knew she'd made a mistake.

"Ah, so you were watching," he said, grinning.

"I most certainly was not," Sarah insisted. "I never sat down myself, except when the musicians took a break. I only just realized that you hadn't made good your threat to claim a dance."

"Threat?" he echoed. "I believe I only *requested* a dance, as proof of your goodwill. And I was waiting for a waltz, Miss Matthews."

"Oh? Why?" she asked. *Was this girl asking the daring questions really herself?*

Again, the raised brow. "If you have to ask that, Miss Sarah Matthews, then it's no wonder the South lost the war."

She felt herself flushing so hotly that it took all her strength of will not to open the fan that dangled from her wrist and start using it. "If we stand here arguing all through the dance, Dr. Walker, we will miss it altogether."

The couples had just arranged themselves on the floor, and the fiddlers had struck only the first notes, but he took her hand without another word and led her onto the floor. In a moment they were gliding over the floor with the rest of the dancers.

Sarah saw Milly, waltzing with Nick, watching her, her smile even brighter than before because her sister was dancing with the Yankee doctor. *Good for you,* Milly mouthed. She probably thought Sarah and Dr. Walker had agreed to bury the hatchet. Sarah smiled back, not wanting Milly to worry that she'd only agreed to postpone the battle, not call it off.

She found to her surprise Nolan Walker was an excellent dancer, better even than the Brookfield brothers, who had probably been taught to waltz in their English nursery. His steps were so smooth he made it easy to follow him, so she was never in any danger of treading on his toes.

"Thank you, Miss Matthews," he said when the last notes died away and the other couples drifted off the floor. "I enjoyed that very much."

She couldn't say she'd enjoyed it as well; she'd been too conscious of his nearness and his gaze trained on her the whole time. "You're welcome, Dr. Walker. You…you're an accomplished dancer," she said, determined to give credit where it was due.

"Surprised?" he asked. "I assure you, Miss Matthews, we Yankees do not all live in caves, coming out only to devour raw fish."

Before she could catch it, her mouth fell open at his gibe. "Are you making fun of me, sir?"

He grinned. "Not at all. I was only teasing you, my thorny Southern rose."

How could one man be so infuriating? "I'm not 'your' anything, Dr. Walker. And now that you've had your dance with me, you must excuse me while I go see if my sister needs any help before she leaves."

"Very well, but don't forget about that talk we're going to have."

His blue eyes dared her to claim she didn't remember what he was talking about, but Sarah was not a dishonest person and she remembered all too well that he'd demanded she tell him sometime why she was so hostile to him.

"Oh, I won't. I'll look forward to it," she said.

He bowed, but Sarah felt his gaze on her as she walked away.

The next morning, Sarah met Nick's visiting brothers outside the church. The newlyweds were not with them, but Sarah hadn't really expected them to be up this early. They were to meet after church in the hotel's restaurant for Sunday dinner. After that, the newlyweds would depart for Austin in a specially hired coach, accompanied by Edward and Richard, who would pay their respects to the embassy branch in the Texas capital before journeying back to the coast and boarding a ship for home.

"A pity my wife's so near her time," Lord Greyshaw remarked as they walked up the steps that led into the church. "She'd have loved your Texas, Sarah." Amelia, Viscountess Greyshaw, was only a couple months from delivering their second child. It had been felt the ocean voyage and overland travel would be too risky for her, and Richard's wife, Gwenneth, had remained at Greyshaw to keep her company in their husbands' absence and to watch over Violet, their younger sister.

"Yes, such mild weather, for late autumn, to be sure," Richard agreed, looking up appreciatively at the blue sky. "At home we'd be gathered around the hearth complaining of the dank cold."

"Oh, it'll get colder closer to Christmas," Sarah replied. "Every few winters, it actually snows. You gentlemen must come again and bring your wives and children."

"Eddie's already taken me to task for not bringing him," Lord Edward said, grinning as he mentioned his son. "He'd like to meet a wild Indian. Oh, dear," he murmured, seeing the shudder Sarah hadn't been able to suppress. "I do apologize. I had forgotten all about the attack. How dreadfully clumsy of me."

"That's all right," Sarah said, gazing behind the church where, on Founder's Day, the Comanches had come galloping across the creek and into the town. "Hopefully, now that we have the fort, it won't happen again. There's a cavalry regiment that patrols the area regularly and in any case, the Comanches are in their winter quarters now, up on the Llano Estacado, the Staked Plains. We'd better go in, gentlemen," Sarah said, as the bell began to toll from the steeple above them. She played the piano for the services every Sunday and knew Reverend Chadwick would be waiting on her to begin the service.

She was relieved to see that once more, Dr. Nolan Walker did not grace a pew. She had never seen him attending services since his arrival in Simpson Creek. *He must be an unbeliever. Just one more reason not to be friendly to him.*

* * *

Sarah would have been surprised to know that Dr. Walker was seeing a patient in his office at this very hour.

"Th-thank you for seeing me at this time, Doctor," said the pale, mousy little woman who'd entered his waiting room. "I—I wouldn't want to come when you had other patients coming and going…."

She'd knocked so softly at his door he almost hadn't heard her from his quarters behind the office. He had only just arisen from bed, the tolling of the church bell having awakened him from the sleep he'd finally achieved at dawn.

"And why is that, Miss Spencer? Surely you have a right to consult a physician as much as anyone else in Simpson Creek."

"I…I don't want anyone to know I'm seeing a doctor," she whispered, eyes downcast. "They might wonder why. I—I'm expecting a child, you see."

He looked at her quickly. If Miss Ada Spencer was pregnant, it was not obvious, as yet. But that explained the reason for the furtive visit, if it was true.

"Are you certain? That you're…ah, with child?" he said, wondering for the thousandth time why women in this day and age spoke of it in hushed tones or euphemisms and couldn't use the correct term for something which was, after all, a natural thing and should be a happy event—unless, of course, a woman was unmarried.

"Yes, I'm sure," she insisted, and told him all the symptoms she had been having.

"I'll need to examine you," he said. "Would you be

more comfortable if there was another woman present? Would you like to come back when you can bring someone?"

Still looking down, she shook her head. "I haven't told Ma," she said. "She'd be ashamed of me. She'd want me to keep to home now that I've 'disgraced' myself. She's in church now, so she doesn't know I'm here."

Was Mrs. Spencer a church-going hypocrite, praying for the heathen in Africa while oblivious to the trouble within her own house? He was familiar with the type, but he hadn't met the woman so he shouldn't assume that was the case. Did Ada Spencer have no friends, then? But perhaps she had no one with whom she was willing to trust her secret.

"I just want to make sure the baby's healthy," she murmured, glancing timidly up at him, then away again.

"Where is the father?" he asked, careful to keep his tone neutral.

"Dead," Ada said, her tone as lifeless as the word. "He died when the Comanches attacked in October."

"I see." Simpson Creek had suffered half a dozen casualties that memorable day he'd arrived. And now there would be a child born who would never know his father because of it, and a woman who might be bowed down with shame the rest of her life. "I'm sorry."

A tear trickled down Ada's sallow face. "He wasn't going to do right by me anyway," she said. "He was leaving town that morning. It was his bad luck he happened to run into those savages."

Nolan remembered the man who'd appeared at

the church, tied onto his horse, who'd lived only long enough to give a few moments' warning of the impending raid.

"And what do you plan to do, Miss Spencer? It's none of my business, of course, but if you stay around town, people will eventually know that you're with child. Have you considered relocating to another town—even another state, where you could say you were a widow?"

Again, she shook her head. "Ma and Pa are old. I'm the only one left at home to take care of them. They won't turn me out, even once they know."

But they won't give her emotional support, either. He sighed, and wished he had a nurse he could call on to be present.

"Very well, let's have a look," he said, opening the door to his exam room and beckoning her inside.

Afterward, he waited for her at his desk in the adjoining room.

"If you're expecting, it's very early," he said, after she came in and sat down. "At this stage, I can't be certain. When did you…that is…" He stopped, aware of the awkwardness of his question and wishing he could just spit it out instead of having to dance delicately around the point. He'd been so much more comfortable around soldiers, saying what he meant without having to think about it so carefully.

"In September," she said, thankfully sparing him having to come up with another euphemism. "It…it was only once or twice…."

Nolan Walker sighed. Obviously once or twice had been enough. It was useless to wish the dead man had behaved honorably and married the girl before leaving her with child and getting himself killed.

She wasn't a bad-looking woman, he thought, though in her present depressed, shame-faced state it would be hard for a man to see her better qualities. How did one go about suggesting to a woman in this predicament that if she held her head high and was pleasant and charming, some good man might well come to accept her *and* the coming baby?

Ah, well. He was a physician, not a counselor or matchmaker. Perhaps he could persuade her to trust Reverend Chadwick with her secret. The minister seemed like a decent man who wouldn't shame this poor woman still further, but could give her good advice. And perhaps in time, she would trust one of her friends enough to enlist another's company at her appointments with him, if her mother wasn't willing once she knew the truth. Ada Spencer belonged to that Spinsters' Club, didn't she? So she must have some acquaintances, at least. He'd feel a lot more comfortable when he needed to examine Miss Spencer if she brought another female with her.

"Very well, Miss Spencer," he said. "If all goes well between now and sometime in the middle of June, I see no reason that you cannot deliver a strong healthy child. I'll need to see you a few times before then, of course."

"The middle of June? That's when my baby will come?" A spark of joy lit the woman's narrow face, and he marveled. Even while she risked disgrace, a woman could find joy in the thought of a coming baby.

"Based on what you told me about when the child

was conceived, yes. Though babies, of course, have a mind of their own and can come earlier or later than when a physician predicts."

"Thank you, Doctor."

"You're quite welcome, Miss Spencer." He rose to indicate the appointment was over, and she moved quickly toward the door.

"Oh, and Miss Spencer," he said, trying to make his request sound casual, "why don't you bring a friend with you next time you come? I'm sure it would be wiser for the sake of your reputation." *And mine.*

She looked back at him, then bolted out the door without another word.

Chapter Four

"My message," Reverend Chadwick began, "is one I have felt compelled to preach today, the subject of forgiveness. Certainly this is a timely subject, in view of the recent national conflict that nearly tore our country in two forever. Maybe the Lord wanted me to speak on this because *one person* present is struggling to forgive another. But really, it doesn't matter whether one person or twenty needs to hear it. I take my text from Matthew Chapter Eighteen, in which Peter is asking Jesus how many times he should forgive his brother."

Sarah winced inwardly. Of all the subjects for the pastor to preach about! And just after she had been thinking that his failure to attend church served as an additional reason why Dr. Nolan Walker deserved neither her forgiveness nor her friendship...

Reverend Chadwick went on to describe how Jesus had decreed one should forgive seventy times seven. "Now, does the Lord mean we are only to forgive four hundred and ninety times? No, dear people, He means *infinitely.* If we don't forgive, we aren't forgiven—simple as that."

Sarah shifted uncomfortably in the pew, hoping the elegant Lord Edward and his kindly brother Richard didn't notice. The white-haired pastor seemed to be speaking straight to her, though he wasn't looking in her direction.

"In fact," Reverend Chadwick went on, "the Bible goes so far as to say if we take our gift to the altar, and discover we have something against our brother, we're to go and make things right with him first."

Very well, then. She had brought a tithe of her profits from her bakery sales to put in the collection plate, but she'd hold on to the coins until she'd had a chance to speak to Dr. Walker. That was the right thing to do. It wouldn't be easy—much would depend on how he responded, but surely Pastor Chadwick's choice of this topic meant that she was to forgive Nolan Walker for serving with the Union Army. She could pay him a visit this very afternoon, after she and the Brookfield brothers met with the Milly and Nick for dinner and she saw them all off to Austin. After all, she was already in town, and had left dinner on the stove for the cowhands, so she didn't have to get back to the ranch soon.

She sighed, at peace with herself now, and admitted she was even looking forward to seeing the blue-eyed doctor and hearing him talk in that outlandish accent again. With some difficulty, she forced her attention back to the sermon.

"Time to go see the newlyweds," Edward murmured, after they had shaken hands with Reverend Chadwick and had spoken with several members of the congregation.

"Yes. I think marriage will be good for Nicholas,

especially marriage to your dear sister," Richard told Sarah. "He's made an excellent choice. Just think, Edward, now there's only Violet for us to see safely married…."

"As she's hardly out of the schoolroom, I hope that will be some time from now," his brother said, but Sarah was no longer listening.

Instead of gazing down the main street of Simpson Creek to her right, toward the hotel where they would meet Nick and Milly for dinner, she had glanced to her left, where a low white picket fence surrounded the doctor's office.

Just as she looked, the door opened. Perhaps Nolan had peered out, seen her emerge from the church and was coming to greet them? Perhaps she could say something to indicate she would like to talk to him later?

But instead of Nolan Walker, she saw a female figure emerge, glance furtively at the townspeople strolling away from church, then turn away and walk quickly down the alley that ran past the side of the doctor's office. A dark bonnet hid her features as soon as the woman turned her head, but in those brief seconds when she had been facing toward the church, Sarah recognized Ada Spencer.

What is she doing there? Doctors don't have office hours on Sunday mornings. Therefore she must have been there for a completely nonmedical purpose. Thinking about Ada's secretive manner, Sarah was suddenly sure the two had been Up to No Good.

She thought back to the summer, when Ada had been giddy with excitement over being courted by that Englishman Harvey Blakely. Blakely had come to try to blackmail Nicholas about his past or, if he wouldn't cooperate, to expose Nick's disgrace in India, but after failing to discredit Nick, Harvey had been the first casualty on the day of the Comanche attack. Ada had been a virtual recluse ever since, and never came to the Spinsters' Club meetings. When she thought about her, at all, Sarah had assumed Ada was still mourning her English beau, scoundrel that he had been. In the excitement of her sister's wedding, Sarah had forgotten all about Ada.

Now, though, it seemed that Ada had set her cap at a new bachelor, and perhaps Nolan Walker was all too willing to meet with the vulnerable woman in his office at a time when they wouldn't likely be interrupted by patients.

They probably hadn't even remained in the office. Behind it was the doctor's private living quarters— Sarah knew this from her long friendship with Maude Harkey, the late doctor's daughter and also a member of the Spinsters' Club who had shared those quarters with her father until his death in the Comanche attack. When Dr. Walker had taken over as town physician, he had been offered the space, and Maude had moved in with a married sister in town.

Sarah's heart sank. Though she had been looking forward to clearing the air with Dr. Nolan Walker, and perhaps more, she knew now she had been right all along about him.

Dr. Walker was nothing but a Yankee opportunist—little short of a carpetbagger. And now, it seemed, he was a womanizer as well, and was engaged in an improper relationship with a woman who had already proven she was more than willing to go to any lengths to have a suitor.

Resolutely, Sarah turned her face away from the doctor's office, and gazed directly ahead of her toward the hotel. She'd go straight home after her dinner with Milly and her new husband. She'd cook a fine supper for the cowhands and perhaps begin planning for her move to the cottage she would be sharing soon with Prissy.

It was a good thing she'd found out about Dr. Walker's true character before she'd made a fool of herself. Perhaps she should warn the others in the Spinsters' Club, she thought, firmly ignoring the ache in her heart.

The time had gone by quickly. Milly and Nick had arrived home December 23, and Sarah welcomed them back with a wonderful supper.

"Oh, Sarah, why don't you stay till after New Year's?" Milly said the morning after Christmas. "It doesn't seem right, your moving out right now. Why not stay till then?"

"It was a wonderful Christmas, wasn't it?" Sarah said. "Your first one as husband and wife," she said, smiling at the couple across the table. "But Milly, I can't keep putting it off. Today's the perfect day. Bobby and Isaiah are already set to load up the buckboard right after breakfast, aren't you?"

Down the table, the two cowhands nodded.

Sarah looked forward to sharing the cottage with Prissy, for her lively and vivacious friend knew no strangers. It would be fun teaching Prissy how to cook and manage a household. And what would it be like, not having to cook three square meals a day for hungry cowboys, and hitch up the horse whenever she had baked goods to deliver?

An hour later, all was in readiness for her departure.

"Now remember, you—"

"Can always come back," Sarah finished for Milly, from her perch on the driver's seat of the wagon loaded with her bed and chest of drawers, as well as a pair of chairs Milly said she could spare. "I know. And perhaps I will, after I teach Prissy a few basic kitchen and housekeeping skills."

"She couldn't possibly be any slower to learn to cook than I was," Milly said. "Now, with the fried chicken, you dip it in the beaten eggs, *then* the flour and spices, right?" She was to cook her first dinner without help tonight, and she'd already admitted she was nervous about it.

"Right. Actually, I'm more worried about teaching Prissy how to launder clothes than the cooking," Sarah said. "She still thinks doing the laundry consists of handing her dirty clothes to the housekeeper. But don't worry, your first supper will be fine."

"Of course it will, darling," said Nick, who'd been helping Bobby and Isaiah load the wagon. He put an arm affectionately around his wife's waist.

Sarah watched them with a certain wistfulness. She was so happy for her sister, yet wondered if she would ever know this happiness herself.

She straightened and nodded to Bobby, sitting next to her and holding the reins, and Isaiah, who waited on his horse beside them. They were coming along to help her move her furniture into the cottage. "We're burning daylight, as Josh would say. I reckon we'd better get going."

By noon, the men had unloaded everything on the wagon, placed it all wherever Sarah and Prissy had directed in the little cottage, rid the house of a mouse that had sent Prissy shrieking in panic out into the yard and departed. Now Sarah and Prissy sat down and enjoyed the sandwiches Sarah had packed for their midday meal.

"It's shaping up well, isn't it?" Prissy said, surveying with satisfaction the room that served as a combined dining area and parlor. They had arranged the round oak table between the kitchen and the couch and chairs, and there was a fireplace along the back wall. Behind the dining room and parlor, a short hallway divided the two bedrooms.

"Small, but cozy," Sarah agreed. "But I just realized something I should have thought of before..."

"What's that?"

"Now that I'm here, I won't have the wagon to deliver my baked goods to the hotel and mercantile. It's a lot to carry, so I'm either going to make at least a couple of trips back and forth to the cottage, or—"

"I could help you carry your pies and cakes," Prissy offered.

"Thanks, but it's not fair for you to have to do that several times a week. I think I'll just go see if Mr. Patterson has a little pull-cart he could trade me for this week's pies." She arose, and took her woolen shawl and bonnet from the pegs by the door. "I need to discuss with him and the hotel owner when I can start delivering again, anyway." She had notified her customers she would not be baking again till after the move. "Do you want to come with me?"

"No, I think I'll work on arranging my bedroom," Prissy said. She stretched and rubbed the small of her back. "I have a feeling my bed's going to feel very good tonight, after all the boxes we've been carrying and the furniture we've been arranging and rearranging. Oh, and while you're there, would you look and see if they have anything lighter for curtain material? Mama's castoff damask curtains are just too dark and heavy for this room, don't you think?"

Sarah nodded her agreement. "I'll look at the bolts of cloth while I'm there. Perhaps a dotted swiss…" Sewing was Milly's area of expertise, but surely she could sew a simple pair of gathered curtains.

It only took her five minutes to walk from the cottage on the grounds of the mayor's property, out the wrought-iron gates and down Simpson Creek's main street to the mercantile. The weather was cool, and lowering clouds in the north promised colder weather still, perhaps even a "blue norther." Might they even have some snow? It was too bad it had not come in time for Christmas, if so…

Distracted by her thoughts, she didn't remember to look out for the warped board that lay halfway between the hotel and the mercantile—

—and suddenly she was falling headlong, her arms flailing in a vain attempt to regain her balance. She cried in alarm as her shawl slid off backward and her forearms skidded along the rough boards. The fabric of her left sleeve snagged on a protruding nail which sliced a three-inch furrow into the tender flesh of her arm, leaving stinging pain in its wake.

And blood. A crimson trickle, then a rivulet welled up from the lacerated flesh, staining the cloth. Dizzy and nauseated at the sight, she closed her eyes, hoping she was not about to faint.

Then there were voices and running footsteps from inside the store, and a pounding on the boards as someone ran up the walk from behind her. "Miss Matthews! Are you all right? I saw you fall."

Sarah recognized the voice of Mr. Patterson, the owner of the mercantile. She heard another voice asking, "Wait, don't try to move her. Can you hear me, Miss Matthews?" She recognized that voice, too—that of the very last person she wanted to have witnessed her humiliation, Dr. Nolan Walker.

Her recognition galvanized her and kept her from giving into the blackness that she might well have surrendered to otherwise. She opened her eyes. "Of course I can. I'm fine. Just…give me a minute."

She opened her eyes, and saw that he was kneeling beside her.

"Can you move your limbs, Miss Matthews?"

"Of course I can," she said again, and to prove it, struggled to sit up.

"Wait. Just lie there a moment, get your bearings." he commanded her, coolly professional. "Lift your head." He wrenched off his coat, and laid it under her head.

"I assure you, Dr. Walker, I *have* my bearings."

He ignored her. "Mr. Patterson, could you please get me some clean cloths and water?"

By now a trio of curious cowboys riding by, and a couple of small boys who'd been shooting marbles across the street, had stopped to gawk at her, and she felt her face flaming with embarrassment. "Please, I don't want to be a public spectacle." She reached out a hand. "And it's cold. Help me inside."

"Very well, just sit up for a moment, don't rush—"

She was not about to act the fragile, swooning belle in front of this man. Paying no heed to his injunction, Sarah used his hand to pull herself to her feet. Then she accidentally caught a glimpse of her bloody sleeve. Her head swam, and the black mist threatened to swamp her again. If only she had a vial of smelling salts in her reticule, as proper ladies did! Suppressing a shudder, she looked away from her injured arm and allowed Dr. Walker to help her into the mercantile.

Inside the store, Mr. Patterson had set out a chair in front of the counter, and Mrs. Patterson bustled about, setting a bowl of water and some folded cloths on top of the flat surface.

She sank gratefully into the chair, and felt the soothing, cool wetness of the cloth the mercantile owner's wife wiped on her forehead, murmuring, "You poor dear, that was a nasty fall!"

"Thank you, Mrs. Patterson, I—I'll be all right," she felt compelled to say, though she still wasn't completely certain.

"You'll want to look away," she heard Dr. Walker saying, as he peeled back the blood-stained, ripped sleeve from her injury. He then took another cloth and soaked it in the water, wrung it out, used it to sponge the blood away. The cut stung like a hundred red ants

were biting her at once, and Sarah bit her lip, determined not to cry out.

Then Dr. Walker patted it dry, and used a long dry
cloth to wrap around her arm, ripping one end of it into
two strips to tie it expertly, binding the bandage.

She had to admire his cool professional manner.
He'd done it all in less time than it took for Mrs. Patterson to stop clucking over her.

"Thank you, Dr. Walker," she said, standing. "I—I
appreciate what you've done. I'm sure it will heal
up nicely now." She'd have to return another day to
see about the curtains and the wagon. Right now she
wanted nothing more than to escape his gaze and that
of the Pattersons and go back to the cottage. She'd
doubted he'd accept payment for his impromptu doctoring, but perhaps she could bring him a cake by way
of thanks.

"It's a blessing he was there," Mrs. Patterson murmured in agreement.

"Oh, I'm not done, Miss Matthews. That's a nasty
gash you have, and it's going to need proper disinfec-
tant and some stitches to heal properly. You need to
come down to the office with me where I can do it
properly."

Her eyes flew open. "Oh, I'm sure that's not necessary," she protested.

"And I'm sure it is. Come along, Miss Matthews,"
he said, tucking her uninjured arm in his.

"But—"

"Best listen to the doctor, dear," Mrs. Patterson was
saying.

"Yes, he's treated wounds on the battlefield, after all," her spouse added.

She felt herself being pulled out the door, willy-nilly. She trusted his medical judgment, but she wasn't sure she was ready to be alone with him, even if she was only a patient to him in this instance.

Chapter Five

His hand under her elbow, and keeping his eyes on her still pale face, Nolan led Sarah carefully down the steps to the street. Behind them, a dog had found the bonanza of apple pie splattered against the wall and on the boardwalk and was happily lapping it up.

It was the coldest day he'd experienced since coming to Texas, but it was still nothing to what the weather would be like in his home state at this time of year. Back in Maine, there might well be a foot of snow on the ground and a bitter wind blowing. Folks would be swathed in heavy coats, hats, boots and knitted scarves. Perhaps he'd miss seeing snow eventually, but right now he savored the warmth of the sun on his face.

Then he felt Sarah shiver.

"Are you cold?" he asked.

"No, I—I'm fine."

Nolan whipped off his frock coat again anyway and settled it around her shoulders over her shawl. She had sand, he thought—real courage and grit. She hadn't given in to her faintness when many ladies would have, but he had to remember she'd just had a traumatic experience and had lost some blood.

Sarah blinked at the gesture, and a little color crept into her cheeks. "Th-thank you."

They said nothing more during the short walk to his office. He ushered her inside, seating her in his exam chair which had a flat surface extending over each arm. He was thankful he'd had sense enough to clean and boil his suturing instruments last night, even though the hour had been late—after he'd finished taking care of a cowboy who'd been cut by flying glass in a ruckus at the saloon. The instruments lay on a metal stand, concealed by a fresh cloth, but he wouldn't bring them out yet.

"I'll be right back. I'm going to put a pot of water on for coffee when we're finished," he said, deliberately not giving her the chance to demur before he walked down the hallway that led to his living quarters. She'd need something hot and bracing when he was done.

Returning, he stepped over to a basin, poured a pitcher of water into it and began to scrub his hands and forearms with a bar of soap, remembering all the times the other field surgeons had made sport of him for what they called his "old maid fussiness" when he was preparing to operate. "I can amputate twice as many legs and arms as you can in half the time, Walker," one of them had boasted. "And I don't use gallons of carbolic, either." News of the use of carbolic acid's role in preventing infection had come from Europe in the last year of the war, but only a few doctors in America believed in it.

"Yes, and you lose most of them to infection days

later," he'd retorted, "while most of mine live to recover. So I still come out ahead."

He felt her curious gaze on him, watching as he scrubbed up and down, the harsh lye soap stinging his skin. Then he poured diluted carbolic acid over his hands. When he looked back while he was drying his hands on a clean towel, though, he found her staring at his open rolltop desk. He'd been looking at a small framed daguerreotype he normally left hidden in a drawer, and when he decided to stroll over to the mercantile, he'd absentmindedly left it out on the desk.

"That's my wife and son," he said, when he could find his breath. "They died the summer before the war began."

Her eyes widened and grew sad. "Oh, I'm sorry," she said quickly, then seemed to hesitate, and he knew she was trying a polite way to ask the question.

"Cholera," he said, sparing her the need.

"Oh…how terrible," she murmured. "You had no other children?"

He shook his head, firmly suppressing the old pain within him. "No. Now you're going to have to be brave," he said, knowing his words would distract her from further questions. He brought the bottle of diluted carbolic acid and a basin to the armrest. Pulling a stool over, he sat, then carefully unwrapped the bandage around her arm. He held her arm over the basin, and caught her gaze.

"This is going to sting," he warned. "You want a bullet to bite?"

He'd hoped his little attempt at humor would make her smile, at least for a moment. but she only shook her head and looked away, putting her other hand to her mouth.

"Go ahead," she whispered.

He poured the carbolic acid over the wound, wincing inwardly as she gasped and clamped her free hand over her mouth.

"Sorry. I don't want you to get blood poisoning or lockjaw from that rusty nail."

After removing the basin, he rolled over the tray of instruments on its stand and unscrewed his jar of boiled catgut suture in alcohol, pulled out a couple lengths and laid them on the stand among his instruments. Then picking up a suture needle, he threaded it.

"This is going to hurt, too, I'm afraid, though not as much as that carbolic."

"Do what you have to do," she said, tight-lipped, her face as white as the unbloodstained part of her bodice.

He bent his head to his task. She couldn't know how much harder this was for him than it had been to suture a soldier's cuts, knowing his touch was inflicting more pain on the very woman he cared about so much. He had to steel himself to ignore her wince each time he inserted the needle into her flesh. Thanks to his experience in battlefield surgery, he was able to close this relatively uncomplicated wound quickly. When he was finished, he looked at his patient.

Her head lay back against the headrest of the chair, her eyes were closed. Pearls of sweat beaded her pale skin.

"I'm done," he said, wondering if he ought to get out

the vial of hartshorn he kept in his desk for swooning ladies. "You were very brave, Miss Matthews."

She opened her eyes and smiled wanly at him. "Thank you."

He saw her dart a glance at the neatly sutured wound before she raised her gaze back to his face.

"This may scar a little," he said, "but not as much as if we'd just bandaged it. And you're going to have to watch it for infection. Any red streaks or swelling or drainage, you come back to see me immediately. I'm going to rebandage it," he said, and took up a roll of linen, which he circled around her forearm and tied by the ends as he had at the store. "Now I'll get that coffee I promised you."

"Oh, but you needn't bother—" she began, but he cut her off.

"No bother, I want some, and I need to see a little more color in those cheeks before I let you out of that chair. If I let you get up now, you'll collapse like a wilted lily." Wishing he could invite her back to his kitchen but knowing it would seem improper to her, he left without waiting to hear any further protests.

He returned a moment later, carrying two sturdy crockery mugs full of steaming coffee.

"I took the liberty of putting sugar in yours," he said. "I didn't know if you take it that way, but you need the sugar for energy right now." Then, a little less certainly, he said, "It's probably a little strong for you. I could get some water—"

"No, it's fine," she assured him. "Josh, our foreman, always says it isn't ranch coffee unless it's so strong the spoon stands up in the cup." She took a tentative sip, then another deeper one before he spoke again.

"Is this a good time to have that talk?"

"T-talk? What talk?" Sarah stammered. She should have known he would take advantage of being alone with her like this to claim the fulfillment of her promise. She could hardly refuse to talk to him, now that he'd played the Good Samaritan and taken care of her wound.

His expression told her that he knew she'd been playing for time to think, that she knew exactly what talk he meant. "The talk you promised me at the wedding, even said you'd look forward to, and have avoided ever since. The talk in which you're going to explain why you don't like me."

"I haven't avoided you," she protested. "I've been very busy at the ranch, what with Milly being off on her honeymoon and all. I haven't come into town except to deliver my pies and cakes, go to church and attend a meeting of the Spinsters' Club."

He raised an eyebrow as if to imply that if she could do all that, she could have made time to talk to him. "So why don't you? Like me, that is. You seemed to like me well enough when we were corresponding, but as soon as you set eyes on me, you no longer did."

Sarah sighed. She was trapped and there was no getting around it. She'd promised to do this and she had to honor her word. She owed him her honesty, at least—but now that it came down to it, and especially after what he'd done for her today, she didn't feel as righteous about her dislike as she had before. Or as certain.

"Perhaps you find me a homely fellow, not much to look at," he ventured, but there was a twinkle in his eye.

She met his gaze head on. "Dr. Walker—"

"Nolan," he corrected her. "We're not speaking as doctor and patient now."

"I'm sure you have some sort of a mirror," Sarah said, "so you know very well you're not ugly." Quite the contrary, she thought, looking into his deep blue eyes and studying his strong, rugged features. She took a deep breath. "All right, but remember you asked to hear this. I didn't like you because you're a Yankee."

Understanding dawned in his eyes. "So you thought well enough of me until I spoke to you."

"Yes, and that's your fault. You never said you were a Yankee. By writing to me from Brazos County, you allowed me to believe you a Texan."

"So you dislike me strictly because I come from the North," he stated. "Doesn't that sound rather arbitrary on your part, seeing as the war's over? As I mentioned, it hasn't prevented the rest of the townsfolk from accepting me. Why is it so important to you?"

Sarah sighed again, steeling herself to the pain of talking about Jesse. "I was engaged to a wonderful man before the war began," she said. "Jesse Holt. He…he died in the war—at least, I have to assume that, since he never came back. The men who did come back said…" She looked down as she struggled to finish. "Sometimes when men were killed, they…they…couldn't be identified."

Nolan's eyes, when she looked up, were unfocused, haunted, as if he was remembering that and worse.

"I loved Jesse," she said simply. "I…I can be your friend, I suppose…that is to say, we don't have to be enemies. But you came in town to court me, isn't that right? How can I keep company with someone who fought with the Union, when they killed my Jesse? And don't tell me that you were just a doctor, caring for the wounded," she said, when she saw he had opened his mouth to speak. *"You wore blue."* All the old grief swept over her, threatening to swamp her, and she bent her head, struggling against tears that escaped anyway. She put a hand to her mouth. "I'm sorry," she said. "I…I thought I was over it."

Now it was Nolan's turn to sigh. "I know," he said, shifting his gaze to the daguerreotype on his desk. "Mostly, I only have pleasant memories about Julia and Timmy…but once in a while someone will walk like her, or a little boy will remind me of him… But I know they wouldn't want me to mourn forever, Sarah."

She noticed he had switched to using her first name, but she didn't correct him.

"It's been over five years now since they died," he said. "I want to go on with my life. I…know it might be too soon for you."

"I wanted to go on with my life, too," she said. "Meet a good man, get married… That's why I agreed to join the Spinsters' Club when my sister started it."

"But you didn't want to meet a Yankee."

She let the statement stand. "You're free to court any of the other ladies in the group, or find someone elsewhere, you know."

"I know," he said. He raised his head to look at her, and it was a long silent moment before she found the strength to look away.

"We're friends, at least. That's something." He gave her a half smile. "Here's some bandages," he said, reaching inside a box and taking out several rolls of bleached linen. "Keep the arm clean and dry and change the dressing every day. Will you come back in a couple days, so I can satisfy myself that it's healing properly?"

She nodded, thinking she could bring him that cake then, and offer to pay him something, also. "Do you have to take out the stitches?"

He shook his head. "No, they're catgut—made of sheep intestines, really—so they'll absorb on their own inside, and the part that's showing will disintegrate and fall out."

She stared at the bandaged wound and shuddered. "Sheep intestines?"

He chuckled. "I'm sorry. I shouldn't have told you that."

Then he smiled at her, and she was so struck by what a compelling smile he had that she forgot all about sheep and their insides.

Chapter Six

"Oh, Sarah, that looks divinely delicious!" Prissy gushed two days later, watching as Sarah put the finishing touches on her blackberry jam cake with pecan frosting. "Will you teach me how to make that one for the New Year's Day party?"

Sarah looked up from her work, pushing back a stray curl which had escaped from behind her ear. "What New Year's Day party?"

"The one my parents are giving. Remember the afternoon party on New Year's Day my parents always gave before the war? The whole town came, and everyone from the nearby ranches. Papa wants to start having it again as a sign that things really have gotten back to normal. I meant to mention it sooner," Prissy said with an airy wave of her hand. "You know, it's really the last *big* social event till spring for the whole town, if you think about it," Prissy went on. "You can't plan on anything big for certain, what with the unpredictability of winter weather, though we might manage something smaller with the Spinsters' Club, if some candidates show up. *Que sera, sera,* as the French say."

What Prissy was saying was true. The Spinsters' Club had been started in the summer, when it was relatively easy for an interested candidate to travel to Simpson Creek. They had a taffy pull coming up, but that was all until at least March.

Oh, well, it didn't matter to her anyway. Even before her sister had founded the Spinsters' Club, Sarah had been a homebody, content to wait on the Lord to provide her a beau if He willed it so.

"But at least all the ladies of the Spinsters' Club will be coming, and the ones who are being courted will bring their beaux. You never know who might bring an eligible man to the party as a guest," Prissy said, still thinking out loud.

"Oh, and I told Mama we'd bring a couple of desserts." It was a typical Prissy-style change of subject. "Why don't you bake your cherry upside-down cake, and I'll make one like this—" she pointed to the one Sarah was completing "—if you'll teach me, of course."

"Sure I will." Sarah vaguely remembered attending some of those extravagant open-house parties the mayor and his wife had hosted in those halcyon prewar years, though she had barely been old enough to put up her hair before the last of them.

Mentally, she readjusted her plans. She'd been thinking of asking Milly if it was okay if she and Prissy came out to the ranch for dinner for New Year's. Now, of course, she'd have to think about what she was going to wear, as well as making a dessert to contribute. Perhaps Milly and Nick would come into town for the party.

"Or maybe you should make the biscuits. I declare, yours are the lightest, the fluffiest…I don't think I'll *ever* be able to make biscuits like that." Prissy let out a gusty, dramatic sigh.

"Oh, I don't know…the ones you made this morning were…um, much better," Sarah told her with a grin.

"You mean they were almost edible this time, as opposed to the lead sinkers I made last night for dinner," Prissy said, with a rueful laugh. "Your sisters' pigs probably wouldn't eat them."

"It just takes practice. You'll be making fine biscuits before long, I promise."

Prissy seemed reassured. "Is that for the mercantile, or the hotel?" she asked, gesturing at the cake.

"Neither. I promised to see Dr. Walker so he could check my wound, so I'm going to take it with me when I go to the office this morning."

"Ohhhhhhh!" Prissy said, drawing the syllable out, her eyes dancing with glee. "So your heart has thawed toward the handsome Yankee."

"It's done no such thing," Sarah said quickly. "At least not the way *you* mean." She avoided her friend's knowing gaze. "It's just the polite thing to do. He was very kind to me that day."

"Hmm," Prissy murmured, clearly unconvinced by Sarah's casual words. "It must be nice to have a knight in shining armor. Oh! You might as well deliver his invitation to him personally," Prissy said.

"Invitation?"

"To the party, silly. Mama had asked me to take the invitations around town this afternoon, but you can save me that stop, at least."

Before Sarah could say anything else, Prissy dashed into her bedroom and was back in a couple of minutes, waving the cream-colored vellum envelope with its handwritten invitation inside. *Of course Dr. Nolan Walker is to attend the party like everyone else.* Suddenly attending the party had become much more complicated. How was she to act around him?

"So what are you going to wear?" Prissy asked.

Sarah shrugged. "I don't know...I suppose you have a suggestion, now that you've seen the entire contents of my wardrobe?"

Prissy giggled. "I think you should wear that lovely red grenadine dress with the green piping. Very festive. And men like red dresses."

"I don't give a fig what color Dr. Walker likes!"

"Ah, but *I* said 'men.' *You* applied my generalization to Dr. Walker."

Caught. Sarah tightened her lips and glanced at the clock on the mantel as she reached for the cake cover. "This is a silly conversation, Prissy Gilmore," she said primly, "and I'm going to be late if I don't leave now."

The sound of her friend's giggles followed her out into the street.

Really, she was going to have to warn Prissy to cease and desist with her matchmaking efforts, Sarah thought as she walked down the street, avoiding ice-rimmed puddles—she didn't want to fall again. She was *not* going to change her mind about Nolan Walker, she really wasn't, and the sooner her friend understood that, the better. She didn't want to be embarrassed at the party. Perhaps she *would* wear the red and green dress, but really, her selection had *nothing* to do with the town doctor… When she'd pointed out he was free to court anyone else, he'd simply said, "I know," so surely that meant he realized she was never going to reconsider her position with him, and he was now considering other options….

She'd said they could be friends, hadn't she? Had she been too hasty to indicate there could be nothing more? Even with all she'd had to do in the last few days because of her move into town, Nolan Walker had seldom been far from her mind.

So intent on her thoughts was she as she turned and strode up the walk that led to the doctor's office that Sarah almost bowled right into a figure descending the steps.

"Oh!" she cried, tightening her grip on the cake plate and looking up at Ada Spencer. "I'm sorry, Ada, I didn't see you. I'm afraid I was lost in thought."

The other woman gave a short laugh. "That was certainly obvious!" Her eyes narrowed as they focused on what Sarah was carrying. "A treat for the good doctor? My, my, he's going to grow fat with all the goodies the ladies of the town are bringing him," Ada said archly. "Why, just the other day I brought him pralines myself. Have a nice visit with Dr. Walker. I must be getting home—we spent far too long chatting, the doctor and I. I don't know where the time went."

Sarah stiffened as the other woman stepped past her and went out into the street. So "all the ladies in town" were bringing treats to the doctor, were they? Or was it only Ada? Suddenly Sarah felt foolish and pathetic carrying the beautiful cake, like a schoolgirl with a silly infatuation. She could turn around now and take the cake back down the street to the mercantile and sell it. Yes. That's what she'd do, and then return to the doctor's office and have him check her wound, as she had agreed.

"Well, good morning, Miss Sarah," Dr. Walker said, opening his door. Through the window, he'd seen her coming up his walk right after he'd just closed the door on Ada Spencer. Surely Sarah's coming was his reward for being patient and kind during Ada's unexpected visit, made under the pretext that she'd felt something was wrong with the baby. It had taken him an hour to calm her and send her on her way, and now here was Sarah Matthews, looking lovely in her loden green shawl and navy holly-sprigged wool dress. And bearing a gift, he thought, spotting the covered plate she carried. *Well, well.*

He saw her start. Clearly, she hadn't been expecting him to open the door before she'd even had the chance to knock.

"G-good morning, Dr. Walker. I…I've come to have you check my arm, if you have the time."

"Please, call me Nolan," he said, guessing she called him "doctor" to maintain a distance between them. "And of course I have time. It will only take a minute. Come in," he said, opening the door and gesturing for her to enter. "And what is that you're carrying?"

Two spots of pink bloomed on her cheeks. "I brought you a cake, to thank you for your kindness the other day when I fell—as well as the dollar I owe you for the doctor visits," she said, pointing to the placard that indicated his prices. She set the cake on a chair next to his inner office door and began to fish about in her reticule.

"Please forget about the fee." He put out a staying hand. "I'm sure this cake will be quite enough in the way of payment, and how thoughtful of you to bring it. May I?" he said, putting his hand on the lid of the cake plate.

"Of course. But I've been told you've been receiving quite a lot of such things," she said, "so it won't be all that special." Her tone strove to be unconcerned, but he heard the disappointment underneath.

His hand stilled and he gazed at the entrance door. He'd seen Ada and Sarah exchange a few words on the walk, and hadn't missed the quickly suppressed dismay which had flashed across Sarah's features. What had the other woman said to her?

"Nonsense," he said, going ahead and lifting the top and staring at the delicious-looking confection it had concealed. "This looks wonderful, Miss Sarah. I've been told you're quite a cook—and now I'll be able to discover that for myself."

She looked at him as if she wondered where he could have heard such a thing or if he was trying to flatter her, but said only, "Well. I hope you enjoy it. But I don't want to waste your time, Dr. Walker. Why don't you have a look at my wound and then I'll be going?"

He followed her into the office, closed the door behind him, then gestured for her to sit in the chair. He began to unwrap the linen roll, noting with satisfaction that as he had instructed, the bandage had obviously been changed from the one he had applied, and once he had completely removed it, the wound itself proved to be free of redness, swelling and drainage. His sutures had held. He pressed a finger into either side of the wound, and was pleased to see that she did not flinch.

"It's no longer painful?"

She shook her head.

"It appears to be healing well," he said. "I want you to continue to keep it clean and dry, and change the bandage every day, and by, say, New Year's Day, you can leave the wrapping off, get it wet and so forth." He saw a flush of color rise in her cheeks again and realized he no longer needed to hold her forearm. He released it.

"Oh, that reminds me," she said, once again reaching for her reticule. "Prissy asked me to give you this for her parents." She held out a vellum envelope.

Curious, he opened it, and saw that it was an invitation to an open-house party at the home of the mayor and his wife on New Year's Day. "A party," he murmured. "Are you going?"

"Of course. I live right on the grounds now, you know, in that little cottage with Prissy."

She'd mentioned her move when she'd been in his office the last time, after her fall. She would have been surprised to know he thought of her every night when he went into the hotel restaurant right across the street from the mayor's house for his supper. If he had been on better terms with Sarah, he would have called to bring her some little thing as a housewarming present, but he hadn't thought she'd welcome such a visit.

"Good. I'll see you there, and I'll bring your cake

dish and cover with me—unless you need them before that?"

She must have thought it was a dismissal, for she arose and said, "No, at the party will be fine. Good day, Doctor."

He couldn't bear for her to leave so soon, but he had no good reason to keep her here—unless she would allow him to share the concern that had been weighing on his mind. He'd thought about waiting to bring it up till he knew her better, but after Ada's disturbing visit, he wanted to speak of it now.

"Please," he said, rising, too. "If you have a minute, may I discuss something with you?"

She glanced at him sharply, her eyes wary. Probably she feared he was going to revisit their conversation about why she would not let him court her. He sat back down, and as he was hoping, she sank back into her seat, too.

"I'm worried about the lady who just left, Miss Spencer. How well do you know her? Are you friends?"

She blinked. "Friends?" She gave a shrug. "I used to think so…I've known her for years, and she was a part of the Simpson Creek Spinsters' Club when it started, but lately…"

Her voice trailed off, and her eyes looked troubled. He wondered if that meant she knew about the baby.

"Why do you ask?" Her tone was curious, but not guarded. No, Ada hadn't told her.

Here was the tricky part. He wanted to make sure Ada Spencer had friends to help support her, but he didn't know if she'd told anyone about the baby she claimed to carry. He was no more certain than he had been at Ada's last visit that she actually *was* with child, and had been troubled to see that once again she'd come alone, disregarding his request to bring another female with her. And she'd seemed even more brittle, emotionally, when she'd come today than she had before.

He took a deep breath. "It's difficult for me to say," he began, "without violating her confidence…but I will say she seems troubled. I—I'd hoped she had friends to confide in." He waited to see what she would say.

She hesitated, but at last she said, "Ada's been keeping mostly to herself lately. She used to seem as carefree as any of us, but…that all changed after that Englishman came to town—the first man who was killed the day of the Comanche attack, remember?"

He nodded. Despite all the horrors Nolan had seen in the war, the image of the arrow-riddled, bloody figure slumping on his horse was a sight he'd never forget.

"They were courting," Sarah said. "She stopped coming to the Spinsters' Club meetings once that began. Afterward, we all assumed she was grieving, but then…" Her voice trailed off and she bit her lip, looking away.

"Then?" he prompted.

"Forgive me, Doctor…Nolan…I, uh…thought that you—that is, the two of you—were…um…"

Her face was scarlet now, and he guessed what she had been thinking. It was exactly as he had feared, and he could guess Ada Spencer had given Sarah that impression.

"I'm not sure what you thought, exactly, Miss Sarah," he said carefully, "but Miss Spencer is my *patient. Only* my patient."

"I…I see."

Did he imagine it, or did she appear slightly less distressed?

"She's going through a difficult time," he said. "I think she's in need of friends, Miss Sarah. I know it's asking a lot, but would you perhaps be willing to…be a friend to her?"

Chapter Seven

He held his breath as he watched her eyes widen in surprise, but to his relief, he saw no immediate resistance there.

"You think she needs my friendship? What makes you think she would accept me as her friend after distancing herself all this time?"

"I don't know why anyone wouldn't be glad of your friendship, Miss Sarah. I know I am." He locked his gaze with hers.

Her lashes dipped low over her eyes. "Thank you, but I'm not sure Ada would feel the same, given the way she's been acting lately. Perhaps you should approach Reverend Chadwick—"

"I thought about that, but I really think she needs to speak to another woman at least to begin with," he said quickly. "All I'm asking is that you try."

She was touched by his trust in her. "And you cannot say what is troubling her?"

He shook his head. "That'll have to come from her, if she chooses to take you into her confidence. If she won't open up to you, perhaps she will to another of the ladies, but please use discretion in who you ask."

Sarah studied him. "Why do you care so much about this?" she asked.

"Because I know what it's like to feel friendless."

She looked as if she'd like to ask him more, but just then the bell over the entrance tinkled, announcing the arrival of another patient. The whimpers of a fretful child penetrated through the door between the waiting room and the inner office.

"Duty calls," Sarah said with a wry smile, rising again. "I—I'll try to talk to Ada. And thank you for looking at my arm," she added, formal once more.

"You're very welcome." He placed the cake inside his rolltop desk and closed the cover over it. No sense giving anyone anything else to gossip about.

She opened the door, and Nolan saw that one of the young married women of the town stood in the waiting room, holding a red-faced, squirming toddler, while another child not much older clung to her skirts.

"Howdy, Sarah."

"Lulabelle, looks like you've got your hands full," Sarah observed.

The young mother gave her a flustered smile before turning to Nolan. "Doctor, Lee here stuck a black-eyed pea in his ear and I can't get it out nohow," the exasperated mother told him.

"Well, bring him in, I'm sure we can remove it," he said, but his eyes lingered on Sarah's graceful figure as she exited.

Because I know what it's like to be feel friendless. His answer reverberated in her mind as she stepped into the street. There were so very many things she wanted to know about him. Why would Nolan Walker ever have been friendless? He'd made friends effortlessly soon after arriving in town, and just look how easily he'd managed to talk her into being friends, if they could not be more than that. Had he meant the loneliness he'd felt when his wife and son had died?

She would have asked him if Lulabelle Harding hadn't brought her child in just then, and she still wanted to know. Perhaps she could ask him about it some other time. And he had never told her what he'd been doing in Brazos County during the time he had been corresponding with her—had he been assigned with federal occupying troops? He must have been. What other reason could he have had for being there?

Sarah had been surprised by Nolan's request that she try to be a friend to Ada. Thinking she should go talk to her now while the resolve was fresh in her mind, she started to turn down the road that led past the doctor's house to the home Ada shared with her parents, then hesitated. If she went there now, Ada would realize she had come straight from the doctor's office and guess that Nolan had put her up to it. She might even jump to the wrong conclusion that the doctor had violated her confidence. And Ada's parents would be there, which meant that she and Ada might not have any privacy to talk.

No, it was best that she encounter Ada casually in town, if possible. Perhaps she could talk to Milly about it? Milly always seemed to know everything about everyone around Simpson Creek, though she did not gossip. But if Sarah were to tell her that she had reason to be concerned about Ada, Milly might have some insight about what could be troubling the woman. Perhaps she would think it was a simple matter of grief over Ada's slain beau and what to Ada had been a promising courtship cut tragically short. Milly and Sarah, however, had learned the truth about the man's character from Nick, who had known Harvey in India.

Sarah thought about riding out to the ranch. She'd love to see her sister, and inquire how she was doing now that the cooking chores were all up to her. Prissy's father had made it clear that Sarah was free to borrow a riding horse from the stable any time she desired.

She cast an eye at the sky. Gray clouds still hung over the western horizon, threatening rain, and by now it had to be nearly noon. By the time she walked back to the cottage, changed into her riding skirt, had Antonio, the Gilmores' servant, saddle a horse for her and rode out to the ranch, it would be midafternoon. And she still needed to stop into the mercantile and hotel restaurant and promise their respective proprietors that she would be baking again starting tomorrow, and Prissy had asked her to look at lighter curtain material for their main room… No, she would not go today.

But she could always pray about the matter, she realized, feeling guilty that she hadn't thought of that first. No matter when she spoke to Ada, it was best to do so after seeking heavenly guidance, not before. She needed to stop using prayer as a last resort, after she had exhausted all her own efforts, and think of it first.

Father, I'm concerned about Ada Spencer. I don't

*know what's troubling her, but You do, Lord. Please
help her to realize You are always with her, wanting
to aid her. Help her to look to You for her needs. And
please show me how to be a true friend to her...*

She found a bolt of white dotted swiss in the mercantile that would be perfect for their curtains. While
Mr. Patterson was wrapping it up, Mrs. Detwiler came
in and made a beeline for Sarah.

"Hello, Sarah! Did you and the newlyweds have a
nice Christmas? How do you liking living in town?
Are you coming to the New Year's Day party at the
Gilmores? Well, of course you are, you're living right
on the grounds."

Sarah had started to ask about the Detwilers' Christmas, but when the voluble older lady chattered right on
as if she wasn't expecting a question in return, Sarah
smiled and said, "Yes, we did, and yes, I am liking it
and yes, of course I'll be at the party."

"Good! I reckon you'll be on the arm of that fine
Yankee doctor. My, you two made a handsome couple
dancing at the wedding. You and he have probably
been sparkin' ever since, haven't you?" she asked with
a cackle of laughter.

Sarah felt herself flushing and shook her head. "No,
Mrs. Detwiler, we're not courting. We just danced one
dance together...."

"Not from any lack of 'want to' on his part, I'll warrant. It was plain as the nose on my face. Now, don't
you let one of your Spinsters' Club friends snatch up
that fine man first," she admonished, shaking a gnarled
finger at Sarah. "You be like your sister—Milly knew
a good thing when she saw it and she didn't dillydally

and let some other woman get close to that handsome Englishman a' hers!"

Sarah marveled inwardly, thinking how disapproving the older woman had been of Milly when she'd founded the Spinsters' Club, and how Nicholas had won her over. "Yes, ma'am, and perhaps when the right man comes along, I'll—"

"You might not recognize it when it happens. I didn't, when my George first started coming to call. You think again about that Dr. Walker, miss. I know what I'm talking about."

"Yes ma'am," Sarah said obediently. It never did any good to argue with Mrs. Detwiler.

When she reached home, she found Prissy stirring a pot over the kitchen stove, and upon inspection found her friend hadn't managed to burn the beef stew Prissy, with Sarah's help, had started simmering before Sarah left the cottage. "Mmm, that's going to be good," Sarah said, sniffing the air.

Prissy grinned. "Perhaps there's hope for me yet." She put down the large spoon. "Sarah, I've been thinking, why don't we invite someone over for supper sometime soon? Wouldn't that be fun?"

Sarah nodded, thinking this might be her opportunity. Prissy could be the very person to help the withdrawn woman open her heart. "How about Ada? She's been through a lot lately, and perhaps she'd be grateful for some company other than her parents—"

Prissy wrinkled her nose. "Sarah, Ada Spencer's been downright *odd* lately. Just the other day I waved hello to her from down the street and she turned and slunk off in the opposite direction. No, I meant someone enjoyable to be around, like your sister and her husband. Or maybe we should invite a couple of the other ladies from the club—or all of them! Let's do it after New Year's Day."

Sarah sighed inwardly. She was all for a dinner party, but this meant she was back where she started, needing to find an excuse to talk to Ada.

The next three days provided no opportunities, either. She didn't encounter the woman while delivering her baked goods, nor did Ada appear in church on the morning of New Year's Eve. It seemed Sarah would have to go to the Spencers' house after all. But now it would have to wait until after the Gilmores' party the next day, for she was going to be busy this Sunday afternoon helping Prissy and her parents get ready for the event.

"Dr. Walker, good of you to come," the walrus-mustached rotund man said, shaking his hand enthusiastically. "Happy New Year!"

"Happy New Year to you, Mayor Gilmore, Mrs. Gilmore," Nolan said, smiling at him and his plump pigeon of a wife, fighting to keep his gaze directed politely on them while he longed to look over their heads for Sarah. "It was kind of you to invite me."

"Of course, of course. Everyone in Simpson Creek comes to our open house on New Year's Day. It's a tradition, you know."

Not only was all of Simpson Creek milling around in the elegantly appointed, brocade-wallpapered ballroom, it seemed as if half of the rest of San Saba County was, too, all of them dressed in their best finery. The scent of rose and lavender water mingled with savory odors of food and the strains of music played by the fiddler.

"Please, help yourself to the some refreshments, sir," Mrs. Gilmore said, gesturing at the overloaded table in the far corner of the room. And there his gaze found the woman he sought, for Sarah was standing next to a huge haunch of roast beef, slicing it for a handful of people who were lined up.

He headed in that direction, but he was intercepted midway across the room by half a dozen people, the last of whom was the mayor's daughter.

"My, aren't you looking handsome tonight, Dr. Walker," Prissy said, her eyes sweeping over him admiringly. "Just wait till Sarah sees you."

He was thankful he had two black frock coats, one for doctoring calls, the other kept for fancy occasions such as this, and that he'd had time to bathe and shave after delivering Mavis Hotchkiss's baby at a ranch west of town. "Why thank you, Miss Priscilla," he said, "You're looking very fine yourself."

She dimpled and fanned herself, then leaned close to sniff the air. "Thank you, sir. *Mmm,* and you *smell* quite handsome, too."

He'd dabbed on some bay rum after he'd shaved. He'd hoped at the time that a certain lady would appreciate it…but his thoughts had been on Sarah, not Prissy. "Miss Priscilla, I didn't know it was possible to smell handsome," he said, amused. "You must have a discerning nose, to be able to detect such a thing over the delicious scents wafting from the food table."

"Oh, go on over there, you know you want to," she

said, waving him on with a knowing wink. "Doesn't our Sarah look absolutely wonderful in red?"

He was glad that with Prissy, at least, he didn't have to pretend he wasn't longing to stand here and continue making small talk. "As you do in gold, Miss Priscilla," he said. "Thanks."

He crossed the remaining distance to the food table, and seeing that Sarah was still busy slicing beef for the guests in the line, took selections from the other dishes on the groaning board, for he had been at the delivery since dawn and hadn't eaten since the night before.

At last he came to the head of the line. "May I have some roast beef, Miss Sarah?"

She looked up from her carving tools. "Why, Nolan, I didn't see you come in. Happy New Year to you."

May the new year bring about a change in your heart. "Will you have to remain at carving table?" he asked. "I was hoping you could sit down and eat with me." He gestured at the small tables scattered around the sides of the room.

"No, I'm only carving until Antonio can come back," she said, "And here he comes now," she said, indicating a liveried manservant approaching with a clove-studded ham. "So, yes, I can sit down and eat with you. As it happens, I've become very hungry, standing here watching the food go by."

He waited while she selected some food, and then they found a vacant table not far from the door.

"I stopped at your cottage to see if I could escort you to the party, but no one answered," he told Sarah when they had settled themselves.

"No, Prissy and I have been here since early morning, helping them get the food set out," she told him.

"So I figured. Anyway, I left your cake plate and cover at your doorstep. Best cake I ever had," he told her.

"Then you'll have to try my Neopolitan cake that's over on the dessert table to see if you still think so," she said. "And be sure and try the pecan fruitcake Prissy made—please be sure and tell her it's delicious, for she needs confidence in her baking skills. Oh, there's Milly and Nick!" She waved at the couple who had just entered the ballroom.

It was foolish to hope to be alone with a particular woman at a party, he told himself. "It looks like marriage agrees with you two," he told the couple when they joined them a few moments later, along with Reverend Chadwick.

"Yes, I quite recommend it," Brookfield answered, grinning. ""How's the doctoring business?" he asked in return.

"For a small town, it certainly keeps me busy. I've already helped usher Simpson Creek's newest citizen into the world today, out at the Hotchkiss ranch."

"Ah, a new baby for the new year," Sarah said, her face brightening with pleasure.

"I trust Mavis had an uncomplicated lying-in?" Milly asked. "That's her fourth, you know."

Nolan had just opened his mouth to answer her when a shrill cry rose over the hubbub of chattering and the clinking of silverware against china.

"So there you are, Nolan!"

Chapter Eight

Ada Spencer pointed at him, her tone shrill. Her other hand fluttered down to her abdomen. She wore a green hooped gown that would have been the height of fashion before the war, but now it looked decidedly out of place. Her mother was a larger woman, so perhaps it had been hers, for it hung loose as a sack on Ada. Her hair had been pinned on top of her head in a parody of an upswept chignon. Her eyes were unnaturally bright. Two hectic flushes of color blotched her pale cheeks.

Antonio, the Gilmore's manservant, hovered uncertainly behind her as if he hadn't wanted to admit her to the party, but he hadn't known quite how to stop her.

Conversation hushed and people turned to stare. The fiddler stopped playing.

Nolan stared, and darted a glance back at Sarah. "Excuse me…" he whispered. "Reverend, perhaps you'd better come with me," he added in an undertone, and started across the room, feeling as if he had blundered into a nightmare.

Sarah rose. If there was trouble from Ada Spencer,

she didn't want Nolan to face it alone. Milly stood, too, and they followed Dr. Walker and the preacher.

"Miss Spencer, what's wrong?" Nolan said, when he reached Ada, "Are you ill? Is it—" He kept his voice down, wishing they didn't have such a large, curious audience.

"Ill? No, Nolan…the baby's just fine, kicking away," Ada announced in tone of brittle gaiety that was audible to at least half the room. Her hand remained protectively over her abdomen. "Naturally, since you and I… well, I thought you would be by to escort me to the party, but you never appeared. And here I find you consorting with another woman!" She stared at Sarah as if she had never met her.

"Ada, we were only talking…Nolan?" Sarah said uncertainly, even as Milly put a cautionary hand on her shoulder.

"Miss Spencer is ill," Nolan said, making sure his tone was firm and would carry at least to the closest fringe of people who were avidly listening. He figured they could inform the rest. "Miss Sarah, Mrs. Milly, Reverend Chadwick, would you mind coming with me? We're going to help Miss Spencer home."

"But, Nolan, I came for the party!" Ada protested, looking over her shoulder at the party behind her. "I haven't wished Happy New Year to anyone, or had any of the food over there on the buffet table, and our child makes me so hungry!"

Nolan felt the blood drain from his face. He fought the impulse to recoil from this woman. "Come with us, Miss Spencer, please," Nolan said in the kindest, gentlest tone he could muster, the kind of voice one used with a fractious animal—or the insane.

"Nolan, we really *are* on a first-name basis aren't we? After all..." Ada glanced meaningfully downward and laughed. Her eerie merriment made his skin crawl.

"We'll take you home. You want to take good care of yourself, don't you?" What must Sarah be thinking? If he'd ever had any hope that Sarah would change her mind about him, it was surely lost now.

They managed to herd Ada out into the vestibule, and while Reverend Chadwick was wrapping Ada's shawl around her shoulders, Nolan turned to Sarah, hoping to whisper that he'd be back later to explain.

But Ada must have seen him out of the corner of her eye, for she whirled away from Reverend Chadwick, fury in her eyes.

"Is it too much to expect you to be faithful to the *mother of your child?*" she demanded. "You stay away from him, you—you—" Thankfully, words failed her then, but she started gathering herself as if she meant to lunge at Sarah.

Nolan and the reverend took a firm grip on the struggling woman, and suddenly Nick Brookfield was there too, helping them, putting himself between Ada and his wife and Sarah.

Nolan wanted to shout at the crazed woman, "Be quiet! You know that's not true!" but all he could do was turn to Sarah, and let his eyes plead with her to understand. "I'll be back as soon as I can," he managed to say, even as he struggled to keep a hold on Ada.

"Now, Miss Ada, you mustn't excite yourself, you

know it's not good for you..." Reverend Chadwick was saying in his soothing voice, but it was obvious she wasn't listening. The mayor, his wife and Prissy hung back at the entrance of the ballroom, their eyes wide, obviously unsure what to do. All the partygoers were gathered behind them, their mouths hanging open in fascinated horror.

Sarah was pale, but to his relief, Nolan saw no suspicion or condemnation in her eyes, only pity as she gazed at the thrashing crazy woman, then back at him. He thought she saw her nod, but he couldn't be sure.

Shaken, Sarah watched the door close behind the three men herding Ada Spencer.

"Well, I never," breathed Prissy, who had come up beside her. "It's not true, is it? What Ada said about a baby—hers and Dr. Walker's?"

"No, I'm sure it's not," Sarah said quickly, though she could not have said why she felt so certain. She didn't know Nolan Walker that well, she reminded herself. Was this why Nolan had thought Ada needed a friend, because she was expecting a baby and had no husband? Or because Ada was losing her mind? Or both?

"No, it's not true," Milly said behind her. "Sarah, let's walk to the cottage, shall we? I think it's time to discuss something with you. You don't want to stay longer at the party anyway, do you?"

"No, I...I don't," Sarah agreed, feeling perilously close to tears. "You don't mind, do you, Prissy?"

"Of course not. If it's all right—" her gaze sought

Milly's permission in addition to Sarah's "—I'll come, too. Mama and Papa will understand."

Revisiting in her mind the October day the Comanches had attacked in the midst of the Founder's Day celebration was hard for Sarah, but she felt relieved when Milly had finished speaking.

"So Ada had just told you and Nick that Harvey Blakely had abandoned her while she was with child when his horse brought him, mortally wounded into town?" Sarah murmured. The saucer rattled as she set down her cup of tea with a shaking hand. "How dreadful."

"And you never told a soul her secret," Prissy breathed. "You're so good, Milly."

Milly shrugged. "It wasn't my secret to tell. I intended to be a supportive friend to her, but I hardly saw her after that. And what with getting ready for the wedding and all..." She threw up her hands.

"I know what you mean," Sarah said with a guilty sigh. "I meant to do the same when she started acting so oddly...."

Milly's brow furrowed. "You know, for a woman who's four or five months along...I wonder if that's why she wore that loose gown..." Her voice trailed off and she refused to elaborate. "Never mind, I was just thinking out loud. It's none of my business."

"Poor Ada," Sarah said, her heart aching as she remembered the wild look in Ada's eyes.

"I think you'd better stay away from her, after how she acted tonight," Prissy muttered.

"But now she needs friends more than ever!" Sarah cried.

"I'm afraid what she may need is an asylum, dear," Milly said, putting a comforting hand on her sister's shoulder, "since Harvey's death seems to have unhinged her mind. And if anyone's foolish enough to believe Ada's wild accusations even a little, it'll be Dr. Walker who may be needing friends."

Sarah stared at her sister. As usual, Milly was right. "I won't stop being his friend," she said. "He's a good man."

"I agree," Prissy said.

Sarah sighed. "What we *can* do for Ada is pray for her," she said.

"You're right," Milly said, and joining hands with her sister and Prissy, they did so, right then, asking the Lord to give Ada a clear mind so she would know what was true and what wasn't.

Nick arrived at the cottage shortly after that to collect his wife, reporting they'd succeeded in getting Ada home, and that Dr. Walker and the reverend had stayed to explain what had happened to her elderly parents. Then he and Milly left, wanting to reach the ranch before darkness fell.

"Looks like almost all the guests have left," Prissy remarked, standing on their porch step after she and Sarah had waved goodbye to Milly and Nick. The drive that curved in front of her parent's large house and the street beyond was now nearly bare of carriages.

"I imagine Ada's outburst put a damper on the festivities," Sarah said. She could imagine all too well that the scene Ada had made would be the talk of the town for a long time to come. *Please, Lord, don't let anyone believe Ada's unbalanced raving.*

"I think I'll go help Mama and Papa finish up for a while. I'll bring back some of the leftover food for our supper," Prissy said.

"I'll come help, too." Sarah reached for her shawl.

Prissy put out a staying hand. "You'd better stay here, in case Dr. Walker comes back soon. I have a feeling he's going to need to talk."

Sarah paced the cottage restlessly after Prissy left, dusting furniture that didn't need it, rearranging things, going to the window to stare out into the gathering dark.

Nolan arrived, looking haggard and careworn, about an hour after the Brookfields left.

"Ada's sleeping. I gave her a sedative and her mother put her to bed," he replied to her wordless question as she let him in. "No, I won't stay that long," he said, when she would have taken his coat. "I just wanted to come and see if you were all right, after what happened, and to explain…."

"I'm all right," she assured him, touched by the anxious look in his eyes. "And perhaps it will make it easier if you know that Milly told me and Prissy about Ada's being…um…with child," she said, feeling herself flush as she spoke about the delicate matter, "and that Ada told her the father was that Englishman, Harvey Blakely. Then the Comanche attack happened and he was killed…."

Nolan sighed, clearly relieved. "Yes, that does make it easier. Then you know there's no truth to what she said about me being the father."

"Of course. Nolan, at least come sit by the fire and have a cup of tea before you go," Sarah insisted. "You look exhausted."

Following her to the settle in front of the fire, he admitted he was. "The reverend and I stayed awhile to talk to her parents after she finally fell asleep."

"How are they?" Sarah asked.

"Worried, of course," he said, giving her a grateful smile as he accepted the cup of tea she had poured. "They've been concerned about her odd behavior for months now, and didn't know what to do—they were too ashamed to speak to anyone about it. I think as much as they were embarrassed to learn that she had sneaked out of the house in that outlandish dress and made a scene at the open house, they were relieved to know there was a cause for Ada's...shall we say, unusual behavior. Reverend Chadwick and I assured them we'd help in any way we can." He took a breath and added, "Your pastor is a good man."

"Yes, he is."

Nolan stared into the fire. "They didn't know about her claim that she's expecting."

"They didn't?" Then her mind focused on the way he had said it. "Why did you put it that way, Nolan— 'her claim'? You don't think she's with child?"

He shook his head. "I didn't want to talk about this, but after what happened, and especially the way she acted toward you, I think the time for silence is over— for your safety, if for no other reason. I examined Ada once in my office, and I wasn't sure she was with child then. I helped her mother get her to bed tonight, and... well, to put it as delicately as I should to a lady, there's no changes to her body that should be there by now, if her story was true."

"There aren't? Then why would she tell such a story?" Sarah asked. "She has to know the truth will come out eventually when there's no baby."

"Because I think she believes it's true. It's my opinion she has what's called a hysterical pregnancy, Sarah. Throughout history some women who wanted a child badly enough have somehow tricked their bodies into displaying some of the symptoms of pregnancy. I don't know if you ever read any English history, but Queen Mary, sister of Queen Elizabeth, suffered from this delusion too, back in the sixteenth century."

Sarah stared at him, trying to take it all in. "Did you tell this to her parents?"

Nolan nodded. "I've urged them to consult another doctor in the closest town, just to confirm what I'm saying. I've told them I'll remain her doctor if they're willing, but her mother must come with her to her appointments."

"Now I understand why you said she needed a friend to confide in," Sarah said. "Nolan, I tried, but I never had the chance to speak to her," she admitted. "I'm sorry."

"No, I'm the one who should be sorry for even suggesting it," he said. "I didn't realize until the scene at the party how brittle her hold on sanity is. It might have been dangerous for you to reach out to her."

"You meant well," she told him. "Nolan, Milly says she might need to be in an asylum."

He sighed again. "It's possible, though I hope not. Mrs. Spencer told me that there's been a history of insanity in the family tree. Her grandmother died in an asylum." Then he studied her for a long time. "Perhaps I shouldn't have told you all that, but after the way she reacted toward you, I thought it was best that you know." His gaze locked with hers. "And I find you so easy to talk to, Sarah."

She looked down, her heart beating faster at the directness of his gaze. "You may trust me not to gossip, Nolan," she assured him.

"I knew that," he said. The clock struck the hour. "And now I must bid you good night." He rose.

She stood up, too, and went to the door with him.

He looked down at her as he opened the door, the planes of his angular face shadowed by the darkness. He smiled.

She had the oddest feeling he had wanted to kiss her. She couldn't have allowed it, of course. They had agreed to be friends, but even if she was willing to forget he was a Yankee, she reminded herself, he wasn't a Christian. The Bible warned against being unequally yoked in marriage, so friends was all they could ever be.

How silly of you, Sarah. Just because a man has a certain look in his eye, that doesn't mean you need to think of why you can't marry him!

So why did she feel a moment of regret as she watched him walk away?

Chapter Nine

Nolan was thoughtful as he made his way back home. He'd been pleased and relieved that Sarah, though she'd blushed and looked embarrassed, was willing to speak with him about such a frank subject. Most women wouldn't have spoken about pregnancy to any male except their husbands. And many women might have believed Ada's ranting.

He'd been surprised by Reverend Chadwick, too. He'd been introduced to the town's preacher when he arrived in town, of course, and became more relaxed when the minister didn't seem inclined to pester him about coming to church. He'd assumed the cleric had written him off as a potential member of his congregation.

But tonight he'd been impressed by Chadwick's overwhelming patience toward Ada. Despite the vile names the madwoman called him as she tried to bite and scratch him and the two other men, Reverend Chadwick had never shown himself the least bit angry or even exasperated with her, continuing to speak kindly and calmly to her as they struggled to take her home.

He'd been a rock of support to her elderly parents, too, when they'd huddled, bewildered and distraught, to hear what Nolan had to say about their daughter's condition.

What a difference existed between Reverend Chadwick and the chaplain who'd served with Nolan. Though the chaplain had been a favorite of the men of the regiment, he'd avoided the captured, injured Confederates he was also supposed to minister to as if they had the plague.

Nolan had once taken him to task about it.

"What an idea, Doctor, that I should treat those rebels as if they deserved the same as our boys in blue!" he'd cried, recoiling at the idea. "Why, at home in Illinois, my wife and I ran an underground railroad station. You should have seen some of the poor creatures who came to our house, running for their lives away from cruel slave owners. And you're telling me that you think I should speak of God's mercy to the very men who held them in bondage?"

Nolan had very much doubted most of the scary, skinny men and boys in the tattered remains of gray uniforms had ever owned slaves, let alone the ones who'd come to the chaplain's home, but he didn't trouble himself to argue with the man. He didn't think wounded, dying rebels would find much comfort in anything that man had to say.

Reverend Chadwick lived in a small house behind the church, so he and Nolan walked together when they'd left the Spencers' house and Nick had gone to fetch his wife.

"That was very troubling," Chadwick said, as they walked. "I'll be praying for her."

Nolan sensed the man was hoping Nolan would say he would pray for her, too, but he didn't want to tell the preacher how little he believed in prayer. "Have you known the Spencers long?" he asked instead.

Chadwick nodded. "They moved to Simpson Creek when Ada was a babe in arms. She was just like any other young lady before that Harvey fellow came to town—happy, but wishing for a beau. It's very sad to see her like this now." He was silent for a few strides. "I'll be praying for you, too, son. That can't have been pleasant, having such an accusation leveled at you in front of all those folks."

"No," Nolan agreed. He was touched by the reverend's caring. Though Nolan didn't think the prayers would accomplish anything, he could still value the kindness of the gesture. "You don't think anyone will believe it, do you?"

"Sensible people, no," the reverend said. "Though there are always a few who are willing to believe the worst rather than the best. But the people around here need a doctor too much to ride that high horse for long. Oh, your ears may burn for a few days until some other topic becomes a nine days' wonder. That's the way of small towns, I suppose."

"I'm surprised you're not telling me the best thing I could do to dispel the rumor would be sitting in a one of your pews every Sunday," Nolan said. He watched for the man's reaction.

Chadwick gave a chuckle. "There are probably better reasons for coming to church than as an antidote to gossip," he said, unoffended. "But you know you're welcome, Nolan. And whether you come or not, I'm always here to listen if you need to talk. You minister to bodies, while I minister to souls—but both can be lonely at times, I think."

Nolan had heard the reverend was a widower, but he thought Chadwick meant more than that.

"But as for church, if you don't come to hear me preach, you might come to hear Sarah play the piano. She's very gifted."

Sarah played the piano? It was something he hadn't known about her. But then, she wasn't one to boast of her accomplishments.

The reverend was watching him with a knowing twinkle in his eyes. "Ah, perhaps I've given you a good reason," he said with another chuckle. "I heard you say you were going to go back and tell her what happened. Perhaps you ought to do that now, son, before it gets any later. She looked worried."

Now, having finished his talk with Sarah, he let himself inside his dark house and reached for the match safe so he could light the lamp on the entry table. His mind turned back to his talk with the reverend.

Even when Nolan had steered the conversation toward the church, Chadwick had never once made him feel that he thought less of him for not attending. Interesting.

His thoughts turned again to Sarah. Before the scene at the party, he had decided to gently pursue her, and gradually try to break down her resistance against him courting her. But now that Ada Spencer had made a public accusation against him, and had included Sarah in her venomous attack, he wasn't sure what to do. Perhaps he should just let things lie for a while until the gossip died a natural death.

He couldn't stop his eyes from searching for her, though, during the next fortnight, as he walked to the hotel for some of his meals and to the mercantile for supplies. But he didn't encounter the shy, golden-haired beauty making her rounds of deliveries to either place.

The number of patients coming to his office had dwindled since the party. He'd gotten some pointed looks by a few townspeople on the street, people he remembered seeing at the New Year's Day party, and two or three times conversations had ceased just as he'd entered the hotel restaurant or the mercantile. He'd tried not to let it bother him, supposing they'd realize they were wrong when Ada Spencer never gave birth, but after his initial warm reception when he'd first come to Simpson Creek, he'd be lying if he told himself their reaction didn't hurt.

But there were still those who either hadn't heard about Ada's wild accusation or needed doctoring too much to care, such as the elderly widow who came in because of catarrh, the near-deaf old man complaining of rheumatism, a young mother bringing in a fretful child with quinsy throat or a cowboy "all stove up" after being thrown from a horse he was trying to break.

He looked up each time the bell at the door of his office tinkled to announce an arrival, hoping against hope it was Sarah coming to visit, but he was always disappointed. At least, if it wasn't Sarah, it wasn't Ada

Spencer, either. He hadn't seen the unstable woman since the New Year's Day party, though he had seen her mother walking past his house with a basket in her hands as if she was doing some errands. He supposed he should call and inquire about Ada's welfare, but he wouldn't go alone, he'd take the reverend with him. It was just common sense.

Finally, curiosity got the best of him one morning when he spotted Prissy coming out of their cottage as he walked by on his way to the mercantile for a new can of Arbuckle's coffee. He waved and called out to her.

"Fine weather for January, isn't it, Miss Prissy? Back home in Maine we'd likely be wading through a foot of snow," he began, wondering how soon he could inquire about Sarah and still sound casual.

"I sure wouldn't want it to be any colder than this," Prissy said, shivering and pulling her coat more closely about her. "Though I would like to see snow, just once. You just never know about winter in this part of Texas—some days it can feel like spring, and then a norther will blow in. But you're not really interested in the weather, are you? You want to ask me about Sarah, so why don't you go ahead and do that?" Her eyes danced with mischief.

He couldn't help but laugh. "As always, Miss Prissy, you see through me all too easily," he said. "How *is* Sarah? I haven't seen her around for a few days."

"That's because she's been out at the ranch almost since the party," Prissy said. "Her sister's found out she's expecting a baby, and she's had a rough time of it with morning sickness. Sarah went out to help with the cooking till Milly's feeling better because she couldn't even brew the coffee without being ill. I've really been missing Sarah—I've had no one to test out my cooking on but Mama and Papa, and Papa says he'd rather eat Flora's—that's our cook—meals until I get a little better," she said ruefully.

"Hmm, perhaps I should pay Mrs. Brookfield a call," Nolan murmured, thinking he could kill two birds with one stone—offer any medical help that the first-time mother needed, and see Sarah at the same time. "If you don't think that would be presumptuous, that is, since she hasn't sent for me."

"You could, and of course it wouldn't be presumptuous, you silly Yankee man, it would be neighborly," Prissy said, chuckling.

Not expecting any patients, Nolan had gone straight home, intending to hitch up his buggy and drive right out there after dinner. But as soon as he'd finished eating, Ed Thompson, who owned a nearby ranch, arrived at his office with a boil that needed to be lanced.

Nolan drove out to the Brookfield ranch after that, only to be told that Sarah had just left the ranch after dinner, for Milly was feeling well enough to cope with the cooking again. Milly Brookfield was radiant with happiness that she would give her Nick a child in the early fall. She thanked Nolan for the kindness of coming to check on her.

He promised to deliver her baby when it came, of course, even while he thought of how Sarah must have ridden back to town while he was eating his dinner, or perhaps while he was attending to Thompson.

It seemed if he was to see her, he must take Chadwick's suggestion and come to church after all. He hoped God—if there was a God, which he very much doubted—wouldn't mind that he was trespassing in His house just to see the golden-haired beauty who played piano every Sunday.

Too bad it was Monday. Sunday had just passed and he would have to wait until it rolled around again. But perhaps he would get lucky and see her before Sunday, and not have to go to church after all. Prissy would have told her that he'd been looking for her—perhaps he could contrive to "accidentally" encounter Sarah instead of attending church to see her. He'd rather not be a hypocrite if he could help it.

But the next day marked the beginning of a disaster, and after that he was much too busy to think about maneuvering a chance meeting with Sarah Matthews, or going to church just to see her.

Chapter Ten

A pounding at the door roused Nolan from a sleep filled with uneasy dreams.

"Sorry to wake you like this, Doc, but please, kin you come out to the ranch?" the distraught-looking man on his porch pleaded, when Nolan went to the door. "I'm Hal Parker's son, Hank. Pa's took real bad with a fever, and he says he kin hardly catch his breath."

"Pa caught cold a week ago," the middle-aged Hank Parker went on while he helped Nolan hitch his horse to the buggy. "He was sneezin' a lot an' didn't seem too bad at first, but now it seems like he jes' cain't shake it. He's achin' all over, feverish and his breath's rattlin' in his chest…we were gonna wait till mornin' t'call you, but he says he can't get no air…"

"No, no, you did right," Nolan assured him, and soon they were on the road heading eastward to the ranch that lay between Simpson Creek and San Saba, Parker riding alongside Nolan's buggy. Nolan feared the old man's condition had gone into pneumonia.

When they arrived at the ranch house, Hank escorted him into the retired rancher's bedroom, where his father lay in the bed, propped up by pillows and surrounded by his anxious old wife, the son's wife and a quartet of sleepy-looking children of various heights. All of them edged politely back against the wall as Nolan entered the room with his black doctor's bag.

Hal Parker labored for each rasping breath. The sound of it filled the small room.

"Pa, we've brought the doc," his son announced, as Nolan went toward the bed, but if the old man heard, he gave no indication.

"Hello, Mr. Parker," Nolan said as he leaned over the bed. "I'm Dr. Walker."

The old man opened clouded eyes and tried to focus on Nolan, then closed them wearily again. "Where's... Doc...H-Harkey?" he managed to say, but the effort sent him into a spasm of coughing when he finished.

"Hal, he's dead," his elderly wife told him loudly. "He died when those Comanches attacked last fall, remember?"

Nolan studied Parker. He was red-faced and clammy, his pulse thready and rapid. His eyes seemed sunken. His mouth gaped wide like a fish's with his attempts to draw in enough air.

Nolan opened up his bag, took out his stethoscope and listened for thirty seconds. Just as he had feared, the moist rattling within the man's chest filled his ears. It was definitely pneumonia.

Mr. Parker's daughter-in-law had already given him willow bark tea for the fever, and to this Nolan added a dose of morphine, trickling the draft in cautiously lest the delirious man choke. He directed the daughter-in-law to sponge him with a cold wet towel.

Nothing they did worked, however, and the old man breathed his last just as the sun was rising over the distant blue hills.

"He's gone," he told the white-faced son, and closed the old man's eyes. The man nodded grimly, unsurprised, and put one arm around his weeping mother, the other around his wife. The children clustered around them, some crying, some solemn-eyed in the presence of death.

"Thank ya. Ya done all ya could," the old woman murmured, tears sliding down the weathered grooves of her cheeks. "Hal's with the Lord now, and someday soon I'll join 'im."

Nolan inclined his head respectfully. However accustomed he was to death, he could never understand this calm, patient acceptance. He was angry when he lost a patient, angry at himself and against an implacable foe that fought without scruples. When Jeff had died despite all his efforts, he'd raged for days, finally seeking oblivion at the bottom of a whiskey bottle but finding no relief.

Death was the end. There was nothing more. When his wife and son had died, Nolan had received no echoing sense that they were alive on any other plane of existence. Nothing he had seen in the war had taught him any different.

"I'll inform the undertaker when I get back to town," Nolan told them, gathering up his black bag.

"And Reverend Chadwick, too, if you'd be so kind, Doc."

Hal Parker's death was Nolan's first since becoming Simpson Creek's doctor, he mused as he drove back to town. The few deaths on the day of the Comanche attack didn't count—he'd only taken over, as any doctor would, when the town's physician had been felled by an arrow.

He tried to be philosophical as he drove back to town. Pneumonia was always a danger to the elderly, especially in winter. A doctor couldn't expect to be in practice and not see death.

The funeral was held two days later in the churchyard, where all the Simpson Creek inhabitants had been buried ever since the town had been founded back in the 1850s. Fortunately it was a mild day—cold enough to require a coat, but without any wind or rain. The whole town attended, for Hal Parker had been one of the first settlers of Simpson Creek. Nolan went too, in part out of respect to the family, but also because he knew he'd see Sarah there. With the loss of his first patient in town weighing on him, the pleasure of some time in Sarah's company would be a comfort, indeed.

She stood near the coffin, her golden hair a lovely contrast to the somber black dress and coat she wore. She caught his eye and nodded slightly as Maude Harkey joined her, then the two began an a cappella duet of "I Know that My Redeemer Liveth." Maude's voice was a reedy soprano; Sarah's clear notes soared above it in perfect pitch, though she sang no louder.

He decided that he'd speak to her after the service— casually of course. But while Reverend Chadwick read a passage from the Bible in which Jesus said He was the resurrection and the life, Nolan became distracted when he noticed that the deceased's widow was absent from the gathering, as was the daughter-in-law. Half of the Parker brood were coughing, and one of them, a little girl of perhaps six, looked especially sallow and wan and leaned against her older brother for support. Had they caught their grandpa's illness?

"I would also ask your prayers, good people, for Hal's widow, who took ill yesterday," Reverend Chadwick announced as he closed his Bible at the pulpit. "Sally Parker is home taking care of her. Under the circumstances, rather than having the usual dinner in the social hall following the burial, we're going to send the food y'all have so generously provided home with the Parkers, so they can get back to the ranch sooner."

It was a very good idea, Nolan thought, though the dinner would have given him a longer time to be in Sarah's company. It seemed like illnesses spread like wildfire among large gatherings in the winter, so he figured it wouldn't hurt if a cold spell kept Simpson Creek folks in their homes for a while. When he'd taken his medical training back east, he'd seen that whenever there'd been a milder winter and people were able to gather together often, there were more cases of chest colds, catarrh and influenza.

When the funeral service was over, some headed for their wagons or their homes down the road, while others lingered in the churchyard to talk. Nolan discreetly made his way toward Sarah, who along with Prissy had just helped the Parker family arrange the covered dishes of food into the buckboard among the children.

"Mr. Parker, if there's anything more I can do, please let me know," he said, before turning to Sarah. He'd be called out to see the little girl soon, unless he missed his guess.

"Thanks for what ya done, Doc," the drawn-faced young rancher said as he climbed into the driver's perch. "No one could have tried harder to save Pa. It was jest his time, I reckon."

Nolan touched the brim of his hat to the man as he clucked to his horses and drove out.

"Sarah, your song was lovely," he said. *Though not as lovely as you.* He supposed Sarah Matthews would be beautiful in any circumstances.

Pink bloomed in her cheeks. She looked down, then back at him. "Th-thank you," she said. "It…it's always been a favorite of mine…I hope it blessed the Parkers…."

Nolan was conscious of all the people passing by them, of Prissy standing by Sarah, trying to appear as if she was not listening. They had probably come together. If only he had some excuse to take Sarah where they could talk.

"I…I hope you've been well…" he said, and thought immediately how ridiculously trite it sounded.

"Yes, of course…I'm usually healthy as a horse," she said, then chuckled. "Oh, my, that didn't sound very ladylike, did it?" she said, glancing at Prissy to include her in the conversation. "Ladies are supposed to be delicate flowers, aren't they?"

He appreciated a woman who could laugh at herself. "There's nothing wrong with having a sound constitution," he told her, and then silence reigned again as he tried to let his eyes speak for him.

Prissy took it upon herself to rescue them. "Dr.

Walker, you *are* coming to the taffy pull the Spinsters' Club is holding on Friday night, aren't you? Seven o'clock, in the church social hall."

"I...I didn't know about it," he said. "I—"

"I hope it doesn't sound like a childish pastime, but it's hard to find things to do in the winter," Prissy said.

He didn't miss the surreptitious nudge Prissy gave Sarah. Obviously she thought Sarah should chime in on the invitation. But Sarah's gaze had strayed toward the road.

"Not at all," he said, wondering about the way she seemed to be sidling away from them—*as if she wants to be away from this place...or me. Does she not want me invited?*

"I confess I have a bit of a sweet tooth, so thanks for the invitation," he said. He wanted to ask Sarah if she would be there, too, but first he had to see what reaction she had to his acceptance of the invitation.

But her gaze remained fixed on the road before her. At last his gaze followed hers, knowing and dreading what he would see.

Ada Spencer was standing at the entrance to the churchyard, glaring at them, her eyes like drawn daggers. Her mother stood next to her, her expression worried, one arm anxiously draped around her daughter's shoulders as if to make sure Ada did not move any farther into the churchyard. She was obviously trying to urge her away, but Ada seemed glued to the spot.

Nolan fought the urge to give in to frustration and struggled to keep his face serene. What right did this disturbed woman have to destroy their peace, to ruin an innocent relationship?

"I'll leave first, and try to draw her away," he whispered to Sarah and Prissy. "I'll talk to you later, Sarah." He strode toward the road, lifting an arm in greeting, "Hello, Mrs. Spencer, Miss Spencer," he called, trying to sound as if he was genuinely glad to see them. "How have you been? Are you feeling well, Miss Spencer?" he said, as he reached them.

Ada smiled a strange smile, then let her coat fall open. She was wearing another oversized dress whose waist tie outlined the curve of her supposed pregnancy. "Oh, I've been feeling *very* well, dear Nolan," she said, in a weirdly cheerful voice that was loud enough to be heard by those still in the churchyard.

"You should call him Dr. Walker, Ada," her mother admonished. "He's a physician, and he deserves respect—"

"Oh, but we've been using each other's given names in private for a long time now, haven't we, Nolan? I suppose it *is* time for me to come see you in the office again," she said, patting her abdomen as she had at the New Year's Day party. "We do want to take proper care of our child, don't we?"

Nolan glanced at her mother, who only grimaced in pained ruefulness.

Why couldn't the woman control her daughter? Biting back the reply he wanted to make, he focused on Ada again. "That would be fine," he said carefully. "As the town doctor, I'm always happy to care for its inhabitants. Be sure to bring your mother with you, all right? I'm sure you'd be more comfortable that way.

Good day to you both," he added, touching the brim of his hat and hurrying past them.

Reaching his yard, he opened the gate, then pretended he had dropped something until he could be sure Ada didn't linger to accost Sarah.

Chapter Eleven

Sarah couldn't stop looking over her shoulder every few yards as she and Prissy walked home, still not sure she wouldn't see Ada following them with some weapon raised high to attack her.

For God hath not given us the spirit of fear, but of power, and of love, and of a sound mind, she remembered from the New Testament, she thought, and felt the fear lift away from her as if someone had removed a thirty-pound sack of flour from her back.

Lord, please heal Ada and restore her sound mind.

They reached the wrought-iron fence that surrounded the mayor's house and grounds. "Thank God that crazy Ada didn't try to follow us, although I'm sure Dr. Walker wouldn't have let it happen," Prissy said, lifting the heavy iron latch that opened the gate. "Oh, I wish something could be done with her so she wouldn't keep popping up like that, when you least expect her! It's positively spooky," she grumbled on. "Why can't her parents see she needs to be in an institution? There ought to be a law."

"I'm sure that poor old couple can't bear the thought," Sarah said. "From everything I've ever heard about such places, it's like putting someone in a cage. You don't hear of anyone ever emerging again in his right mind."

Prissy rolled her eyes. "That may well be true, but I think you're being entirely too generous about this," she said. "Next, you'll say we need to keep praying about it."

Sarah grinned, for she had indeed been about to say that very thing. "Of course I wish Ada weren't acting like this—for Dr. Walker's sake, if not for mine. He looked so tired today at the graveside, so sad. I'm sure losing a patient must be very hard on him."

Prissy sighed. "See, you do care about him! Sarah, what Nolan Walker needs is a good *wife* to encourage him, to see that he eats properly, make sure he gets his rest."

The picture Prissy had painted of Sarah as devoted wife, caring for Nolan, was a very appealing one. But she couldn't dwell on it, because Prissy wasn't done.

"When are you going to get off your lofty perch and let yourself love him?" she went on. "That excuse that he's a Yankee's wearing a little thin by now, don't you think?"

Sarah stared at her as they had reached their little cottage and went in. She hung up her coat with a sigh, then took Prissy's coat and hung it up, too. "Dr. Walker and I *have* become friends. But how can he and I be anything more if he's not a believer? The Bible warns about being unequally yoked, you know."

Prissy groaned exasperatedly. "Sarah Matthews, if

you gave that man the *slightest* bit of encouragement, he'd be sitting in the front pew every Sunday morning, and you know it."

"Having him come to church with the wrong motive is not the answer," Sarah said. She knew she sounded prim and she didn't want to, but if Nolan came to church, she wanted it to be for the right reasons.

"Maybe he'd start off coming to see you, but while he was there, he'd have to hear the preaching," Prissy pointed out. "That's the way *I'd* do it, anyway."

Sarah sighed again. Could Prissy be right?

"You don't mind me inviting him to the taffy pull, do you?" Prissy asked. "I mean, I wasn't inviting him for my sake, but you were distracted by seeing Ada staring at you, which I didn't realize at the time, and I—"

"No, I'm glad you did," Sarah assured her. She couldn't deny she'd be glad to see Nolan there. Unless someone brought some unattached male guests, she and the other Spinsters would be watching the ones who were courting bill and coo with their beaux, something that was becoming harder and harder to do without feeling a very human envy. "With no family here in town, he probably doesn't take very much time to enjoy himself," Sarah murmured. "And perhaps he and one of the other Spinsters will discover a liking for one another…" She busied herself with lighting the stove and putting the teapot on top of it, activities that didn't require her to look Prissy in the eye.

Prissy gave a low whistle. "Sarah Matthews, you can just stop saying such silly things that you don't even believe. I'm not fooled for a minute."

Sarah couldn't help but smile. "I'm glad you always tell me the truth, Prissy," she said, and gave her friend an impulsive hug. "We'll see what happens. Now, why don't we get back to your cooking lessons? If your mama and papa are coming to supper tomorrow night, we'd better see if you can make some edible dumplings, and then we need to do a bit of housekeeping."

"Ever the taskmaster," Prissy groused good-naturedly.

Nolan didn't show up at the taffy pull. Sarah told herself it didn't matter, that she hadn't been expecting him to, and tried to keep herself from watching the door every time it opened to reveal a new guest's arrival. She even had a good time, laughing and singing with the others as they stretched and pulled the sugary, sticky confection into pieces of candy. A wiry ranchhand from Cherokee glued himself to her side during the early part of the evening, and he was pleasant enough company, but when he left later without asking if he could call on her, she was only relieved.

Had Nolan been called out to see a patient, or had he decided a taffy pull was just too childish for a professional man such as himself to bother with? Perhaps he wasn't interested in her after all.

In actuality, Nolan had been summoned back to the Parker ranch that morning, for both the little Parker girl and her grandmother, Hal Parker's widow, were abed with the same high fever and coughing that had felled the old rancher. Hank Parker's wife was staying out of bed by sheer will to take care of them, for she was feverish and coughing, too.

By nightfall he'd forgotten all about the taffy pull, immersed as he was in the struggle to save the old woman and the child. He stayed out at the ranch for twenty-four hours, alternately medicating the grandmother and the granddaughter and helping the younger Mrs. Parker sponge both of them down. He finally sent the exhausted young wife off to bed and instructed her worried husband to heat up some of the broth left on the stove for her. By morning, the little girl seemed as if she would survive with some careful nursing, but the old woman had followed her husband into death.

He drove home the next day, aching in every joint, as weary and discouraged as he'd ever been in the war after hours in the casualty tents.

But when he arrived back at his office, there was already a man sitting on a horse in front of it, waiting for him. There would be no rest for him yet.

He visited two ranches and three houses in town that day, and all of the patients he saw were suffering from the same chills, fever, coughing and body aches. He dosed them for their fevers and coughs, instructed their families on nursing them and giving them lots of water and nourishing broths and reassured them the best he could. He advised the still-healthy inhabitants of each house to stay home so as not to spread the contagion.

Of the patients he saw that day, only two were advanced in years, so with any luck the others would recover. But it was clear that Simpson Creek was in the throes of an epidemic. And all of them had been at the funeral of Hal Parker.

Each time he returned to his office, someone else was waiting to bring him to another sick person, or had left a note in his door that he was needed at such-and-such a house. He wished he could split himself into several doctors, so he could be in more places at one time, or at least had a trained assistant who, in his absence, could dispense medications, or take care of someone until he could get there. A nurse—yes, that's what he needed. A nurse. Or several nurses.

He finally fell into bed without eating supper, for he was too tired to make himself anything and it was too late to walk down to the hotel restaurant. He slept dreamlessly until the sound of church bells woke him the next morning.

Got to tell Reverend Chadwick he ought to call off Sunday services until this epidemic dies down, he thought groggily. People didn't need to be congregating in small places, spreading the sickness. If there was a God, wouldn't He understand?

He'd barely completed the thought before the sound of his office bell jangled him fully awake. Apparently he wasn't going to have time to have a proper breakfast and shave before his patients needed him again.

"I declare, I've never seen so many cases of the grippe," Mrs. Gilmore said Wednesday afternoon over dinner. Sarah and Prissy were dining with them, as they did at least twice a week. "Why, just in town yesterday I heard of half a dozen people down with it."

Sarah thought of Milly. They'd just been together at church Sunday, but perhaps she ought to ride out to the ranch this afternoon and check on her and Nick. If they were fine, she was going to tell them not to come into town, she decided. A woman with child didn't need to be exposed to sick people.

Before she left, she'd set a pot of vegetable soup to simmer on the stove, enough for their supper and to take some down to leave at Nolan's office. The poor man was likely working such long hours that he probably wasn't taking the time to eat properly. But could she trust Prissy to mind it so that it didn't boil down to nothing and scorch the soup into a charred mess? The girl could be so forgetful sometimes….

"And someone said it's really bad down at Burnet," Prissy's mother went on, helping herself to another serving of scalloped ham. "I'm going to have to write your Aunt Vira, Prissy, and make sure she's all right. She lives in Burnet, you know," she said to Sarah.

Sarah did know, for Mrs. Gilmore spoke incessantly about her older sister Vira. It sounded as if the woman was quite a character, and a hypochondriac to boot.

"Speaking of Vira, I stopped by the post office on my way home, and there was a letter from her," Mayor Gilmore announced, breezing into the dining room, late as usual, and waving an envelope.

Seizing the envelope, his wife dropped her fork on her china plate with a clatter and tore it open. She held out the unfolded page for a moment until her eyes found their focus, then scanned the page.

Sarah saw the color drain out of her normally florid cheeks.

"Oh dear," she murmured, and stared at the page again.

"Mama?" inquired Prissy. "Is Aunt Vira sick?"

"No, but she says everyone else in Burnet is, so she thought it best to come here for a visit. She plans to stay until the influenza's all gone from down there. Anson's going to bring her, she says."

"Mama, you've got to write and tell her not to come!" Prissy cried. "It's no safer here, with people falling ill left and right."

"I can't," her mother wailed. "You know Vira—she never waits to hear an answer. She's probably already on the way!"

"Nevertheless, Martha, we ought to try," Mayor Gilmore said. "There's probably more risk of her bringing the contagion here than of her contracting it in Simpson Creek. Write out what you want to say after dinner, and I'll see if we can send a telegram—or if the wires are not working, maybe I can pay one of Andy Calhoun's boys at the livery to ride down with the message."

"Well, if you're not able to stop her, it'd be fun to see Anson, at least," Prissy said. "I've been writing him to persuade him to come visit with his mother ever since we started the Spinsters' Club, but he kept giving me excuses. I think the idea of all those single women scared him," Prissy said with a giggle. "You'd like him, Sarah."

"Didn't I meet him a long time ago? Before the war?" Sarah asked. She had a hazy image in her mind of a boy with dark brown hair some six years older than her who'd taken delight in tormenting the girls at a church picnic.

"That's right, you did—I remember now. Oh, he's changed since then," Prissy assured her. "Last May when we went down to Burnet to welcome him home from the war, I swan, he'd grown a foot taller while he was away," Prissy enthused. "And that military bearing…" She pretended to fan herself. "If he wasn't my cousin…"

Sarah laughed at her friend, and then everyone was quiet as the clatter of horses' hooves and carriage wheels on the driveway outside reached their ears.

Mayor Gilmore got to his feet and peered out the window. "Well, you needn't bother writing the message. She's here, she and Anson. And from the amount of trunks and boxes, she means to stay for a while."

Chapter Twelve

With an excited shriek, Prissy sprang up from the table. She ran to the window to confirm her father's words, then out of the dining room, her shoes clattering on the flooring of the hallway. Mayor Gilmore and his wife hastened after her in a more decorous fashion. Sarah followed them, lingering in the doorway, not wanting to intrude too soon on a family reunion.

"Aunt Vi! Anson!" Prissy called, running down the steps. The young man assisting his mother out of the landau had his back to them when Sarah reached the doorway, but Sarah could see that he was tall and solidly built. Aunt Vira was plumper than her sister, indeed quite rotund, and possessed of at least two chins. She was dressed in a matching violet coat and bonnet which clashed violently with the maroon wool dress beneath it.

Sarah saw the old woman look up to see her niece rushing at her, but before she opened her arms to her, Aunt Vira pressed a rumpled lacy handkerchief to her mouth and gave a gusty sneeze.

"Oh, my dear girl! Martha, Herbert! I certainly hope

you have a roaring fire going, for I declare, I've never been so chilled in all my born days!" she cried, embracing Prissy, and then her sister. "Anson put a hot brick at my feet when we left, but it didn't stay hot very long, I can tell you. And that road! My poor bones have never been so rattled about in my body! I felt as if my brain was about to shake right out of my skull!" She sneezed again.

"I told Mama the trip would be hard on her, and that we should keep to home, but she insisted on coming," said the young man, who had finished giving Antonio directions on stabling the horses and had now come to join his mother. "Why, cousin Prissy, you're looking all grown up!" he said with raised eyebrows.

Sarah understood instantly why Prissy had hinted that her cousin was handsome. With those dark eyes and hair and that broad-shouldered frame, she could well imagine he could make quite an impression on the Spinsters' Club if he stayed long enough.

"Oh, pooh, I don't look any different than I did in May when we came to see y'all," Prissy pouted prettily, and her cousin gazed down at her, enchanted.

As long as there were women like Prissy, Sarah thought with amusement, there would always be Southern belles.

"But who's this?" Anson said, tearing his gaze away from Prissy and toward Sarah.

Prissy didn't seem to mind relinquishing the spotlight. "Aunt Vira, Anson, this is my best friend, Miss Sarah Matthews. Sarah, my aunt, Mrs. James Tyler, and my cousin Anson."

Anson strode forward and bowed to Sarah. "Miss

Matthews, I am charmed to meet you," he said, turning the full force of his smile on her. *"Charmed."*

Sarah could no more have stopped the smile which spread across her face at this fulsome greeting than she could stop breathing, but even as her eyes catalogued his features, she was thinking how Nolan's angular face appealed to her more.

"Mrs. Tyler, Mr. Tyler, nice to meet you," Sarah murmured.

"Oh, no, that won't do, Miss Matthews," protested Anson smoothly. "Please, call me Anson."

Aunt Vira smothered a cough before saying, "And where do you live, Miss Matthews? Are you visiting with Prissy?"

"That's the best part, Aunt Vira!" Prissy interrupted. "She lives right there," she said, pointing beyond the older woman toward the cottage, which was nearer to the road. "With me! Mama and Papa are letting us use the old cottage!"

Vira Tyler's jaw dropped open. "Whatever for? Why would you choose to live away from your dear mama and papa, niece? That makes no sense."

Prissy giggled. "Oh, Aunt Vira, we're just across the lawn from the big house!"

"Actually, it makes perfect sense, Vira," Mayor Gilmore put in smoothly. "Martha was at her wit's end trying to teach Priscilla all the housewifely arts when our daughter would much rather think of feminine fripperies, but her friend Miss Matthews seems to have perfected all the skills and virtues that a young lady should know to manage her own house. So we thought it a fine idea to let them live in the cottage for a while, where Miss Matthews can teach her all these things. I fear we have been too indulgent with our only daughter, Vira, but she learns willingly from Miss Matthews."

Unseen by her parents and her aunt, Prissy rolled her eyes at Sarah before interjecting, "Aunt Vira, she's teaching me how to cook! I've learned to make delicious stews and light-as-a-feather cakes and mouthwatering fried chicken and—"

"Yes, yes," Vira Tyler said, waving one hand and dabbing her forehead with her handkerchief in the other. She sneezed yet again. "That's wonderful, dear niece, and you must tell me more later, but right now, I need to get inside by the fire. I am chilled to the bone, I tell you! If there's been a colder day this winter, I can't remember it."

Sarah saw Prissy's parents exchange a look. Though overcast, the weather had been very mild for January. Without another word, they helped Aunt Vira into the house.

Anson tucked Prissy's arm in his as they strolled toward the house. "Perhaps you'd like to demonstrate your newfound prowess in the kitchen for me while I'm here, cousin."

"What a good idea! We'll make a party of it! I'll invite the ladies in the club who have not yet found a beau, and—"

"*Whoa*, cousin! What's wrong with just the three of us, you, me and Miss Sarah?" He winked at Sarah over his shoulder. "I believe I'd like to become better acquainted with your friend, not be subjected to a passel of females all aiming their wiles at me at once."

Prissy let out a peal of laughter. "Why, Anson, who's

to say our friends are going to fall all over you, you conceited thing? And if you hadn't interrupted me, I was going to say I'd be inviting Nolan Walker, our new town doctor. He would like very much to court Sarah, but she's still making up her mind about him—"

"Prissy, you're talking about me as if I weren't here," Sarah complained. "And I'm very sure your cousin isn't interested in my personal business," she added with a quelling glare at her friend. Prissy could be such an artless chatterbox at times!

Anson was about to mount the first step up into the house, but at that, he let go of Prissy's arm and turned around to grin at her. "Oh, but I *am* interested, Miss Sarah. A man likes to know at the outset if he has a rival."

Sarah took a step back, unsure how to politely discourage Prissy's cousin's flirtatiousness. Perhaps, if she had not met Nolan first, she might have found Anson Tyler's confident charm appealing. The thought startled her—she had insisted she wasn't interested in Nolan, and yet again she found him preferable to another man?

Even as she made this startling realization, Prissy gave her cousin a light, playful slap on the cheek. "Now you *stop* that, Anson! You'll frighten Sarah away, and she'll move back to the ranch, and Mama and Papa will make me live in the big house…."

Anson raised his hands in mock surrender. "All right, all right," he said. "I hope I haven't offended you, Miss Sarah? I promise to behave myself during my stay here. Pax?"

Sarah smiled in spite of herself. "Pax."

"Wonderful," Prissy said. "You must be hungry, Anson. I'm sure Flora is putting dinner together for you at this very moment. Let's all go inside and chat. You can tell us what's become of all those handsome boys you mustered out with, Anson."

"Y'all go ahead," Sarah told them. "You'll want to spend some time with your relatives, and I have some things to do."

"But—"

"I'll be back by supper," she assured them. "Prissy, I'm sure you'll want to show Anson our cottage—could you just check on the soup I'm going to put on the stove to simmer?"

Sarah headed for the stable, where she requested Antonio saddle the horse she usually borrowed. Then she went to the cottage, where earlier she had diced some carrots, onions and the remains of some chicken they'd had last night, added some dried beans she'd soaked overnight and some pepper, salt and dried chilies and mixed it all in a pot of chicken stock. Then she set it on the stove to simmer before changing into her riding clothes.

Within half an hour she was riding toward the ranch.

She found Milly in her kitchen, stirring her own pot, but hers held chili. The room was redolent with the savory, spicy smell.

"Oh, I was just thinking about you!" Milly cried, rushing forward to embrace her sister. "I heard someone ride up, but I thought it was just one of the men coming in from the pasture. They're all out checking fence and tending stock, but they'll be so glad to see you!"

Roses bloomed in Milly's cheeks once again, Sarah noted, and if she could stand the smell of chili cooking, she must be feeling better.

"You'll stay for supper, won't you?" Milly burbled on. "I'll have one of the men ride back with you, or you could even stay the night…I'm so happy to have some female company after all these men!"

Sarah shook her head. "I'm sorry, I promised I'd be back at the cottage for supper." She told Milly about Prissy's aunt and cousin showing up unexpectedly, but didn't mention one of the reasons she wanted to get back was to deliver soup to Dr. Walker. "I really just came to see how you were doing, to see if everyone was well."

Milly blinked. "Fine as frog hair split three ways—even me," she said with a grin, patting her abdomen, "though I've had to let out my dresses in the waist a bit. Good thing I'm handy with a needle, hmm?" She studied Sarah more closely. "Why shouldn't we be well?"

"The influenza's getting really bad in town, Milly," Sarah told her. "Several folks have come down with it since old Mr. Parker died. I see Dr. Walker's buggy going back and forth all the time, and it seems like there's always a horse or a wagon parked in front of his office. I came to tell you as long as everyone's healthy out here at the ranch, you'd better not come into town. No sense in risking your health, Milly, especially now that you're expecting."

Milly frowned and her shoulders sagged. "But I was

just planning to go to mercantile, now that I'm feeling better," she said. "Bobby's grown out of all his shirts again," she said, referring to their youngest cowhand. "And what about church on Sunday?"

Sarah was thoughtful. It was now Wednesday. "You'd better stay home, Milly. Send one of the men to the mercantile if you absolutely have to have something, or send them to me. As for church, I'm sure the Lord will understand."

"Well, at least sit down with me for a few minutes and have a cup of tea and some of these cookies I made," Milly said, pointing to a crockery jar on the table. "Tell me all about Prissy's aunt and cousin. The middle of January seems like an odd time to come for a visit."

Sarah nodded. "The influenza's hit Burnet very hard, so she wanted to get away from it, I expect." She thought Prissy's aunt was coming down with something, too, what with the way she couldn't stop sneezing and coughing when she arrived, but she didn't mention it, not wanting to worry Milly.

"And is her boy Anson as ornery as ever? I imagine he's all grown up now, isn't he?"

Sarah nodded. "He's grown a foot since he went away to war, and filled out some. He's quite the handsome charmer now."

"Ohhhhh?" No one could inject such a depth of meaning into a single syllable and a lifted brow as her sister.

"He tried flirting with me, but I indicated I wasn't interested," Sarah said loftily, pretending a great interest in brushing a cookie crumb off her bodice. "Though I imagine the Spinsters' Club ladies will be."

"Why?" Milly said, ignoring Sarah's second remark for the first. "Because of our Yankee doctor?"

To her dismay, Sarah felt a blush spreading up her cheeks. "Of course not. I don't know why you and Prissy keep trying to pair us off."

Milly only smiled.

"We agreed to be friends," Sarah said, "and then he didn't even show up at the taffy pull, and hasn't mentioned it since. Though I imagine it was because he was so busy taking care of all those sick folks," she admitted, determined to be fair.

"And how's Ada?" Milly asked.

Milly had been to the Parker funeral, but she had left before Ada had shown up and glared at them. Sarah told her sister about the incident, finishing with "But I haven't seen her since, fortunately."

"You be careful if you do," Milly said. "I'll pray for her."

The grandfather clock in the parlor struck the hour. "Goodness, it's getting late," Sarah said, rising. She wanted to return in time to deliver that soup to Nolan so he'd have it before he was ready for his supper. "I've got to be going. Please tell Nick and the men I'm sorry I didn't get to see them...."

As much as she cared about Molly and the rest of the ranch's inhabitants, she felt pulled back to Simpson Creek as if by a magnet. For that was where Nolan was.

Chapter Thirteen

No light showed through the windows, either in the doctor's office or the connected house in the back as Sarah strode up the walk in the gathering dusk. Setting the heavy pot of soup on the step, Sarah walked around the yard toward the back, her high-button boots crunching the dead brown grass. A quick glance around showed the buggy parked, its traces empty, but just to be sure he hadn't ridden the horse, she stepped into the small barn and found his chestnut gelding in his stall, busily devouring his oats. The beast looked up, snorted at her, then dipped his head to his feed once more.

Had Nolan already gone down to the hotel for supper? A glance at the watch pinned to her bodice had told her it was only five, but perhaps he'd missed the midday meal and had gone early. She'd knock, just in case.

Repeated knocking produced nothing but an answering silence. She was about to turn and go, but on an impulse, stooped to peer through the waiting room window.

In the dimness she could make out the shape of a

man sprawled in one of the chairs, his feet propped up on another chair, shirtsleeved arms splayed out limply beside him. Nolan's mouth gaped open slightly.

It was his utter stillness that alarmed her. Through the window she could not see any rise and fall of his chest, any movement of his jaw that would indicate Nolan Walker was alive. Oh dear, what if he had died, a victim of the very epidemic he was trying to combat? Could the influenza work that fast? Perhaps it could, if someone was utterly exhausted from his work, as Nolan must be.

With a cry of alarm, she tried the knob and found it unlocked. Maybe she was not too late. Perhaps if he was still breathing, and she summoned aid—Reverend Chadwick would be the closest—they could get him to bed and nurse him back from the brink… She crashed into the room.

The "dead" man came instantly awake, throwing himself into an upright position before his blue eyes were even fully opened.

"Are there wounded, corporal?" he barked out. "How many? How bad off? Are we in retreat? How close are the rebels?"

She uttered a shriek of surprise and jumped back at his rapid-fire questions and sudden violent movement, even as relief flooded over her that he was not dead or dying. "Dr. Walker—*Nolan*—it's me, Sarah Matthews," she said. "The war is *over*, remember? You're in Simpson Creek, Texas."

She watched him guardedly as Nolan struggled to focus on her, saw when the realization hit him that he'd been dreaming, and when recognition dawned in his sharp blue eyes.

"Ayuh," he said, his voice thick with his "downeast" accent and the remains of sleep. He stood up. "Of course. I...I dozed off for a moment. Just needed a catnap... What time is it?" he asked, rubbing his eyes and then his chin.

"Going on five-thirty."

He blinked, reminding her of an owl.

"Wh-what are you doing here, Sarah? You—you're not ill, are you?" he asked, a touch of anxiety in his voice. He peered at her closely. "Or are you here for someone else?"

"No, I'm not sick, and I'm not here for anyone else," she said, seeing the weariness lining his face, and his pallor. "But you're going to be soon if you don't start taking better care of yourself, Nolan. I—I brought you some soup," she added.

"Soup?" he muttered, looking confused as his gaze fell on her empty hands.

"I left it on the step." She went out to get the pot.

He was alert enough by the time she came back in to open the door for her. "But why—?"

"Because I guessed that you might have been so busy that you weren't taking time to go to the hotel for a proper meal."

"You'd be right about that. I was going to walk down there, after I shut my eyes for a minute...that was an hour ago, I think." He lifted the lid and sniffed the pot's contents, gazing into the mixture of chicken, vegetables and broth like a child might look at a gingerbread house at Christmas. "*Mmm,* still warm." His face relaxed from its tense lines and his mouth broadened into a smile. Then his stomach rumbled, loudly, and they both laughed.

"Sarah, I think you arrived just in the nick of time and probably saved my life," he said. "Will you come into the kitchen and have a bowlful with me?" He took the heavy pot from her and set it on the chair beside him.

She looked at him, wanting to say yes, but knowing it wouldn't be quite proper to be alone with him in his private quarters. She didn't want to keep Prissy waiting for their supper, either, though her friend still hadn't returned from the big house when Sarah came in from the ranch.

"I...I have to get back to the cottage," she said. "Prissy will be waiting for me, and we're to have company, Prissy's cousin." She explained again about the unexpected arrival of Prissy's relatives from Burnet, but unlike when she had told her sister, she told Nolan how Vira Tyler had seemed to be in the early stages of an illness.

"Of all the fool things to do!" he snapped. "The newspaper editor was just telling me today how he's had word that the influenza's hit Burnet badly, and Prissy's aunt's came from there, probably bringing it with her. You must stay completely away from her, Sarah, do you hear? You and Prissy both."

His sharp tone took her aback. "I—I'll try, Nolan, but I don't know if Prissy will. It's her aunt, after all," she said, her tone mildly reproving.

He sighed. "I'm sorry," he said. "I didn't mean to sound as if I was issuing orders. It's just that this influenza's the most virulent I've ever seen, and in case that's what she's got instead of an ordinary catarrh, I don't want your health endangered. Or Prissy's either, for that matter."

The caring in his tone, and blazing from his blue eyes, touched something deep in her soul.

"There are a lot of people stricken with it around Simpson Creek?"

He nodded, his face grave. "There've been a handful of deaths already between Simpson Creek and San Saba," he told her. "People who woke up feeling well enough, just a bit tired, who've been on their deathbeds by the next morning. Mostly old folks, though I've seen plenty younger who were hard hit. It starts with the same sneezing and coughing that you said Prissy's aunt is doing. And like anything contagious, it spreads quickest when people are gathered together. I'm going to have to speak to Reverend Chadwick about canceling church services till this is over."

Her mouth fell open. "Canceling church?" she repeated, aghast at the idea. "How could coming together to pray and sing be harmful?"

His brows knit together and his eyes grew stormy. "Everyone coming to gather in that little building is the very worst thing that could happen. It would only help the sickness spread," he said, as if incredulous that she would have to ask.

He shrugged. "We physicians don't know how illnesses like this spread, only that they do when people congregate together like that. There's no need to make my job that much harder."

The condescension that flavored his Yankee voice

lit a spark of irritation in her. "You might consider that the town coming together to worship could make your job easier," she said.

"And how could *that* possibly be?" he demanded.

"We could pray for you, and for those who were ill," she said. "Or haven't you ever heard of praying for the sick?" There—she could be patronizing, too.

He blinked. "Yes, of course, and I used to believe in it," he said.

"'Used to?'" How could she have forgotten that however friendly they had become, they were poles apart in matters of faith? "You think it's impossible that the Lord could care about an influenza epidemic in a little Texas town?"

His face softened, and his gaze fell. "I…I'm sorry, Sarah. I don't mean to quarrel with you. I fear I'm too tired to remember my manners. Please forgive me."

"Of course," she murmured, seeing anew the lines of weariness that creased his forehead and cheeks. "And I'm keeping you from eating the soup. But before I go, I had another reason for coming," she said. "Prissy wanted me to invite you to come down to the cottage for supper tomorrow," she said. "I imagine you and Anson would have a lot to talk about, since you both served in the war, though of course he was a Confederate. I hope that's not a problem for you?"

In actuality, she thought it might be more of a problem for Anson, so she'd have to make sure he was prepared to be civil to their Yankee doctor.

"And we were going to ask a couple of the Spinsters' Club ladies, those that aren't attached to anyone…" She didn't say other females were being invited to discourage Anson from flirting with her, for she thought Nolan's presence might be sufficient to accomplish that.

His expression told her that he realized the significance of her inviting him somewhere, but it was followed by one of regret.

"I thank you for the invitation," he said, "but even if I weren't on a call when suppertime comes, I have to tell you I think any social gatherings are ill-advised right now, for the same reason I believe church should be postponed for a while."

Her gaze met his, and she saw the pleading for her to understand in those blue depths.

"I suppose you're right," she said with a sigh. "Very well, if Prissy hasn't already invited the other ladies, I'll tell her not to. But I suspect she's afraid Anson will be bored, and go home to his farm, leaving Vira with them for too long a visit," she confided. "Why don't you just come, if you're not on a call? We'll leave the invitation open. You have to eat, and so will Anson," she pointed out reasonably. "We'll understand if you don't stay late afterward, I promise."

"I really think you ought to go back to your ranch till the threat is over."

"I just came from there," she said. "I told Milly not to come into town, since she's expecting, but I can't go running back to the ranch every time something happens."

He sighed. "Very well, I'll be there if I'm able, Sarah. And thank you again for your thoughtfulness," he added, gesturing toward the soup.

Sarah had only gone as far as the millinery shop,

which lay midway between the doctor's office and the cottage, though, when she saw Prissy and Anson coming toward her. Even in the gathering darkness, she could see their faces were grave.

"I'm sorry, did you get impatient waiting on me for supper?" she called. "Didn't you see the note I left that I was delivering some of the soup to Dr. Walker?"

Prissy shook her head. "No, it's not that. We've come to fetch the doctor."

"What's wrong?" Sarah asked, stopping stock-still. She had a feeling she already knew, however.

"Mother's taken very ill, Miss Sarah," Anson told her, his flirtatious manner gone as if it had never been. "She began having shaking chills while we were eating, and Aunt Martha put her to bed with a hot brick at her feet. She woke up with a high fever just a little while ago. And she's short of breath."

"Flora said her forehead was so hot she was afraid the sheets would catch fire," Prissy said, her eyes wide in the shadows. Since both the Mexican housekeeper and Prissy had a penchant for dramatic exclamations, Sarah didn't take the statement at face value, but she knew the situation was serious.

"Mama's staying with her, sponging her forehead and trying to get some willow bark tea into her. Oh, Sarah, please say you found Dr. Walker at home."

Sarah nodded, reversing her direction and beckoning for them to follow. Poor Nolan. He probably hadn't even had time to eat a bowl of the soup before he'd be forced to leave his home once more.

Chapter Fourteen

Too hungry to bother reheating the soup, which was at least still tepid, Nolan was just lifting the first spoonful to his mouth when the bell at the door tinkled yet again.

Smothering a most unphysicianly curse, he let the spoon drop with a clatter back in the bowl and got to his feet. If it was anything less than a dire emergency, he promised himself as he trudged down the connecting hallway that led to the waiting room, he was going to tell whoever had come he'd be along in a few minutes after he'd finished his meal. A doctor had to eat, like everyone else. Or perhaps, if he was required to go some distance, he could put some soup in a big mug and gulp it as he drove. It was better than nothing.

When he recognized Sarah's anxious face in the window, however, thoughts of his interrupted meal fled.

He opened the door quickly. "Sarah? What's wrong?" He saw that Sarah was flanked by a worried-looking Prissy and a somewhat younger man he didn't recognize—her cousin from Burnet?

"Oh, Nolan, I'm so sorry to bother you again so soon, but on my way back to the cottage, I met Prissy and her cousin on their way here. Prissy tells me her aunt's taken very badly since I went out to the ranch this afternoon. Oh…sorry," she added, with an apologetic glance at the other man on the steps. "This is Mr. Anson Tyler, Prissy's cousin. Anson, Dr. Nolan Walker."

"Mr. Tyler," he said, acknowledging the other man, and pretending not to see how Anson Tyler had stiffened at the sound of his voice.

"Please, will you come to the house, Dr. Walker? Aunt Vira's burning up with fever, and she's short of breath—" began Prissy.

But Anson Tyler was putting up a hand to stop his cousin's flow of words. "Prissy, we won't be needing this man's services after all," he snapped, his body rigid, his voice shaking with indignation. "You didn't inform me the man was a Yankee. I won't have him touching my mother, do you hear? I take it there is no other physician in Simpson Creek? I'll escort you ladies to the house, and then I'll saddle a horse and ride for San Saba. There must be a doctor there we can trust."

Nolan felt his temper kindle at the stiff-necked rebel's foolishness. If not for Sarah's and Prissy's presence, he might well have told Anson Tyler to come back when he was prepared to be sensible and closed his door on him.

But before he could say anything, Nolan saw anger storm over Prissy's normally cheerful features. She rounded on her cousin, stamping a tiny booted foot as she exploded. "Anson Tyler, don't be a fool! The war is over and Nolan Walker is a fine doctor!" She shook her small fist at him.

Then Sarah chimed in. "Anson, it would take you an hour or more to saddle up and ride in the dark to San Saba, longer still to return with its doctor, even assuming you could find him. What would you do if you found him gone, out tending some sick person there? You'd lose time your mother may not have!"

Prissy turned her back on Tyler and stepped closer to Nolan. "Please forgive my witless cousin, Dr. Walker—we'd be very grateful if you'd come see what you can do for my aunt."

Sarah looked as if she would very much like to box Tyler's ears, but she turned her pleading gaze on Nolan, too. "Please?" she murmured, and he knew in that moment he could refuse her nothing. He waited for consent from Anson Tyler, though. He could see pride and loyalty to the lost cause of the South warring with filial love and practicality, and he saw the moment the latter virtues won.

"Very well, Priscilla, Sarah, perhaps you're right in this matter," he conceded. "Under the circumstances, I will set patriotism aside *for the moment*—" he said, his dark eyes warning Nolan "—and let this Yankee sawbones see what he can do for my mother. But take care, Yankee—I'm putting you on notice that we'll not accept any stinting in her care."

Nolan set his teeth to prevent a contemptuous retort, saying only "If you'll excuse me, I'll just get my bag."

As he retraced his steps down the passageway, he

heard Prissy snap, "Anson Tyler, if you don't stop being such an *idiot*, I'm never going to speak to you again!"

Nolan grinned. Texas women might appear fragile, but they had backbones of steel, and they didn't suffer fools gladly.

Sarah waited with Prissy, Anson and Mayor Gilmore in the parlor at the foot of the stairs while Mrs. Gilmore accompanied Nolan up the stairs to the guest room where her sister lay. They were gone, it seemed, for an eternity; when he returned to the parlor alone, his face was bleak.

Anson had jumped up when he came into the room. "How's Mother doing? What do you think about her chances, Dr. Walker? You didn't leave her alone, did you?" he asked, with a trace of his previous suspicion.

"She's sleeping at the moment, sir. Your aunt is staying with her while I speak to you. I've given her something for the fever and the cough."

"You can save her, can't you?" Anson pleaded, his eyes wide with dread.

Prissy patted his shoulder soothingly. "If anyone can, he can, Anson."

"I don't know," Nolan said honestly. "Tonight will be critical. Much depends on the lady's constitution."

Sarah thought Anson looked even more frantic when he heard those words. Prissy had already told her that Aunt Vira suffered many ailments, and her heart wasn't strong. The excess weight she carried probably wasn't helpful, either.

"Have you applied a mustard plaster? The doctor in Burnet swears by them," Anson said eagerly.

Nolan shook his head. "I haven't, but when I arrived, the housekeeper informed me she had. I left it on—it will do no harm."

"How about a purgative?" Mayor Gilmore suggested. "Calomel syrup?"

Again, Nolan shook his head. "A lot of physicians use it, but I see no value in a medicine whose chief ingredient is toxic mercury."

"How about bleeding her?" Anson said. "Surely you've thought of that."

Sarah thought she detected a flash of impatience in Nolan's face, but it was gone too quickly to be sure. His next words, uttered flatly, though, tended to confirm what she'd seen.

"The option crossed my mind, yes, but it's my belief it only weakens the patient," he said. "Some of my fellow doctors did it during the war, when they could think of nothing else to do. Their patients died, for the most part."

"But—surely there's something you can *do?*" Anson demanded indignantly.

"Mr. Tyler, in the Hippocratic oath, physicians are instructed 'First, do no harm.' I realize it's difficult to wait out the hours, but I've treated her fever and her cough, and propped her up on pillows so she can breathe more easily. It's called supportive therapy. I will continue to watch over her. After that, it's up to the patient."

"And up to the Lord," Sarah said, startling herself when she realized she had spoken out loud. "I've been praying...I'm sure we all have been," she said, looking around the parlor at the others. "Perhaps we could send for Reverend Chadwick."

"I'll send Antonio," Mayor Gilmore said, getting heavily to his feet. He appeared relieved to have something to do. Anson sank back into the chair, nodding in acceptance.

Nolan's eyes met hers, and in them, she saw gratitude that she had calmed those in the room with her words.

Lord, please, if it's Your Will, save Mrs. Tyler and show Nolan that You are indeed the Great Physician. Help him to realize that You are present, working alongside him.

He was awake, but in that not-fully-focused state in which one part of his mind watched the labored rise and fall of the elderly woman's chest and heard the whistle of her breathing, while the rest of his mind roamed free, visiting the past, pondering the future, when some slight sound—a rustle or the creak of a floorboard behind him—brought him to full alertness.

He turned, and saw Sarah standing there, a candle in its holder in one hand, a plate with a covered bowl in the other.

A glance at the clock told him it was midnight. "Sarah? Sarah, you should not be here," he said softly, rising with the stiffness that long stillness brought and coming to meet her. He'd thought she must have gone back to the cottage long since and be fast asleep.

She came into the circle of light provided by the lamp on the bedside table. "I couldn't sleep," she confessed in a whisper, her gaze going to the woman on the bed. "How is Mrs. Tyler?"

"About the same," he said. "Soon it will be time to give her some more of the willow bark tea, if I can arouse her enough for her to safely swallow. She was cooler for awhile, but now her fever's climbing again. What is this you're carrying?"

"I got to thinking about how you never did get to eat your supper," she said. "I thought I'd warm up some of that soup and offer to sit with her while you eat it."

"Dear Sarah," he said, smiling at her in the flickering light. "You are determined to feed me, aren't you? I'm so tired I'm almost past the point of hunger, but this will be very welcome," he said, taking the plate from her. He saw that there were also sandwiches next to the covered bowl of soup. "But come back into the anteroom, here, and sit with me while I eat. I don't want you exposed to her illness any more than you have already been."

She hesitated. "But Mrs. Tyler—"

"Will be well enough for a few minutes," he finished for her. "I'll be able to hear any change in her breathing from here," he said, gesturing her into the adjoining room, where a small table and a pair of chairs stood.

"Who came in, after I came upstairs?" he asked her. "I heard the door open and close, and voices."

"Reverend Chadwick," she told him. "He's downstairs, keeping a prayer vigil. He said to call him if you needed him."

He absorbed the fact. "He's a good man. Did you tell him what I said about canceling church services?"

She nodded. "He said he'd pray about it tonight. If he does decide to cancel them, he could put out the word around town, but there's always a chance people from the outlying ranches wouldn't hear and would show up anyway."

"But there'd be fewer of them. Did the Gilmores and Mrs. Tyler's son go to bed?" he inquired in between spoonfuls of soup. "Prissy, too?"

She nodded.

"That's good. They're going to need their rest tonight, in order to be strong enough to combat this influenza if and when it strikes them. After being around Mrs. Tyler so closely today, I fully expect one or more or them to come down with it," he told her. "Especially her son, who's been around her from its onset."

"I'll be here to help take care of them," she told him, her gaze meeting his steadily.

She was as brave and selfless as any of the sturdy male assistants who'd served with him in the battlefield tents, he thought, though slender and dainty. No wonder he was falling in love with her.

"I don't want you ill, Sarah, but I may have to take you up on that. So you'd best go now and get some rest yourself, in case I have to call on you for nursing care."

"I will in a minute, Nolan, but before I go, I have a

question for you, something I've been wondering about for a long time now."

"Yes?" He could not imagine what it was, but her lovely face was serious.

"Will you tell me what were you doing in Brazos County, after the war, when you wrote me from there?"

Chapter Fifteen

She saw his blue eyes widen a bit, and thought he was going to assent, but then, from the other room, she heard Mrs. Tyler cough and utter a little moan.

To Sarah's disappointment, he shook his head.

"It's too long a story. There's no way I could summarize it in a few short sentences and send you on to your rest." Then he reached out and took her hand. "But I promise I *will* tell you one day, Sarah, when all this is over. I want to tell you about it."

She would have to be content with that for now.

"All right, Nolan. I'll say good night. Prissy and I will go back to the cottage to sleep, but Mrs. Gilmore told me there's a bellpull by Mrs. Tyler's bed that will summon Flora if you have need of anything. We'll see you in the morning. The guest room's been made ready for you down the hall," she added, pointing. "When I relieve you in the morning, you can sleep."

He shook his head wearily. "I'll have to go back to the office in case anyone else is seeking me."

She nodded, realizing she had forgotten in the last

few hours that many others in and around Simpson Creek were also suffering from the influenza epidemic. How could one doctor take care of all of them? When could Nolan rest?

Her fears must have shown on her face, for he reached out a hand and cupped her cheek. "Don't worry, dear Sarah," he said, in that flat downeast accent she was coming to love. "We doctors learn to doze in chairs, eyes closed, but with our ears attuned to any change. I'll manage. Now go sleep—doctor's orders."

She managed a weak smile at his words and left, sure she would never sleep a wink for worrying.

For God hath not given us the spirit of fear...

She fell asleep praying.

Sarah woke the next morning with Prissy shaking her arm. "Come on, we've got to go to the house."

"Is your aunt—?" Sarah could not put her dread into words.

"She's no better—no worse, either—but Mama and Papa both came down with fever and chills during the night." Prissy's eyes were wide with anxiety. "Anson's wild with worry."

Sarah dressed hurriedly and followed Prissy out of the cottage. On the way, Prissy explained that Nolan had gone back to his office to get more medicine for them and would be back as soon as he could.

Going up the walk into his office, Nolan noticed that there was already a sign posted in front of the church:

SUNDAY CHURCH SERVICE CANCELED
UNTIL FURTHER NOTICE DUE TO INFLU-
ENZA OUTBREAK. PLEASE PRAY FOR
THOSE SUFFERING.

A good, sensible man, the reverend.

Once inside, Nolan bent over his open black bag,
replenishing his supplies of willow bark extract and
morphine, conscious of the need to hasten back to
the Gilmores'. He hadn't been surprised to learn that
the mayor and his wife had come down with the first
symptoms of influenza during the night; it often took
hold quickly like that and this was apparently quite
a virulent epidemic. He was concerned for them, for
neither was young nor of a particularly sound constitution, and Prissy had mentioned her mother had a weak
heart just as her aunt did. Both the mayor's wife and
her sister, he suspected, were subject to dropsy. Perhaps
Mrs. Gilmore and Vira Tyler would benefit from a little
digitalis.

He sighed. There was so little in his bag that really
helped with influenza. He could treat fever and pain,
but after that, it was up to the body to recover—or
not. He refused to buy the patent medicines that were
advertised in the newspapers as the answer to every ill.
He knew they contained little but flavoring and opium
or alcohol. Nor would he use the drugs his colleagues
had relied on but which he knew to be dangerous, such
as calomel.

He was running low on morphine. Simpson Creek
wasn't big enough to boast a druggist's shop, but perhaps he could persuade Anson Tyler to use some of

his nervous energy to ride to San Saba's chemist for some—it would give the man something to do besides pacing the floor outside his mother's room and glaring at Nolan.

A movement at the window caught his eye and he turned his head, but before he could focus on it, it was gone. It may have been only a bird perching on his windowsill, but might it be some patient peeking in to see if he was present before he knocked?

There was no one at the door, however. Going to the side yard where the window was, he looked down the street and was just in time to see a female figure in a green dress disappearing into the Spencers' house.

Had Ada been spying on him through the window? He felt a flicker of annoyance, then pity for the madwoman.

He thought for a moment of going to inquire at the Spencers' to see if they were well, and by so doing make it plain to Ada that she had been seen, but he decided against it. He needed to get back to the Gilmores' house, and didn't have time today for Ada and her pregnancy fantasies.

He didn't wish influenza on his worst enemy, but the thought occurred to him that if Ada Spencer contracted it, he'd at least have the opportunity to examine her— properly chaperoned by her mother, of course—and prove once and for all she was not with child.

For Sarah and Prissy, the day blurred into a nightmare of sponging the feverish Gilmores and Mrs. Tyler with cool water, changing their sweat-dampened sheets and covering them with blankets when the chills rattled their teeth. They made sure the patients were propped up with pillows to help their labored breathing. They emptied basins. Sarah was glad when Nolan sent Anson after some additional morphine, for his constant barging into his mother's sickroom to check on her condition was making Prissy jumpy as a cat.

She supported both women and helped Prissy hold her father in a leaning position while Nolan thumped their upper backs rhythmically. This was called chest percussion, he told them, and helped loosen the mucus that congested their lungs.

It was clear to Sarah from the first, though, that the two women were taken worse than Mayor Gilmore. Though he coughed hard enough to rattle the windows, at least he *could* cough and clear his lungs, while the women both seemed unable to mount a defense against the rattling congestion in their chests and their raging fevers. Though Prissy's father complained of a pounding headache and stabbing pain when he breathed, they only moaned weakly, while he finally drifted into a peaceful, snoring slumber. He was, in fact, asleep when the sun rose the next morning and both Mrs. Tyler and Mrs. Gilmore died within minutes of one another.

Sarah held Prissy while she sobbed, her own tears blending with those of her grieving friend's. Though it had been years since her own mother had died, she clearly remembered the knifelike sorrow that had lacerated her then.

A stricken, pale Anson joined them in the parlor, followed by Nolan. Sarah released Prissy into Anson's embrace.

Nolan caught Sarah's gaze, his eyes somber. "I'll

go notify the reverend," he said. "I'm sorry, Sarah, but I've had word of another influenza patient in town. I'm going to have to go there, but I'll come back when I can."

Numb, Sarah nodded dully.

Flora entered the room, her own eyes already swollen from crying. "Senorita Matthews, I've closed the curtains and hung a black wreath on the door. If you will write the message, I will send Antonio to the telegraph office to notify Senorita Prissy's brothers in Houston and San Antonio of their mother's passing."

Prissy pulled away from her cousin. "They won't be able to come in time. I wouldn't want them to risk their health coming here, anyway. Tell them to stay at home and I'll write when I can."

Sarah saw Anson wince, and guessed he must be wondering if Prissy would eventually blame his mother for bringing the fatal illness into their home, even though there were so many already ill here in Simpson Creek.

"Prissy, why don't you come lie down for a while?" Sarah murmured, urging her friend toward her old bedroom. "As soon as I compose the telegram, I'll sit with your father, and Flora will take care of what's needed for your mother."

To Sarah's surprise, Prissy let herself be put to bed.

The rest of the day, Sarah remained by the mayor's bedside, with Flora and Antonio assisting in his care. She stepped away only to take a little nourishment brought by the housekeeper at noontime. She hoped it wouldn't be left to her to tell the mayor his wife had died, but in the afternoon Mr. Gilmore's fever soared, bringing delirium with it. He was incapable of asking questions.

She was left with a new fear—would he die, too? How would Prissy survive losing both her parents and her aunt?

Nolan returned at five, and was invited to join Sarah and Prissy for a simple cold supper in the dining room of the big house while Anson sat with the sleeping mayor. Now dressed in mourning, a hollow-eyed Prissy ate little and said nothing.

Anson came into the room when they were almost finished.

"Your father's awake, Prissy, and clearheaded. He's asking for you and about your mother," he said. "I—he saw my black armband and asked about it, so I told him…about my mother. I think he's guessed about Aunt Martha, but he'll want to hear it from you."

Prissy rose, looking almost relieved now that the time had come to share the burden of grief with her father. Sarah rose also, intending to go with her as support, but Anson put out a staying hand.

"I'll go with her, Miss Sarah. You look exhausted. Finish your supper, and keep Dr. Walker company." All hostility toward the Yankee doctor appeared to have vanished in the wake of Anson's grief.

Gratefully, she watched Prissy and her cousin go, then turned back to Nolan, only to find him studying her.

"He's right, you know," he said. "The old sergeant who was my surgery assistant would say 'you look as if you've burned all your wood.' Sarah, you must get some rest tonight."

Sarah managed a tired smile. "Thank you, Doctor, but no more so than you. Who was the new influenza patient you went to see today in town, may I ask?"

His brow furrowed. "I'm afraid it's your old friend Mrs. Detwiler."

She uttered a cry of alarm, and would have jumped to her feet, but he took gentle hold of her wrist.

"Sarah, there's no need for you to go charging out of here to nurse her, too. Her family is taking care of her very capably, and she doesn't seem to have a very bad case."

"But she's old…" Sarah said, still gripped by fear for the feisty old lady who had been so opposed to the Spinsters' Club but who had become her and Milly's close friend this past year.

"I imagine if you were to call on her tomorrow you would find her much improved, unless I'm sorely mistaken," Nolan said. "She's already been through the worst of it, and her daughter only just contrived to sneak out to ask me to call on her, just to be certain."

Sarah felt her lips curve up in a smile in spite of the exhaustion that threatened to swamp her. "That sounds like her. Perhaps if I organized the Spinsters' Club ladies, we could provide nursing during the epidemic for those who aren't blessed with families like Mrs. Detwiler's…" she said aloud. Her mind already raced ahead to think how it could be done.

"Sarah, I've been so impressed with how you've shouldered the responsibilities here," he said. "Prissy would have been lost without you. You're quite a lady, do you know that?"

She could only stare at him, for she had felt totally inadequate to the demands and sorrows she had faced this day. She only knew Prissy and her family had needed her, and she was there.

"When I met you," Nolan went on, after taking a sip of the coffee Flora had brought them, "I heard you were a very talented cook but got the impression Milly always made the decisions. It was Milly who ran the ranch, who started the Spinsters' Club…"

"She did," Sarah agreed, not sure what he was getting at.

"I think she will be quite proud to hear what you've taken on here," he said. "But I must tell you, the very first thing I had to learn as an army surgeon was that I could only concentrate on one patient at a time. No matter what they brought in after I had begun to remove a bullet or—well, you can imagine, there were worse injuries—I had to finish what I was doing before I could take on something else."

"What are you saying?" Sarah asked him. She was sure his point must be plain, but her exhausted brain was too tired to glimpse his meaning through the fog that surrounded it.

"Prissy isn't as strong as you," he said simply. "She's just lost her mother, and her father won't be healthy again for a long time. She's going to need to lean on you in the next few days and weeks."

She could only stare at the table, her gaze unfocused, as realization dawned of what Mrs. Gilmore's death would mean. "Prissy won't be able to stay in the cottage—she'll have to move back into the house to look after her father." Her shoulders sagged in discouragement. "I can't stay there alone, so I'll have to move back to the ranch. How can I help her then? Poor Prissy—so much for her learning independence and the housewifely arts. Flora manages everything in the house." Secretly, Sarah felt a little sorry for herself, too. She'd enjoyed living in town with Prissy. And she loved her sister, but Milly didn't need her as she once did.

"I hope you don't have to move back to the ranch, Sarah," he said. He looked as if he wanted to say more, but he didn't. "Nothing needs to be decided tonight. As soon as Prissy retires for the night, please, I want you to, also."

Chapter Sixteen

On the day after Prissy's mother's funeral, Anson left to take his mother home to Burnet to be buried.

During the farewells in the courtyard, Anson said, "Dr. Walker, would you mind if I spoke to Miss Sarah for a moment?"

Sarah saw Nolan blink in surprise, but after darting a glance at Sarah to see if it was all right with her, he nodded slowly.

Anson took Sarah by the elbow and steered her just out of earshot of the others.

"Miss Sarah, I hope you'll forgive me if I speak frankly, since I'm about to leave," he said, gazing down at her, his dark eyes earnest. When she said nothing, he went on. "I—I'm sorry we didn't get to know one another better, that I didn't meet you before you met that Yankee doctor." He nodded toward Nolan, who stood by Prissy's father, who was still so weak he'd been pushed outside in a wheeled chair. Nolan was trying very hard to keep his eyes averted from them, Sarah could tell, but there was a certain tenseness about him that told her he was very aware of them.

She wouldn't have been female if she wasn't at least a little flattered by the ruefulness that tinged the eyes of Anson Tyler, who remained handsome even in his grief. She couldn't help wondering, if she hadn't already met Nolan, if she would have found Anson more appealing. But it was no use pondering the matter. She *had* met Nolan first, and because of that, her heart was already occupied.

"Anson, I—" she began, struggling to find the right words, but he interrupted her quickly as if to spare her.

"But I know I'm leaving you in good hands," he said. "I've come to respect your Dr. Walker. He's a good man, even if he *is* a Yankee."

The admission touched her, for it represented a complete reversal of his earlier, automatic enmity toward Nolan.

"Thank you, Anson. And I believe there's a wonderful lady out there, just waiting for you to find her. Perhaps you ought to come back to Simpson Creek some day—she could be part of our Spinsters' Club."

"Maybe I will." A spark of the charm that was so much a part of Anson Tyler reappeared in his eyes.

Once Anson had departed, and Nolan had helped Prissy's father back inside, Nolan took his leave, for he had many ill people to attend to.

Mayor Gilmore called his daughter and Sarah into the parlor.

Sarah was braced for this talk. Prissy's father would express his thanks for her help nursing the family and for what she had taught his daughter, tell Prissy he needed her in the house and offer Sarah the help of

Antonio and the use of the wagon to move her things back to the ranch.

Mayor Gilmore cleared his throat and dabbed at red-rimmed eyes with a rumpled handkerchief. "Sit down, both of you girls," he said, then waited as they did so. "Your mother was so proud of you, Prissy—proud of how sweet and lovely you are, and especially about all you'd learned in the short time you and Sarah have been living in the cottage. But a little bird told me—" his gaze now wandered to Flora, who stood by the door in case she should be needed "—you thought it was your duty to reside again in the house and take care of your old papa. I want to tell you that I don't feel it's necessary."

"But Papa," Prissy protested, surprised. "Of course I'm going to move back in! I want to look after you!"

"Your mother would not want you to give up all you were learning just to keep an old man company day and night. Flora and Antonio will still be here, and with you living just across the grounds, you're close enough to take suppers with me whenever you like—even cook the meals yourself—right, Flora?"

"Oh, *sì,* senor, I would enjoy the two senoritas taking over the cooking whenever they wish," Flora agreed.

"I have to face the fact my little girl has grown up, just as her brothers did," Mayor Gilmore said, dabbing at his eyes again.

"Oh, Papa, you're the best father a girl could ever have!" Prissy said, throwing her arms around his neck.

Sarah saw a proud tear trickle down the mayor's cheek as he hugged his daughter. "And you're the best daughter. But once this blasted influenza lets up, I need to get back to governing the city, eh? I've got a reelection campaign to run this spring, remember?"

"Oh, Papa, as if any man in town wouldn't vote for you!" Prissy cried.

"Assuming there's anyone left to vote," he added, shaking his head sadly. "At the funeral, I heard Mr. Patterson died the day before yesterday, and Andy Calhoun the day before that."

"And Miss Mary, the millinery shop owner," Prissy said. "And Pete Collier, Caroline Wallace's fiancé. Poor Caroline! Their wedding was to be in March!"

"Reverend Chadwick looks worn to a frazzle," Sarah murmured, mentally saying a quick prayer for the gentle old shepherd of their church.

At least word from the ranch was good, Sarah thought, reaching into her pocket to feel the note Milly had had Isaiah drop off this morning. No one at the ranch had been ill, and she had to think it was because they'd stayed away from town. Isaiah had waited outside while Sarah had written a note back to Milly, then gotten back on his horse and rode out again.

Mayor Gilmore stifled a yawn. "Why don't you girls plan on coming for supper tonight? I've asked Flora to make your favorite tamales, Prissy."

"Wonderful, Papa! We'll be there, won't we, Sarah?"

"Good, good. Right now, though, your old papa is tired and needs a nap."

"That was very generous of your father," Sarah murmured as they walked back to the cottage.

Prissy sighed. "He's being so brave."

Sarah agreed. Even as she mourned for the dead and fretted about the continuing ravages of the epidemic, though, she felt a sense of being reprieved. She would not have to move back to the ranch—*away from Nolan,* her heart whispered.

The thought stopped her short. Hadn't she decided that no matter how she admired his fierce dedication to healing, he was not for her, because he was not a man of faith? But her heart didn't seem to be listening.

"What shall we do this afternoon?" Prissy asked. "I feel as if we've been cooped up in the big house forever. I don't want to sit in the cottage and just think about how I miss Mama. But it's not a good time to go visiting, and all the shops are closed…."

"I had an idea," Sarah told her, remembering the thought she'd first broached to Nolan at dinner after Prissy's mother and aunt had died. Perhaps now was the perfect time to transform her thought into action. "Let's go brew a pot of tea, and I'll tell you all about it."

Prissy thought her idea was wonderful. By suppertime they had visited all the Spinsters in town who weren't already nursing family members or mourning a loss, like Caroline, and enlisted their aid. Then they called on Nolan to inform him. And so the Spinster Nursing Corps was born.

Nolan's first impulse, when he found Sarah and Prissy waiting at his office after he returned from yet another call upon a new influenza victim, was to forbid Sarah to have anything to do with nursing the sick.

She'd done more than enough already in her care for the Gilmores. She was too sheltered, too fragile...*too precious to him*. He did not want her exposed again to the ravages of influenza.

Yet he realized even as his mouth opened to form the words that he couldn't forbid her to do this. He had no authority over her. She'd accepted him as her friend, but he was nothing more to her, and she'd do this thing with or without his blessing, he could tell by the determined jut of her jaw and the warlike glint in her eyes. He couldn't very well permit Prissy to nurse the sick and not allow Sarah to do so, also.

And he had to admit he desperately needed help. Each day brought word of new influenza cases. There were so many down with it in and around Simpson Creek that it was no longer practical to remain at the bedside of each one until they passed the crisis and either gradually got well or developed a fatal pneumonia. He needed capable assistants whom he could trust to watch over feverish patients and dose them with medications according to instructions, and who could judge when it was necessary to summon him back to the bedside. In short, he needed nurses, and here were two young women saying they wanted to be just that, and had enlisted others, too.

He met with them at his office just after sunrise the next morning, and smiled in spite of his fatigue to see the row of earnest-looking young women. All of them were clad in dark, practical clothing, either actual mourning or somber-hued skirts and blouses.

"Good morning, ladies. I'm thankful you're here, and I applaud your dedication to your community and your willingness to place yourselves at risk. You do understand, don't you, that you could be putting yourself in a position to contract the infection?"

To a woman, they all nodded, their faces solemn. His eyes lingered on Sarah, who nodded again, almost imperceptibly. He could imagine what she was thinking—*if I didn't catch it nursing Mr. and Mrs. Gilmore, or Mrs. Tyler, surely I'm not going to.*

"Very well, then, before I send you out," he said, "we shall just cover a few basics, with which some of you may already be familiar." Then he spoke of providing warmth for patients who were chilled, but not over-blanketing them, which slowed down the body's natural cooling mechanism, the specific diet for those able to eat, the brewing of willow bark tea, accurate dosing of the morphine and laudanum he would send with them.

"In regard to these medicines, it is not a case of 'if a little is good for the patient, a lot is better,'" he cautioned the would-be nurses. "These drugs can be deadly if not properly used, so you must adhere strictly to the guidelines I have given you for indications, amount and frequency."

He saw them all taking it in. Sarah and some others took notes.

"Lastly, the most important preventative measure you can take for your own health is to *wash your hands vigorously with soap and water* after touching a patient. If they're able to follow instructions, tell them to cover their coughs and sneezes. And get the proper rest and nourishment. If you fall ill yourself—" He could not look at Sarah as he said those words. Visions of his wife and son, dying so quickly and miserably in the cholera epidemic, swam before his brain. Once again he wished he could forbid her to expose herself to this danger.

He cleared his throat with difficulty. "If you fall ill yourself," he began again, "then someone must nurse *you*, so do not allow yourselves to become exhausted or go without eating and resting. You must let me know immediately if you develop chills, fever, headache or sore throat—promise me, ladies?"

There was an answering chorus of yeses.

"Very well then. We shall move on to assignments. In some cases, I will send you out in pairs if there is more than one family member ill at a residence. In other cases, only one of you will go. Miss Harkey and Miss Thompson, I'd like you to go to the Fedders' house, where both Mr. and Mrs. Fedders are ill. Miss Jeffries, to the Hotchkiss ranch. Miss Shackleford, to Mrs. Brenner..." He allowed himself to look at Sarah again, toying with the idea of asking her to accompany him on calls as his assistant, a way of keeping an eye on her and making sure she did not overtire herself in her zeal to help. But he knew it might cause talk, and worse, she'd see right through his claim of needing a nurse to accompany him and resent his ploy.

"...Miss Gilmore and Miss Matthews, to the Poteets—both the sheriff and his wife are ill."

At this point the bell over the door tinkled, and Nolan looked up to see Reverend Chadwick entering, wearing his care like a heavy frock coat.

He didn't wait to be greeted. "Dr. Walker, I'm sorry to interrupt, but you're needed at the Spencers."

"Ada's ill?" Sarah asked, before Nolan could form the question. "Or is it…"

He knew she was trying to ask whether it was influenza, or her supposed pregnancy, but didn't know how in front of the other ladies, some of whom still believed Ada's story.

"Both her parents have come down with the influenza," the minister said. "Miss Spencer seems…well enough…"

Nolan guessed Chadwick didn't want to add *physically, at least.*

Sarah and Prissy exchanged glances, as did the other ladies. Ada had been their friend and part of the Spinsters' Club, after all, before she had started acting so strangely.

Nolan rubbed his chin. "Well, then, that means a change of plans. I was going to keep you, Miss Bennett, and you, Miss Lassiter, in reserve, to take over when the others need to be relieved or if new cases should arise, but instead I'll need you to come along with me to the Spencers."

He sought and found Sarah's gaze. She would understand why he dare not have her come to the Spencers, after the way Ada had acted toward her at the Gilmores' New Year's Day party. He sensed that her thoughts mirrored his. What might her parents' illness—or worse, their deaths—do to Ada Spencer's already troubled mind?

Chapter Seventeen

Nursing Sheriff Poteet and his wife was much harder than taking care of the Gilmores and Mrs. Tyler had been. At the Gilmores' luxurious, stately home, at least, she and Prissy had had Flora and Antonio to assist them and take over when they needed to rest or take their meals. Here at the sheriff's far humbler abode, which was actually connected to the jail, they were completely on their own, and had only each other to rely on.

They soon developed a system—Sarah kept vigil by the ailing lawman and his wife, dosing them with willow bark tea and morphine and bathing them with tepid water, while Prissy kept chicken broth simmering on the cookstove and boiled the soiled bedding over a fire outside; then they traded off. In the evening, Prissy would go home to check on her father, who continued to progress slowly in his convalescence. During the night one girl slept on a pallet in the small kitchen while the other sat between the beds of the sheriff and his wife, and they'd switch in the middle of the night.

Sarah had not forgotten the middle-aged sheriff's complicity a few months ago with those who would have persecuted the former slaves now working as Matthews Ranch cowhands, but she could not find it in her heart to hold that against him as he struggled for each breath. Each paroxysm of coughing turned his lips blue, a ghastly sight against the florid heat of his face. The once-paunchy man looked sadly diminished in his nightshirt.

"I'm gonna die, ain't I?" he rasped on the third full day they had spent there, after a spasm of coughing left the pillowcase blood flecked.

The sight of the crimson spots made Sarah queasy, but she steeled herself to ignore her churning stomach. She couldn't help the desperately ill man by giving in to squeamishness. "Sheriff, you've got to keep fighting," Sarah said, sponging his sweaty brow. "If we can just get this fever down…" But she feared he was right. He kept coughing, but it didn't seem to relieve the increasing rattling in his lungs.

"Better send fer th' Rev'ren'…got a lot to atone for…I ain't always been the best sheriff I coulda been. Git Mabel in here, will ya?"

"I'll go fetch him, Sarah, and leave a message for Dr. Walker, too," Prissy said. She had just come in the room with a couple of sheets she'd dried in front of the fireplace. Snatching up her cloak, she strode back through the door that led through the jail to the street. Thank God there were no prisoners awaiting trial in either of the jail's two cells. The criminals must be either holed up for the winter or had heard of the influenza outbreak and decided to give Simpson Creek a wide berth.

Sarah noticed Sheriff Poteet hadn't asked for the

doctor. He'd already given up hope, and probably nothing further she said about his recovery would sound convincing.

"Sheriff, your wife's already here—she's sick, too," Sarah reminded him, moving aside so the ill man could see his wife lying on the trundle bed across the room. With some effort, Mrs. Poteet turned on her side and faced them, a tear trickling down her gaunt cheeks.

"Robert, you…got t'…hang on, y'hear?" she said, in between her own spasms of coughing. "I need you… Simpson Creek needs you."

"Dunno…if I can, Mabel," the sheriff mumbled, as his eyes drifted shut. "You been a good wife…"

Those were his last words. He drifted into insensibility and was unaware of Reverend Chadwick's arrival or his bedside prayers. He lasted until sunset. Nolan arrived just as he heaved his last breath.

Out of the corner of her stinging eyes, while she and Prissy did their best to comfort the new widow, Sarah saw Nolan close the sheriff's eyes and cover the body with the bedsheet. She kept Mrs. Poteet shielded against her body while Nolan, aided by Prissy, carried the sheet-covered form out of the bedroom and into the office so the ill woman would not have to witness her husband's removal whenever it took place. Nolan had told her the town's undertaker could hardly keep pace with the number of victims the influenza epidemic had claimed.

When he was done, Sarah left Prissy with their remaining patient and went outside with Nolan into the winter darkness. Fatigued by her ordeal and the overheated bedroom, she'd been craving fresh air and news of the "outside world," as she had begun to think of Simpson Creek, but she longed to spend a moment with Nolan even more.

Their breaths formed clouds in the chill night air.

"Sarah, you look so tired," he said, stepping close and smoothing away an errant strand of hair that had plastered itself to her forehead. "Are you sure you're getting your fair share of rest?"

His fingers felt blessedly cool against her aching head, and it was all she could do not to lean into his caress. Her head pounded and she was too tired to examine the significance of his touch, and why she appreciated it so much.

She nodded. "Oh, Prissy's doing her share and more. In fact, I caught her trying to let me sleep through my shift. She said she couldn't bear to wake me." She gazed up at his earnest face, lit only from the kerosene lamp shining through the jail window. "I wanted to ask you about the Spencers, Nolan. How are they? Is Ada still well?"

His gaze fell, and she knew before he spoke what his answer would be. "Mr. and Mrs. Spencer died this morning, Sarah."

She couldn't stifle the gasp. "Both of them? But what of Ada? Is anyone with her? She didn't catch it, did she?"

Nolan shook his head. "The last time I saw her, she was as she has been, physically hale but still insisting she is pregnant."

Something in his eyes alerted her. "The last time you saw her? What do you mean? Where is she?"

He shrugged. "I wish I knew, Sarah. Mr. Spencer

died first, then his wife, and when I told Ada her mother had expired, she ran out the door, shrieking, and I haven't seen her since. The reverend has a couple of neighbors out searching for her, but though they've caught glimpses of her, running behind houses and dodging down alleys, they haven't been able to get close to her. It's as if she's become a wild creature... We left the house open—I hope when she gets cold and tired enough, she'll come back and take shelter."

Even in the shadows, she could see his eyes were troubled.

"Poor Ada," she murmured. "What will become of her? At least, when her parents were alive, she had a reason to stay around home, people to watch over her and love her...."

He rubbed his forehead. "I wish I knew what was best to do. I'm going to have to speak to the reverend as soon as I can to learn if she has any relatives who could be sent for. If not, I'm afraid an institution may be the only answer."

"How awful." She had a sudden sense of how blessed her own life had been, how relatively carefree, and shivered.

He misunderstood. "You're cold. Let's go back inside," he murmured, gesturing toward the door, but he stopped with his hand on the doorknob. "Sarah, now that the Spencers have died, either Miss Bennett or Miss Lassiter are free to take over here. I believe I'd better send for one of them to relieve you and Prissy—"

Sarah couldn't hide her dismay. "No, not tonight, Nolan, not when Mrs. Poteet's just lost her husband. She's used to us. It wouldn't be right to turn her care over to someone else when her grief is so new, so raw."

"Tomorrow morning then," he said firmly. "I won't have you overtaxing yourself, Sarah. You…you're too important to me."

She froze in the doorway, caught by his words and the intensity in his eyes. "Nolan…"

He raised a hand to ward off her objection. "I know, I know. We agreed not to speak of this. But I won't let you endanger yourself any more than you already have, Sarah."

Her eyes stung with unshed tears. Her throat felt thick with words she wanted to say. "I…that is, thank you, Nolan. For caring about my welfare."

"I would do more than *care*, Sarah. You know that."

Impulsively, she reached out a hand and touched his cheek, bristly with the beard he hadn't taken time to shave this morning. "Yes. I know, and I—" She caught herself, not wanting to blurt out something she hadn't thought through. "We'll talk, Nolan, when this is over…."

He covered the hand that still cupped his cheek. "Yes, we will. It seems we're always postponing our talks."

"You can send Faith or Bess over tomorrow morning, and Prissy and I will go home and rest, I promise. Mrs. Poteet needs us with her tonight."

He gave in with a sigh, perhaps recognizing she was right.

When he had gone, Sarah returned to the bedroom where Prissy sat with Mrs. Poteet. Nolan had given the woman a sleeping draft, and she snored softly now, her breathing still labored and congested, but clearer than it had been yesterday. Her fever had been down all evening. Mrs. Poteet would recover, Sarah realized, though in her grief, there would probably be times the sheriff's widow would wish she had died, too.

Prissy studied her in the lamplight. "Go lie down for a while, Sarah," Prissy said. "I'll sit up with her. You look done in."

She wanted to argue, to point out that her friend looked just as tired, but she ached in every bone, and her head was throbbing. Maybe a few hours of sleep was a good idea. "As our old foreman Josh would say, I feel tired as a mule that walked a mile in spring mud. But—"

Prissy interrupted. "I'll come wake you when it's your turn, I promise." She made shooing motions with her hand. "Now *go*."

Nolan laid down the straight razor and rinsed the remaining soap from his face, then straightened and studied his image in the mirror above the basin to make sure he'd hadn't missed any spots.

After restocking his black bag, he'd slept straight through the night, for no one had come to summon him. It was the first time he'd had a solid night's sleep since the influenza had struck. Was it too soon to hope the epidemic was starting to abate?

He'd stop first by Miss Bennett's to ask her to relieve Sarah and Prissy, and then he'd drive around in his buggy, checking on all his influenza patients to make sure they were recovering. Pneumonia was always a threat in the wake of influenza, especially if a person tried to rise from his bed too soon....

Then he heard the light thudding footsteps running up the stairs, followed in short order by pounding at his door.

He grimaced. *No, the epidemic isn't over yet,* he thought, striding down the hall to his office. This would be yet another frantic relative of a new influenza victim, reporting that his wife, or her pa, or grandma, or child, was coughing and feverish....

Through the side window, he saw that it was Prissy standing on his porch, her shoulders heaving with her efforts to catch her breath, her eyes wide in her flushed face.

He threw open the door. "Prissy, is Mrs. Poteet worse?"

She shook her head, still panting. "Nolan, you've got to come! I-it's *Sarah!*"

Chapter Eighteen

"She's coughing and her forehead is so hot…and she says her chest and her head hurt…"

"Sarah?" An icy fist seized his heart and squeezed it. *No, it can't be.* He'd just seen her last night, and while she was clearly fatigued, her eyes had been clear and she hadn't mentioned any discomfort… But it was often thus, he reminded himself. A person went to bed merely tired, and woke up ill. Sarah might not have recognized the first symptoms, the aching bones, the throbbing headache, as being anything more than fatigue.

"When did it start?" he demanded, mechanically throwing on his coat and spotted his doctor bag where he'd left it by the door, his mind racing ahead.

"She took over for me at Mrs. Poteet's bedside about midnight, and she didn't mention anything…but when I woke up this morning, I heard this steady rattling from the floor in the bedroom… It was her chair, Nolan, shaking from the force of her shivering in it!"

"I'll go to Sarah," Nolan told Prissy as they rushed out of the office. He had grabbed an umbrella from the tall hook on the wall as he left and handed it to Prissy. Big fat raindrops had begun to fall, and one landed with chilly precision on his left ear.

"Would you run home, please, and tell Flora to pre-pare a sickroom for Sarah, then go to Miss Bennett or Miss Lassiter—whoever's closer—and tell her to come to the Poteets' to take over there as quickly as she can? You may return home as soon as your replacement's arrived, but be sure to bathe and change your clothes before you come in contact with your father—we don't know what might trigger a relapse."

"Do you want Antonio to hitch up the carriage to bring Sarah down to the house?"

Nolan nodded as they reached the street. "I could carry her there quicker, but getting drenched in this cold rain is the last thing she needs. Tell him to hurry!"

They ran their separate ways in what was now a downpour. Fear lent wings to his feet, and in his head-long rush, he skidded into an icy puddle between the hotel and the mercantile, lost his balance and fell flat in the mud. Heedless of the mud that now splotched both coat and trousers, he picked himself up and rushed on.

Within seconds of arriving at the Poteets', his eyes confirmed the truth of Prissy's report. Sarah lay propped up on the Poteets' horsehair sofa in their sit-ting room, swathed in a thick blanket, her eyes slitted open and dull with fever. A hectic flush bloomed on each cheek.

Her teeth chattered against themselves. "C-c-*cold*," she muttered when the sound of his footsteps caused her to open one eye a trifle wider. "Tell N-Nolan... sorry."

She doesn't even recognize me.

"I *am* Nolan, sweetheart," he said, "and you have nothing to apologize for. I'm going to take good care of you," he told her, leaning down close so she could see him. "You're going to be fine, sweetheart," he promised, though he had no idea if he was telling the truth or not. He reached out a hand and touched her forehead, intending only to brush away a lock of damp, dull gold hair plastered there, but it was like touching the inside of a pot from which boiling water has just been poured.

He wanted to wrap another blanket around her, scoop her up in his arms and run out of the house, but the rain still drummed steadily on the tin roof overhead, and he forced himself to remain calm and wait for the promised carriage. Reaching in his black bag, he pulled out his stethoscope and listened for a moment, hearing the rhonchi, abnormal whistling sounds, and rales, a noise that proclaimed congestion in the breathing passages.

"Do you think you could drink some willow bark tea?" he asked her. "I'll just go set the kettle on the stove."

"I'll...t-try...but wh-what...about Miz...P-Poteet...?"

"I'll check on her," he promised, but he put the kettle on to boil before he did so.

The sheriff's widow opened her eyes when he peeked into the bedroom. They were reddened and puffy from weeping and her sallow features wan, but the light of full awareness shone from them.

"Doctor..."

"How are you today, Mrs. Poteet?" he said, forcing himself to come to the bedside and inspect her more closely when all he wanted to do was go back to Sarah.

"Better...." she rasped. "Sorry...Sarah's sick now...."

He had left his stethoscope in the other room, but he could tell even without it that her breathing was much less labored than it had been yesterday. Sarah and Prissy had nursed her back from the brink, and now it might cost Sarah her life.

"I'm going to take good care of her," he promised again. "You just rest, Mrs. Poteet. With some watchful nursing, I believe you'll be just fine. Miss Bennett or Miss Lassiter will be here in a few minutes to help you."

Sarah had fallen into slumber by the time he returned with the tea. He had to shake her awake to take it, and when she drank the hot brew, her teeth rattled against the crockery cup. *Where is Antonio with that carriage?*

Oh, God, make him hurry! He was hardly conscious of addressing the Lord, whom he had not talked to since his wife had died—except when he had prayed, in vain, that Jeff be made well. *And please heal Sarah. Don't let her die like You did Julia and Timmy, please...*

While he waited, he laid Sarah out more fully on the couch, yet keeping her propped up so she could breathe, and pushing up the sleeves of her blouse, bathed her arms, her face and her neck in tepid water to bring down the fever. Sarah seemed barely aware of his efforts, her only reaction to shiver as the heat of her skin evaporated the moisture left by the cloth almost before he could dry it. Was he winning against the heat that burned within her, or merely keeping pace with the inferno?

"Please, Lord, let her live. Take me instead," he prayed aloud, willing the carriage to appear, along with one of the other Spinsters.

It seemed an eternity before the creak of wheels and the slowing *splosh* of hoofbeats heralded the arrival of the mayor's brougham.

For Sarah, the day passed in a series of confusing, unfocused images—being swaddled in blankets and carried outside, the rhythmic turning of carriage wheels, the soft touch of feminine hands as she was undressed and placed in sweet-smelling, warmed sheets, of Nolan's "Downeast" accent as he barked out orders for cool water, another blanket, willow bark tea. She heard Prissy's voluble chatter, too, shrill with fear, Flora's melodious Spanish…and was that Milly's worried voice? But how could that be? Hadn't she firmly told her sister to stay on the ranch, away from the contagion that plagued Simpson Creek?

She was aware of each breath rattling in her lungs, shaking the thick fluid that threatened to smother the life-giving air, the knifelike pain with each inhalation that stabbed into her ribs like thin spears heated over a fire, the paroxysms of coughing that racked her body until she had to stop and gasp for air so she had the strength to cough some more, the headache that was like a white-hot hammer pounding on a red-glowing anvil, producing multicolored sparks that flared against her eyelids. Her throat felt like a raw wound that had been rubbed with salt, too sore to swallow the liquids that she nevertheless sucked down greedily whenever she was awake enough to take them. She had to have water, for her skin felt like the parched sand of the desert, and then, in the next instant, she felt as if she lay in a snowbank, with more feathery-cold flakes drifting down on her, her skin turning blue against the icy crystals.

Then the fever soared even higher, and the voices around her faded, and other voices and figures swam hazily into view—her mother, her father, smiling at her. She saw a figure standing with them, and wondered if it was Jesse, her dead fiancé, and whether she would see him soon.

Then she looked closer, and saw that it was not Jesse—the Figure that stood between her father and mother was much taller, and wore a long robe so dazzlingly white between them that she couldn't look at Him, but she knew who He was. He smiled, too, but He held up a nail-scarred palm.

"Not yet."

And she knew nothing more for a while, sinking back now into a dreamless sleep.

Later, the voices she knew swirled around again— the voice of Reverend Chadwick, praying and reading aloud from the Psalms, and Prissy's voice, saying she'd heard that, sometimes, the only way to decrease a fever for a woman was to cut her hair as close as possible to the scalp. The idea was so horrifying to her that she raised up, swinging and shrieking, until she heard Nolan's voice promising they wouldn't cut her hair if she'd only calm down, for her frenzy was raising her fever still higher.

Then darkness fell—for the first time? the second? the third?—and the light in the room was reduced to the glowing circle cast by the single lamp on the bedside table. Her bones ached as if someone was grinding them to powder, inch by inch. At intervals, liquid was trickled down her throat. Sometimes the liquid was bitter, and though the pain slid into the background then, the sleep that followed was full of horrifying images—of the terrifying, war-painted faces of attacking Comanches splashing across Simpson Creek on their Paint ponies, of arrow-studded, bloody bodies of the Indians' victims….

"Are you praying, Reverend?" she heard Nolan's voice, the vowels flat and harsh, demand. "Why isn't she getting better? Why isn't your God doing something to bring her out of this? Doesn't He care?"

"Are *you* praying, son?" came Chadwick's gentle answer. "We all need to be praying, I think."

"Oh, He doesn't want to hear from me, Reverend, I promise you. If He did, He wouldn't have let Julia and Timmy die in that horrifying way."

"'Julia and Timmy?'"

"My wife and son. They died in a cholera epidemic. Have you ever seen someone die of cholera, Reverend? You'd never—" she heard his voice catch "—forget it…"

Is Nolan crying?

"Easy, son, easy…it's going to be all right," she heard Chadwick say, his rusty old voice soft and soothing.

"No, it won't, Reverend," Nolan snapped. "It wasn't all right for them, or for so many of the men I tried to save, men in blue *and* gray—I didn't care! It wasn't all right for Jeffrey Beaumont… No, He doesn't listen when *I* ask. I'm nothing to Him."

He expected the preacher to challenge him on his last remark, but instead Chadwick asked, "Who's Jeffrey Beaumont, Nolan?"

"A colonel who was brought to my tent during one of those last battles, after the war should have been long over, but it wasn't yet. He wore gray, Reverend—I cut away what was left of his uniform and found a minié ball had penetrated his spine. He couldn't move his legs. He begged me to let him die, but I wouldn't listen. Maybe I should have…"

"So he lived?"

She heard Nolan's short, harsh laugh. "He lived. Long enough for them to threaten to haul him off to Libby or someplace like it where he'd just lie there, helpless, until some fever took him. I held them off at gunpoint one time, and told the pair who came for him I'd send them both to perdition before I'd let them take him. Jeffrey and I had become friends by that time, you see."

"Yes, I can well imagine," the minister said. "I'd want such a staunch defender as a friend, too."

"He told me he knew he was going to die, but he just wanted to get home to Texas. I couldn't imagine what difference that made…I hadn't been home to Maine since the war broke out and I'd seen so many states by then I couldn't even remember where I was by that time. I told him that he wasn't going to die, that with some devoted nursing care he could live out his life in a wheelchair, though it was sure he'd never walk again. He told me there was no one at home who could do that for him—his parents were dead, you see—but he wanted to make it to Brazos County. He said he'd die happy if he could take his last breath under that big cottonwood tree on the bank of the Brazos River that flowed past his land."

"So what happened?"

"About the time I was sure they were going to court-martial me and ship him off to prison by force, the war ended, and I resigned my commission and told Jeffrey Beaumont I was taking him home. So I rode with him on the train, and took care of him. Sometimes I had to defend him against arrogant Federals who wanted to take his seat on the train—for I had to purchase extra space for him so he could lie down. Other times, once we left the train and were traveling over the road, he had to tell suspicious Southerners that the Yankee with him was trying to help him reach his home."

So that's what he'd been doing in Texas, Sarah thought, and felt guilty about all the times she'd imagined him being part of the occupying troops, or some sort of carpetbagger....

"So you took him home," the minister's voice gently prodded.

"Yes. I took him home to Beaumont Hall, his plantation on the river. And I met his cousins and his elderly aunt, who wept on my shoulder and thanked me for bringing him home. We were there for weeks, and he was doing well. He could still use his hands, even if his legs were becoming withered and contracted, despite my efforts to exercise them and massage them. He'd gotten used to his chair on wheels, and the necessity of accepting help with so many everyday things...." Nolan's voice trailed off as if he was remembering.

A moment passed, and then he went on. "The girl he loved chose to marry another man, a man who could walk and ride and give her children, and he didn't become bitter—he accepted it with such grace and generosity...he even gave them his blessing." Again, the bitter laugh.

"He sounds like a very good man."

"He was. A better man than I'll ever be, Reverend."

"'Was'?"

"Was," Nolan confirmed. "He died, Reverend. A fever took him, and nothing I did made any difference. Not even when I prayed for him. He died just as he wanted to, under that cottonwood tree on the banks of the Brazos River."

Chapter Nineteen

"So that's how you came to the great state of Texas," Pastor Chadwick murmured, when Nolan finished speaking.

"Yes," Nolan said. He lowered his gaze to Sarah, lying so flushed and still, her eyes closed, her perspiration-damp hair confined in a dull yellow braid lying beside her on the pillow. He wondered what she would have thought of his tale. "Jeff was the brother I never had, and a better friend than any I'd met among those wearing blue."

"And yet, once your responsibility to your friend, the Confederate colonel, was ended, you didn't return east to your home."

Nolan shrugged. "Oh, I could have gone back to Maine, I suppose—a medical college there had already sent me word that they'd love to have a physician of my experience teaching medicine. I'm sure my experience as a battlefield surgeon would have benefited the medical students. But Maine didn't feel like home anymore."

"So you remained in Texas," Chadwick prodded gently.

Nolan shook his head. "By that time, I'd grown to love Texas…her vastness, her big sky, her interesting, warmhearted people with their drawling accents…Jeff told me about mountains here, and tropical palm trees, and deserts, and it made me curious. I'd like to see the rest of it someday." He sighed. "I knew Jeff would never be the one to show me. He had been growing more frail for a long time, but rather than admit to myself that he was going to die, I buried my head in whatever books and newspapers were available…."

He glanced back at Sarah then, for it was the part of the tale where she began to be the reason for his stay, but she just lay there, her shoulders rising and falling beneath the sheet, her breathing harsh and labored. Pearls of sweat beaded on her forehead. As soon as he finished telling this saga, he would have to see if he could rouse her enough to sip some more fever-reducing tea—perhaps verbena this time.

Chadwick's eyes remained bright with interest, so Nolan went on. "And in one of those newspapers, I saw an advertisement for the Simpson Creek Society for the Promotion of Marriage."

Chadwick's lips broadened into a smile. "Ah, the Spinsters' Club. The advertisement piqued your interest?"

In spite of the apprehension that held him in its icy grip, Nolan chuckled. "I admired their pluck in seizing the initiative, to advertise for what they wanted— husbands—rather than staying meekly at home and waiting for them to simply show up on their doorsteps.

I thought if one of these spirited women would have me, she might make a good doctor's wife, and I'd take it as a sign that I belonged here. I sent an inquiry. And in a couple weeks or so, Miss Sarah Matthews started corresponding with me."

He'd lived for those letters, he remembered. He'd imagined meeting and marrying Miss Sarah Matthews, and bringing his bride up to meet his friend at Beaumont Hall. But the visit was not to be—Jeff died, despite Nolan's care and desperate prayers, and once he was gone, there was no real reason for Nolan to remain at Beaumont Hall. The "Spinsters' Club" had invited him and a couple other candidates to come for Founders' Day. He'd ridden southward, knowing Sarah Matthews would be as beautiful in person as she was interesting in her letters, and hoping she would not hate him because he was a Yankee.

"Thank you for telling me, Nolan," the preacher said, rising stiffly. "It's getting late, so perhaps I'd better be going, though of course you can send me word at any hour if you need me."

"Thank you, Reverend. Be careful going home tonight—Antonio said the temperature had dropped, so watch for icy patches in the street."

"I'll do that, thanks. And know that I'll be praying."

Nolan rose with him. "When you do, perhaps you could ask that no one else will need a doctor around here tonight." He wasn't sure he'd be willing to leave Sarah's side, not even if the most experienced doctor in the world could take over.

"I'll do that, son—"

Just then, a harsh, gutteral cry erupted from the woman on the bed. Her spine arched like a tightly drawn bow.

"She's having a seizure!"

Sarah's slender frame threw itself into a racking series of alternating contractions and relaxations. The bed frame thudded in a horrible rhythm against the wall with the force of the convulsion.

Nolan's hand dived to her forehead, and flinched as he felt the heat there. She was as hot as if the very sun had taken up residence within her.

"Dear God!" Chadwick cried.

"Help me turn her on her side, Reverend!" he said, fearful that Sarah would choke.

Prissy ran into the room, perhaps drawn by the noise of the bed shaking, and screamed when she saw Sarah convulsing.

"Prissy! Go out and see if there's ice in the rainbarrel—or in a water trough in the stable. I need it to get her fever down!" Nolan wasn't even sure if she could get it in time to help her friend, but he sure couldn't think with Prissy's shrieking reverberating in his ears.

He was dimly aware of the preacher trembling and sinking to his knees on the other side of the bed, his hands clasped, his head bent.

The seizure went on for an eternity, though in actuality it probably only lasted thee minutes. Then her body sagged in limp exhaustion and a faint pink crept back into Sarah's chalky, blue-white lips. Nolan felt engulfed by hopeless despair flooding through him. It was never good when a fever soared so high the patient convulsed.

He was going to lose her. Perhaps he should have let Prissy cut her hair…

"Reverend, please, pray harder!" he whispered desperately. It was all he knew to do.

Chadwick raised his head, the silver hair gleaming in the lantern light. "*You* pray, too!" he commanded, his voice gentle but strong as granite.

"But I can't… He doesn't listen to me," Nolan protested, knowing he'd said it before. Hadn't the old preacher been listening?

"Hogwash!" Chadwick retorted, his eyes burning a hole into Nolan's soul. "He's *always* heard you. Sometimes the answer is 'wait.' Sometimes it's 'no,' and we won't know this side of Heaven why that is, but He's always heard you, son. The answer may be 'no' this time, too, but it sure doesn't hurt to ask Him—and it would help *you*. I know our prayers together would be stronger than any I can say alone—and stronger still if you believed in the One you're talking to."

Nolan felt his knees bending as if of their own volition, and he sank down by the bedside opposite Chadwick and bowed his head, too.

"Lord, please," was all he said at first, but he knew he couldn't leave it at that. "I don't have any right to come to You, I know that," he went on, his voice hoarse and ragged with the desperation of his need, "but the reverend here says it's all right to ask. I'm begging, even. Please save my Sarah. Take me, if You want to, but please heal her. I…I'll accept Your decision if the answer is no—at least, I'll do my best to—but please save her. I guess I've never *not* believed in You…but I just didn't think You cared one way or the other about me or anyone I loved. Reverend Chadwick says You do care, and I've got to believe that. Please, Lord, save Sarah...." He felt the tears, thick in his throat, hot on his face.

"Nolan, I've got ice!" Prissy shouted from the stairway, and ran into the room, her breath heaving her shoulders. She carried a huge bowl of chunks of ice. Her fingers were wet and blue. She'd apparently broken it out of the rain barrel or trough and fished it out with her own hands.

Nolan rose. "Get me some thin cloth, please—handkerchiefs, rags, whatever you have."

Prissy ran from the room and returned with a two or three delicate lawn handkerchiefs. He wrapped the cloths one layer thick around the chunks so that the ice wouldn't directly touch Sarah's skin, and with Prissy helping him, he stroked the ice over Sarah's forehead, her arms, her neck.

His prayers were silent now, but he continued them. *Lord, please, save Sarah. You are the Great Physician, after all. I'll do anything You want, just save her, please.*

Will you serve Me, Nolan? No matter what happens?

Yes, Lord. I'm Yours, from now on.

Gradually, he felt a peace descending, relaxing his shoulders, quieting his pounding heart. He let his forehead relax against the side of the bed.

He must have dozed for a few minutes, for he awoke to Prissy gently shaking his shoulder.

"Go lie down for a while, Nolan. You're exhausted."

He shook his head vehemently, his gaze flying to the

motionless figure on the bed. "No, I can't, she might have another convulsion—"

"No, she's cooler now, see?" Prissy said, as he reached out a shaking hand to touch Sarah's forehead to verify her words. "I'll watch over her, and I won't close my eyes even for a second, I promise. I'll call you if there's *any* change, no matter how small."

He wanted to argue, but he was too fatigued to form the words, and let her lead him to the guest room down the hall.

Sarah felt like a swimmer who had dived deep into a silent, bottomless pool, now rising slowly to the surface, but not by any efforts of her own, for she was too weak to use her arms to propel herself upward. As if from a great distance, she heard Nolan pleading for her rescue. And then Someone was calling her, telling her to let go, to float to the surface.

Her head still throbbed, her throat remained like sandpaper, but the inferno within had banked its fires. She lay there for an endless time, trying to recall where she was, and what she'd been doing before her body had betrayed her and surrendered to illness.

She had been at the Poteets' home. The sheriff had died. Nolan had been there… She remembered her insistence on staying the night to help the widow, and her first suspicions that all was not right within her….

Tentatively, she opened an eye, squinting against the flaring light of the candle.

"It's about time you came around, Sarah. You've given us all quite a scare," Prissy said.

* * *

Prissy had just finished helping her brush her hair, wash her face and put on a pretty robe when Nolan entered the room the next morning.

"See? I told you that she was better," she crowed, grinning.

"So you did," Nolan said, his gaze fastened only on Sarah. "How do you feel, sw—Sarah?"

He'd been about to call her *sweetheart*. The thought sent hot color racing up into her cheeks and her gaze dropped shyly into her lap against the earnest intensity of his blue gaze.

"Like a butterfly left out in the desert after it's been trampled by a maddened bull," she confessed, smiling and raising her eyes to him again. "I hurt *everywhere*, Nolan, but not as bad as I did yesterday. And I can't seem to get enough to drink," she added, glancing longingly at the water pitcher on her bedside stand.

He took the hint, and poured her a glass of water, sitting down in the nearby chair as if his knees were suddenly wobbly.

"Thank God," he breathed, his eyes suspiciously wet.

"Ah, the senorita is much improved today, *sì?*" Flora called out as she entered the room, bearing a tray of steaming broth. "I expect she might be ready for some soup, eh? You eat that, Senorita Sarah, and I will bake you my best *pan dulce,* no?"

"Yes, *please,*" Sarah said. "I can't think of anything I'd like more."

Flora turned to Prissy, saying, "Mees Prissy, your papa wants to see you. Probably he wants to hear how

Mees Sarah fares, eh? Shoo now, I will stay with her," she added, nodding toward Sarah and settling into a chair.

She had appointed herself as her duenna, Sarah realized, amused, because after a glance in the mirror Prissy had brought, she thought she could hardly be considered a female in need of being chaperoned, with her bloodshot eyes, her hair in a lank braid and her skin pale as milkweed blossoms. She wished she could have had a bath, she thought, even though she realized she would have been too weak to get in and out of it.

"Sarah, I…" Nolan seemed unsure of what to say, which he had never been before. "I…well, I thought you should know that seeing you like this is an answer to prayer."

She blinked. "I heard you," she said, even as she realized the fact. "Thank you…"

"I meant every word," he told her. "Even if you… well, if you had not…not survived, Sarah…" He looked away, as if he needed to collect himself. "I said I would believe. But I asked Him to save you, and He did. And now that He has, I'm going to need your help on this road of believing, Sarah."

She reached out her hand to him.

Chapter Twenty

It was a week before Sarah felt strong enough to leave the big house for their little cottage on the Gilmore grounds. During that time Nolan came to check on her twice every day, morning and evening. At first he seemed fearful when he came into the room, as if he worried that the progress she had made since his last visit—eating solid food, initially getting out of her sickbed, being able to sit up in a chair for longer and longer periods, descending the stairs to eat in the dining room with Prissy and her father—had been only a dream, and he would find her once again lying helpless and insensible, burning with fever. But as each day drew to a close, she grew stronger and coughed less. The bone-deep aching ceased. The anxious look in his eyes each time he beheld her faded.

He stayed only briefly in the mornings, for although the number of new cases in and around Simpson Creek was decreasing, those whom influenza held in its awful grip were still very ill, and some of them died. Every morning Nolan saw the undertaker and his assistant digging new graves in the church cemetery. And of course, the more ordinary business of a small town doctor continued, as he treated illnesses, broken bones, headaches, belly pains and wounds.

Sarah slept much during the first few days after passing the crisis, letting her body regain its strength. Then sometimes she was wakeful during the night, and she passed those hours praying for those she loved and reading the books Prissy would bring her from her father's library.

In the evenings, after his house calls were finished, he left a notice on his office door that he could found at the mayor's house, and came to spend a few hours with Sarah, cheering on her progress and telling her about his day. Sometimes Prissy sat with them, sometimes she left them discreetly alone, though she was always nearby.

They spent time, during his evening visits, reading the Bible together and discussing what they had read. He had questions, and she did her best to answer them, though sometimes she had to suggest Reverend Chadwick might be able to explain a point of doctrine better than she could.

The day came when she was finally strong enough to make the short journey across the grounds to the cottage, leaning on Prissy for support. When Nolan came that night, they celebrated with a meal that Prissy had cooked of Sarah's favorites, fried chicken, blackeyed peas, biscuits and apple custard pie.

Nolan was pleased to see that Sarah's appetite, which had been poor when she first left her sickbed, had returned and she was enjoying her food. The pink was returning to her cheeks, too, and the golden gleam to her lovely hair—thank God they hadn't cut it.

"That was wonderful, Prissy," Nolan praised, when he finished his dessert. "You've turned into quite an excellent cook."

Prissy beamed with pleasure. "I *have* come a long way from the girl who couldn't figure out how to light the oven, haven't I, Sarah?"

"That you have. Pretty soon you won't need me at all," Sarah said with a laugh.

Prissy chuckled. "Not so fast! Nolan, she still has to sit there and help me figure out how to get everything ready at the same time," she confessed, rising. "And now why don't you two go over and sit by the fire, while I redd up these dishes?"

Nolan was glad to comply, and assisted Sarah to the horsehair couch. He suspected Sarah only pretended to need to lean on his arm, and the knowledge that she liked doing so warmed him inside.

"Is that a new dress?" he asked, indicating the flower-sprigged lavender dress she wore. "It's beautiful." *You're beautiful,* he thought, loving the way her green eyes glowed at the compliment.

She nodded. "Milly brought it by—though I distinctly remember telling her to stay at the ranch until the epidemic was completely over. But she said she'd had time on her hands out there on the ranch, so she made this to celebrate my recovery."

"I haven't seen any new cases today," he told her, "and no one awakened me through the night. I think this epidemic is finally on the wane. I believe among those who still have it, all should recover."

"Thank God."

He nodded his agreement. "And thanks to the Spinster Nurses," he said. "I appreciate you organizing them to help. But you know what I *did* see today, Sarah? Buds on the trees! And Mrs. Detwiler has crocus and tulips beginning to poke up through the soil in her flower beds! And it's only February! Back in Maine, the ground would still be covered in a foot of snow!"

Sarah laughed. "I like your appreciation for our Texas weather, Yankee doctor. Let's see if you're still so enthusiastic about Texas summers."

It was an unspoken acknowledgment, he thought, that he had come to stay. Her amusement lit her entire face.

Then her expression sobered. "Nolan, have you seen Ada around town?"

He nodded. "In the mercantile, just today. She was dressed in mourning—not the loose garments she'd been wearing lately."

Nolan saw the spark of hope light her eyes. "Did you speak to her? Are you saying she's returned to her right mind?"

He hated to douse that spark. "Yes, I spoke to her. I asked her how she'd been feeling lately, and she announced that the influenza had caused her to lose our baby, though she knew I'd be relieved to hear it."

"Oh, *Nolan!*" she cried, putting out an impulsive hand to touch his arm in sympathy. "Did anyone hear her?"

"Only the three ladies gossiping by the pickle barrel. I don't think I've met them. They gave me scandalized looks as I departed."

"Surely Mrs. Patterson set them straight after you left," she declared with a confidence he was far from feeling. "I know she was one of others who realized Ada's stories were moonshine from the start."

He sighed. "I don't know if Mrs. Patterson even heard them. She seemed more than a little absent-minded when I paid for my purchases. She even called me Doc Harkey."

Sarah remembered Mr. Patterson had been one of the influenza victims. "The poor woman. She and her husband were married for thirty years."

The clock on the mantel chimed nine times, and Nolan rose. "It's late. I'd better go."

"I'll walk you to the door."

He had hoped she'd say that. "Do you think you'd feel strong enough to go to church with me on Sunday?" he asked, when they reached the shadowy vestibule.

Her face lit with pleasure. "Oh, Nolan, are they holding services again?"

"I told the reverend I thought it'd be safe by then. He told me to tell you not to worry about the music just yet—we can sing without the piano this week." He couldn't imagine a better way to start attending church again than with her sitting in the pew next to him.

"I have three days to gather my strength, then," she said with a grin, for it was Wednesday evening. "Shall I meet you there?"

"No, I thought I'd pick you up, and then we'd have dinner in the hotel and perhaps go for a buggy ride afterward, weather permitting. We can look for more signs that spring is on its way."

Her eyes sparkled, though he wasn't sure if it was

at the prospect of escaping the indoors, returning to church or spending time with him. He hoped it was at least a combination of the three.

"I can hardly wait," he said, meaning it. At church, the town of Simpson Creek would finally see them as a courting couple. Perhaps that meadow west of the creek would be the perfect setting for their first kiss.

"Oh, Nolan, neither can I!" she exclaimed, and before he knew what she was about, stood on her tiptoes and kissed him.

Ah well, if his Sarah decreed their first kiss should be now, who was he to want to postpone it till Sunday? He returned her kiss with enthusiasm, savoring the honey sweetness of her mouth.

When they drew apart at last, he looked down at her and said, "Good night, sweet Sarah."

"Until Sunday," she whispered.

She dreamed of Jesse that night, her fiancé who'd never returned from the war.

She faced the gaunt, hollow-eyed figure in the ragged gray remnants of a uniform.

"It's time," she told him. "I loved you, but now I have to go on." She was relieved to realize she didn't feel guilty.

That was what it meant to fall in love again, she realized. Now that she loved Nolan, her love for Jesse Holt was relegated to a memory, a reality that was no more, just as his time on earth was no more.

Sarah woke at dawn the next day, conscious of a bubbling energy surging through her. It was high time, she thought, that she began baking again. She could barely suppress a happy hum until a sleepy-looking Prissy entered the kitchen and poured a cup of coffee.

"Being in love agrees with you," Prissy observed with a wry smile. "It's about time." Sarah had told her about the plans for Sunday, and while she hadn't spoken about the kiss, she thought her friend may well have guessed, judging by the knowing look in her eyes.

"Now, don't overdo it," Prissy said an hour later, as she was leaving to check on her father. "Remember, Nolan told us about the danger of a relapse."

"I'm fine," Sarah told her. "A little baking will hardly exhaust me." She wouldn't tell Prissy that she meant to deliver them, too.

By noon, she had dropped off her first armload of baked goods at the hotel restaurant, and was planning to return to the cottage just long enough to pick up several pies for the mercantile, which lay in the opposite direction.

Coming out of the hotel, Sarah ignored the lone cowboy lounging in front of the Simpson Creek Saloon. Probably suffering from spring fever, she mused absently, for the day was warm enough to be March rather than February. Perhaps he'd been given an errand in town, and he was lingering, reluctant to return to his duties…

"Sarah?" The voice came from the direction of the solitary cowboy.

She stared, transfixed, into the lean, beard-shadowed face of Jesse Holt.

Chapter Twenty-One

For a moment she forgot to breathe. It couldn't be. It was what she had prayed for for so long. She took a step forward, another, then stopped, expecting the figure in front of her to dissolve into nothingness as he had done in her dream last night. She'd been ill, and she'd dreamed about Jesse. Perhaps that was why she was now transferring Jesse's features, Jesse's *voice*, onto the figure on the bench. If she just waited for a moment and blinked a few times, surely he would fade away again.

Her mind had played tricks on her like this before, when the war was newly over and she had begun to realize that the continued lack of letters and his failure to return meant Jesse was really dead. She'd seen his face in every dark-haired, dark-eyed stranger, and thought for a few precious heartbeats it was Jesse, until a closer look disappointed her each time.

But this hallucination had risen to his feet, his heavy canvas duster flapping in the breeze. He moved slowly forward, pulling off his hat, as if he too were in a dream.

"Sarah Matthews, is that you?" the man repeated again, using Jesse's beloved slow drawl. "Don't you know me, Sarah-girl?"

"Jesse? Jesse Holt?"

A smile spread across the lean, beard-stubbled cheeks. Jesse's smile. "The very same."

She tried nonetheless to hold on to the reality she had known for almost a year now. "You can't be Jesse, mister. Jesse Holt is dead. Jesse never came back from the war."

The stranger masquerading as Jesse had the grace to look ashamed. Taking his eyes off her face, he stared at the line he was toeing in the mud in the street.

"Yes, well, I'm sorry about that. I never meant to make you wait that long. I can tell you're surprised to see me. How are you, Goldilocks?"

She had never liked this nickname Jesse had given her, but his use of it established beyond all doubt that the man walking toward her, so near now that she could almost reach out and touch him, was really her long-lost fiancé Jesse Holt.

"Where have you been?"

She was surprised at the surge of anger she felt within her, and she could tell by the way his eyes widened, then narrowed, that he was, too, for he lost his confident grin for a moment. But then he found it again.

"Well, now, I'll tell you all about that, Goldilocks, I promise I will. What are you doing in town? I thought I'd find you out on your pa's ranch. As a matter of fact I was just waitin' for my horse to have a shoe replaced down at livery yonder, and then I was goin' to ride out and surprise you." He must have remembered his unshaven face, for he added, "Though I 'spose I should've made a stop at the barbershop first."

She remained speechless, and he tried another tack, maybe thinking she needed more reassurance that he was no imposter. "How's your pa? And that sweet sister of yours—Milly, isn't that her name? Is she bossy as ever?"

"Our father's passed on. Milly's married and she and her husband live on the ranch," she said stiffly.

"I'm sorry about your father," he said. "So Milly's got the ranch. What about you? You—you're not married, are you?" He lost that perfect assurance for just a moment.

"No, I'm not married," she said. "I'm living with Prissy Gilmore in a cottage on the grounds of the mayor's house." She didn't jerk her head backward to indicate it; Jesse had grown up in Simpson Creek just as she had and he would remember where the mayor's grand house stood.

He blinked, and looked as if he'd like to ask why. "Don't that beat all?" he said at last. The wind ruffled his hair at that moment. "Hey, you must be gettin' cold, aren't you?" He looked around him as if deciding something. "Why don't you invite me in for a cup of coffee and I'll tell you what I've been doing since the war's been over?"

She stiffened. "I don't think that's a good idea. Prissy's not there right now." She assumed Prissy had not returned from checking on her father, but she wouldn't have invited him even if she had been certain Prissy was there. Too many months had gone by, and now he had appeared without a word of warning, out of the blue. Later, she promised herself, she'd examine why the thought of Jesse in her house no longer appealed to her. Once, she knew, she would have invited him in and been glad that Prissy's absence gave them the privacy to exchange a kiss or two.

He chuckled, rubbing the back of his neck as he glanced behind him at the saloon. "And I reckon it wouldn't be fittin' to invite a lady into the saloon, either, to tell you my tale. Say, does the hotel still have that restaurant? Let me buy you dinner."

"No thank you, I'm not hungry," she said. It was the truth. Her stomach was churning.

"Coffee, then. You can keep me company while I eat. I've been on the trail since mornin', and I'm hungry enough to eat a longhorn steer, hide, horn, hoofs and beller."

Even as she smiled automatically at his joke, she decided he deserved to be heard out, at the very least. They'd once been engaged to marry, after all. And sitting together in a public place was certainly better than inside the cottage.

"All right," she said, and led the way back into the hotel.

Jesse drank a swallow of coffee to wash down the mouthful of roast beef he had chewed. "Right after we were taken prisoner, we were sent to Camp Chase in Columbus, Ohio. We figured we could escape from there and then it'd only be 'bout a hundred miles to the Kentucky border, but before we could do that, they transferred us to Johnson's Island in Lake Erie."

"Was it awful there?" Sarah asked. "We heard horrible things about Libby Prison...."

He shook his head. "Not so bad, except in the winter, when those winds came whistlin' outa Canada. We about froze our Southern hides off. Then in September of '64, a bunch of us tried to seize one of the boats that made stops at the islands, and pretty near got away with it too, but we found out we'd been betrayed and had to hightail it to Canada instead."

"You've been in Canada since the year *before* the war ended?" Sarah cried, unable to hide her indignation. "Why didn't you make your way back to the South, or at least write me from Canada?"

"Now, don't go soundin' all righteous, Sarah," he said with a flash of irritation as he speared another hunk of beef. "We had good reason to lay low. There were spies swarmin' all over northern Ohio and southern Canada lookin' for us, and the war was goin' bad. Someone might've intercepted my letter. We figured there was no use bein' cannon fodder in a lost cause and decided t' wait out the war where it was safe."

While other boys in gray kept dying. "Well then, where have you been since then? The war was over last April."

He sat back, studying her, grinning. "You look good, Sarah."

She recognized a dodge when she heard it. And what nonsense. Her mirror had told her only this morning how pale and thin she looked after her battle with influenza, but then Jesse Holt always had been a silver-tongued rascal.

"Livin' away from that bossy sister must agree with

you," he said with a wink. "I'm glad I didn't have to ride out there and argue my way past that dragon. She never did like me, you know."

No, she hadn't known that, but it was just like Milly to have left her sister to make up her own mind. Sarah bit back the impulse to defend her sister and kept waiting, unwilling to be distracted.

The waiter returned to their table. "More coffee, folks?"

Sarah shook her head. Jesse said, "Sure, and we'll have some of that chocolate cake when we're finished. We're celebratin', you see.

"Where have we been, you asked," Jesse said, after the waiter had gone. "Well, while we were in Canada, we worked here and there, did a little a' this and a little a' that, to keep food in our bellies…."

"'We'?"

"Me and the boys from Johnson's Island who escaped together. Some of 'em were officers, some enlisted, but once we got outta that prison, we were equals. An' we figured it was time to get even with those Blue Bellies that put us in that blasted cold prison. So we've been makin' our way back t' Texas, stoppin' t' make life miserable for the Yankees whenever we could." He winked. "We've found it can be mighty profitable, mighty profitable indeed. And quite amusin'."

Mystified, she stared at him. "Jesse, whatever do you mean?"

He smiled that lazy smile again. "A little raiding, a holdup or two of stages bringin' the payroll to those blasted Federal troops who got no business occupyin' our fair state, a bit a' rustlin' of carpetbagger cattle…"

Sarah felt her jaw drop. "You're an *outlaw?*"

He laughed. "Nah, nothin' like that, Sarah. I told you, we're only harrassin' Yankees. We don't bother honest Southerners. High time we made up for all those years those b—those Yankees stole from us."

While she was still staring at him, her mind reeling at what he was so proudly telling her, he reached out and seized her hand, which had been clutching her coffee cup, and leaned across the table, his eyes intense.

"Sarah, they stole those years from *us,* from you an' me. If they hadn't tried t' bully the South, you an' me'd be married for three or four years with a passel a' kids. With your pa dead, I could've taken over the ranch and we'd have been sittin' pretty, yes siree. You know that's what would've happened."

Yes, they'd have married, she thought, but she was no longer sure she would have been happy. She pulled her hand away from his slowly, trying not to seem as if she was repelled by his touch.

"Jesse, the war is *over*," she said. "The other men from Simpson Creek who survived came home and took up their lives again."

"Aw, Sarah, we were cooped up for so long, we were just havin' some fun before we settled down," he protested. "You always used to like havin' fun, so I figured you'd understand."

She felt her temper spark. "Jesse, I wore *mourning* for you. Your poor mother died thinking she'd see you in Heaven. You couldn't have written to say you were *alive?*"

Finally, he had the grace to look ashamed. "You know I never was much for book learnin'," he said. "I think I gave that schoolmarm we had—what was her name? Miss Russell?—most of her gray hairs. But I never meant to make you sad, Sarah, honey."

He looked at her with puppy-dog eyes, a look that used to melt her heart. "I'm here to make it up to you, Sarah. Run away with me, and we'll get married, and I'll introduce you to th' boys. We'll have a fine life— you'll see. A couple of 'em are married, too, or they have lady friends here 'n' there that ride along with us from time to time."

She couldn't believe her ears. "You think I'd even *consider* leaving with you to live an outlaw's life, always on the run?"

"Aw, Sarah, we have a grand time, livin' high off the hog. We're free to do whatever we want, whenever we want. We eat the best food, drink the best wine—our ladies are drippin' in jewelry and fancy clothes. But I'm willin' to leave it all if you insist."

"'Leave it all'?"

"Sure. That's how much I love you, sweetheart. If you don't want to live free as a bird, I'll come back and have that ranch with you. We'll let Milly stay there, too, of course, but it ain't fittin' for no lady to be runnin' a ranch anyway."

"I told you, Milly's married now," she managed to say, in the midst of the temper that was threatening to boil over into angry words. "I think her husband might take exception to that idea."

"We'll buy him out, then," he said grandly. "They can go find some other ranch. I know you always set great store by that old place."

She was conscious of the handful of other diners in the restaurant, and remembered again that her mother said ladies did not make a scene in public.

She folded her hands in her lap and looked away. "I'm sorry, Jesse. I loved you, and I prayed every night during the war for your return, but now—"

He straightened. "*Loved* me? You don't love me any more? There's someone else, isn't there?" he demanded, his narrowed eyes twin smoldering fires.

She looked away from his glare. She didn't want to tell him about Nolan, didn't want to hear his reaction to the news that his former fiancée was in love with one of the very Yankees he hated so much, especially since she and Nolan hadn't even had the chance to explore their new feelings for one another yet. But she wouldn't lie, not about the relationship that had come to mean so much to her. She just wouldn't say any more than she had to.

"Yes," she said. "Yes, I'm sorry, there is. I wish you well, Jesse. And now I'd best be getting home." She rose. The encounter—preceded by her busy morning of baking—had exhausted her, and she just wanted to reach the sanctuary of the cottage and lie down for a while.

Chapter Twenty-Two

Nolan whistled as he walked across the muddy street toward the hotel. It had been a busy morning, but a good one. All of his influenza patients seemed to be on the mend, and there continued to be no more new cases. And just as the sun rose, he had helped usher a new baby into the world. He couldn't wait to tell Sarah about it.

He glanced over his shoulder at the cottage, which sat diagonally across from the hotel, wishing he could drop in and see her right now, then decided against it, hoping Sarah was following his instructions and resting.

No, instead of knocking on Sarah's door, he'd have his dinner and then return to his office, where he'd restock his bag and "redd up" the office, as Prissy would say. Perhaps he'd even get a chance to catch up on his professional reading.

He was still whistling as he walked through the hotel lobby and into the restaurant, nodding a greeting at the waiter as he headed for his usual table by the window, but then he stopped stock-still.

Sarah was just rising from a table against the wall, and as he watched, the rangy-looking saddle tramp who'd been sitting opposite her jumped up, too, and grabbed her hand with a familiarity only a man who knew a woman well would dare.

Had he been completely wrong about Sarah Matthews? He'd thought she loved him, too. Was it possible she had other suitors, just as in love with her as he was?

"Sarah, you can't leave like this," the man said in a disbelieving voice, his rough features stricken. "I left the boys and came all this way to see you—I even offered t' leave 'em for good, and you're going to just walk out?"

"Jesse, *please*," Sarah said in a low, distressed voice, pulling her hand away. Her back was to Nolan so she hadn't seen him, so he remained where he was. "Don't make this harder than it is. Please just accept what I've told you, and go on your way. But I beg you, if I ever meant anything to you, leave those bad men and start your life back on an honest path. I don't want you to die like outlaws do, from a bullet or at the end of a rope."

The man gave a harsh bark of laughter and his features hardened into something ugly. "Leave them? You make it sound like I'm some homeless cur, Sarah, going along with anyone who'll spare me a crumb. Sarah, I'm the *leader* of the Gray Boys gang. Me, Jesse Holt—the leader!"

Jesse Holt. Wasn't that the name of Sarah's fiancé, who'd died in the war? Apparently he hadn't died. Had Sarah known that all along? Had they met in secret before, and now were becoming bold enough to meet in a public place?

"And I was willing to give all that up for you," the man went on, his face hardening into an angry mask, "but you're throwin' it back in my face and tellin' me you've fallen in love with someone else. Who is it, Sarah? That's what I want to know, and I think I have a right."

He *hadn't* been wrong about Sarah. He didn't know where this Holt fellow had popped up from, or if Sarah had known he was still alive, but obviously Holt didn't mean anything to her anymore, because she loved *him*.

By now, everyone in the restaurant was staring, townspeople and travelers alike. While Sarah had spoken quietly, Holt hadn't bothered to keep his voice down, so everyone in the room was now absorbed in the dramatic scene.

Sarah's voice shook, but her stance was no-nonsense as she said, "It's none of your concern anymore, Jesse. Goodbye."

The saddle tramp thrust his hand out as if he meant to stop her by force. It was time to step in.

"Is this man bothering you, sweetheart?" Nolan said, coming forward and placing a proprietary hand on her shoulder.

Sarah half turned and jumped, clearly startled. "*Nolan!* I'm glad you're here. Please, just take me home." Her face was flushed dully red with misery as she reached for his arm and took hold of it.

He looked down into her eyes, hoping she read the love in them. "Of course." Then he looked back at

Holt, making sure the man wasn't going for a gun. He wasn't, but if looks could kill, Nolan knew he would have been sprawled on the floor.

Clearly conscious of his enthralled audience, Holt's face screwed itself into a mask of scorn as he looked him up and down. "*This* is the fellow you left me for? This Yankee swell in a frock coat? How could you, Sarah? Your ma an' pa must be rollin' in their graves, knowin' their daughter's cozy with a Yankee."

"That's enough," Nolan snapped. "The lady's leaving, and you're not to bother her further."

Holt cocked his head and drawled, "I declare, he talks funny."

A few of the onlookers chuckled.

Nolan clenched his fists, but Sarah's hand tightened on his wrist. "Please, let's just *go.*"

They turned and started for the door, but Holt wasn't done.

"You'll be sorry, Sarah! This whole town's gonna be sorry you threw me over!"

Nolan felt her shaking as they hurried across the road. Fortunately, Prissy still hadn't returned to the cottage, for Sarah managed to hold it in only until they crossed the threshold before she threw herself into his arms in a torrent of tears.

"Oh, N-Nolan!" she cried, her whole body heaving with her sobs. "He j-just appeared out of n-nowhere!"

"Did he come here to the cottage, looking for you?" Nolan asked, chilled at the thought of that man knowing where his Sarah lived.

"N-no..." she said against his coat as he held her,

her voice thick with tears. "I was coming out of the hotel—I'd delivered some baked goods, you see…"

So she hadn't been resting as instructed, but Nolan hadn't the heart to reprove her about overexerting herself.

"…And he was sitting outside the saloon," she continued, still shaking. She told him how Holt had escaped to Canada during the latter part of the war and had been running with a gang of outlaws ever since returning across the northern border. "He thinks it's all right because they're 'only stealing from Yankees,'" she cried. "Oh, Nolan, he's *nothing* like the sweet young man I loved before he went to war!"

"Ssssh, sweetheart," he soothed, still holding her and resting his face against her hair. "War has a way of changing men, and frequently not for the better. But it's over now. You're safe."

"But you heard him! He didn't just threaten me, he threatened the whole town!" she wailed. "What are we going to do?"

"We won't have to do anything," Nolan assured her. "Those were empty threats. Some men don't take rejection very well, that's all."

"But it's so unfair, Nolan! I mean, I'm glad he's not dead, but he never sent a word to tell me he was still alive! And then to show up out of nowhere, almost a year after the war was over, and get angry because I'd gone on with my life. Can you imagine, Nolan, he tried to talk me into running off with him!"

Nolan wanted to growl in rage at the thought of that saddle tramp inviting Sarah to join him on the run. He was relieved to see that Sarah was no longer weeping, but angry.

"Or if I wouldn't do that," she went on, pulling away to pace back and forth, waving her arm in a furious gesture, "he very nobly offered to give all that up and take over the ranch!"

"I reckon Nick Brookfield would have something to say about that, as well as Milly," he said drily. "Just picture Holt trying to waltz in there and persuade Milly to give up her ranch."

She gave a watery laugh and swiped a hand at her eyes. "She wouldn't even need Nick to defend it," she said. "She'd get out the shotgun herself."

"That's the spirit," he told her, stroking her cheek. "Now, don't worry about Holt anymore. Likely as not he's already ridden out of Simpson Creek and you'll never see him again."

"I hope you're right," she said, twisting a fold of her grenadine cloth skirt.

"You weren't tempted—even for a moment, before he told you what he'd been doing?" he asked her curiously, then wished he could call back the question as soon as he asked it. He had no right to probe her heart like that.

But Sarah apparently didn't mind. She shook her head, her eyes unfocused as she seemed to look within herself. "Not for a moment," she told him. "There was something about him that had just changed too much. And he wasn't *you,* Nolan." She went back into his arms and offered her lips for a kiss, and he was more than glad to take her up on it.

"But Nolan," she began when he let her go at last, "seriously, what if it wasn't an empty threat?"

He sighed. "Perhaps you shouldn't go anywhere alone for a while, even in the daytime," he said. "If I can't be with you, take Prissy."

"I meant his threat to harm the town," she said. "After all, the sheriff is dead, and his old deputy, Pat Donovan, has never been up to anything more than whittling while he guards someone already locked up."

It was a sobering thought. Nolan sighed. "I'll speak to Prissy's father. Now that the flu epidemic is over, we need to remind the mayor the town needs a new sheriff."

The next morning, Sarah, accompanied by Prissy in accordance with Nolan's request, headed to the mercantile to deliver the pies and cakes she'd baked yesterday.

"I feel silly asking you to come along like some sort of guard, Prissy," Sarah said as they walked. "It's not as if it's even likely I'd see Jesse between the cottage and the mercantile, even if he did stay in town. And I don't think he'd do anything more than ignore me, anyway."

"Oh, just think of me as someone to help carry your wares," Prissy said cheerfully. "Papa was wanting some peppermint drops at the mercantile anyway. And besides, it couldn't hurt to be careful—why, you could have knocked me over with a feather last night when you told Papa and me about Jesse showing up alive, and then acting the awful way he did."

"Yes, it was the last thing I ever expected," Sarah said. "I was never so glad to see Nolan in my life!"

"See, I told you that he was the one for you," Prissy said smugly as she held open the door of the mercantile to let Sarah in.

As they entered, Sarah spotted Mrs. Detwiler and Mrs. Patterson with their heads together at the counter.

"Good morning, ladies," she called out. "Good to see you up and about, Mrs. Detwiler, after your illness. Mrs. Patterson, I have some baked goods for you."

Both ladies jerked upright at the sound of Sarah's voice, looking so guilty Sarah knew they must have been talking about her. She felt a sinking in her stomach as if she'd eaten one of Prissy's early practice biscuits.

"Good, Sarah, I'll be glad to have them," Mrs. Patterson said quickly, trying to assume a businesslike manner. "It's been so long since anyone dared venture out, even if they were well, and now they're starting to ask where your cakes and pies have been. Of course, I told them you'd been very ill yourself...."

"Sarah, I was about to come see you," Mrs. Detwiler said, as if perhaps she realized Sarah saw through Mrs. Patterson's chatter. "There's something Mrs. Patterson and I thought you ought to know—"

Sarah raised her chin as Prissy quietly laid her share of the baked goods on the counter. "That Jesse Holt is alive and came to town yesterday? Yes, I'm aware. We ran into one another."

Both women looked distinctly relieved at not having to break the news to her.

"I imagine that was quite a shock, seeing him alive after all that time," Mrs. Patterson said, peering curiously at her through her spectacles. "You didn't have any idea? He never wrote to tell you?"

As if the whole town wouldn't know if I'd received a letter from him, Sarah thought, remembering that Postmaster Wallace loved to gossip as much as the women did. "No," she said quietly. "But of course I'm glad he isn't dead, even if our lives have gone in different directions."

"Then you don't mind that he and Ada Spencer were cozyin' up with one another?"

"Jesse? And *Ada Spencer?*" Prissy exclaimed, while Sarah was still trying to find her voice.

"They met in front of the mercantile yesterday—I saw it from that very window," Mrs. Patterson said. "I thought he looked familiar but then Ada came along and went flyin' into his arms and squealin' in delight, callin' his name."

"Well, she knew him, too, of course, before the war," Sarah reminded her. "We all knew Jesse—we'd grown up together."

"Well, they came in here for a while, seein' as it was a mite chilly outside still, and stood and talked for the longest time. I heard bits and pieces here and there—"

"You don't need to tell me, Mrs. Patterson. I've already wished Jesse well, but explained that I've come to care for another very much—"

Mrs. Detwiler interrupted, "And that 'another' is Dr. Walker, isn't it? Took you a while, but you always were a smart girl. I'm right happy for you two."

But Mrs. Patterson was not about to be distracted. "Then you won't mind that Ada practically threw herself at him, and Jesse Holt looked mighty pleased to catch her," Mrs. Patterson said, as if Sarah hadn't hinted she'd heard enough. "Miz Powell, the cook at the hotel, said those two took supper there last night, and Ada was all gussied up," Mrs. Patterson said with a cackle that would have put one of Milly's hens to shame. "Not a sign of mourning on that one. Scandalous! And when they were done eating, Miz Powell said, they went off down the street arm in arm."

Sarah couldn't help but wonder if Ada had told Jesse about her recent "pregnancy."

"Ada's had a rough time lately," she said, aware that both ladies were waiting for her reaction and hoping this would satisfy them. "Perhaps she and Jesse would be good for one another." *And perhaps Ada can persuade Jesse off the outlaw trail.*

Mrs. Patterson kept staring at Sarah with speculative eyes.

"That'll be five dollars for the baked goods, as usual," Sarah said at last, reminding the proprietress why she had come. She didn't want to think about Jesse or Ada anymore, not when she had Sunday to anticipate, when she and Nolan would go to church together and then for dinner and a buggy ride.

"And Papa would like a half pound of peppermints," Prissy piped up.

Chapter Twenty-Three

"This is indeed a day of celebration," Reverend Chadwick announced, beaming from the pulpit as he looked out over the congregation. "Our first service since the influenza epidemic has abated, thanks to the goodness and mercy of the Lord…"

There were several calls of "Amen, preacher!"

"Thanks also in no small part to our dedicated physician, Dr. Nolan Walker," Chadwick continued, gesturing to where Nolan sat in a pew close to the front, with Sarah, Milly and Nick Brookfield and Mayor Gilmore and Prissy, "and his dedicated corps of nurses, also known as the Simpson Creek Spinsters' Club. Would you stand, Doctor, and you ladies, too, that we may show our appreciation?"

They did so, to the sound of loud applause, but to Sarah's surprise, Nolan raised his hand as if he wished to speak.

"Dr. Walker, you have something to say?"

"Yes, indeed I do, Reverend. I want to add my thanks and admiration to these devoted ladies," he said, gesturing next to him, where Sarah and Prissy stood, then around the pews to indicate Faith Bennett, Bess Lassiter, Maude Harkey, Jane Jeffries and Polly Shackleford. "Doctoring is my duty, and I accept it gladly, but these ladies *volunteered* to nurse the sick, going above and beyond anything that could have been expected of them and exposing themselves to the danger of contagion—" He caught Sarah's gaze then. His eyes glistening, he seemed to have trouble going on.

"And we are very glad Miss Sarah survived her brush with death," Reverend Chadwick finished for him. "Thank you, ladies, Doctor." They sat down to more applause. "And now we should remember those who the Lord chose to call home in the epidemic," the preacher went on, "so that we may pray for their families—Mr. Parker, Mrs. Gilmore, her sister Mrs. Tyler..." As he began to speak, the steeple bell began to toll, one tinny bong for each name. "Mr. Patterson, Mr. Calhoun, Sheriff Poteet, Pete Collier—who had so lately come to live with us—Mr. and Mrs. Spencer..."

The preacher kept reading the list of the dead. But Sarah heard a muffled sob from the back of the church, and thinking it was Caroline Wallace, who'd been Pete Collier's fiancée, turned around. She was surprised to see that the weeper was Ada Spencer, garbed in deep mourning, sitting with a black handkerchief to her eyes. None other than Jesse Holt sat beside her.

Their gazes met, and Jesse smirked at her.

They must have come in late. Quickly, Sarah turned around again, glad that Nolan hadn't noticed her looking. But Milly had followed her gaze, and Milly's wide-eyed, shocked face reminded Sarah that she had much to tell her sister.

Sarah told herself it was nothing to her if Ada wanted to put on mourning only when it suited her, and have Jesse Holt console her. At least Ada was no longer claiming she was pregnant, and accusing Nolan of fathering her child. Nolan was a much better man than Jesse had ever been, and Nolan loved her.

And then she felt ashamed for allowing herself to be distracted by less than spiritual thoughts in the Lord's house, and resolved to keep her mind on the hymns and the sermon to follow.

"Let us now stand and sing the first hymn. Mr. Connell, if you will lead us? I'm sure Miss Sarah will be back at her piano next week…."

For the rest of the church service, Sarah threw herself wholeheartedly into worshipping God and being thankful for Nolan's presence beside her, thankful too that he seemed to be thoroughly enjoying the singing and listening carefully to the preaching.

"Would you and Nolan like to come out to the ranch for Sunday dinner?" Milly asked afterward, as the congregation filed out and spilled down the church steps onto the lawn. "Now that I'm feeling better, I'm finding I love to cook. I'd like to show you how accomplished I've become."

"Could we make it another Sunday?" Sarah asked. "Nick's taking me to dinner at the hotel, and then for a buggy ride."

"Of course we can!" Milly exclaimed with a pleased grin. Then, seeing Nolan had been buttonholed by Mrs.

Detwiler to discuss her grandchild's teething woes, she pulled Sarah aside out of the earshot of others.

"If you're not coming to the ranch, then you'll have to tell me now when Jesse Holt reappeared like Lazarus coming forth from the grave!" she said in a low voice. "Why didn't you warn me? I nearly swooned in surprise when I turned around and saw him. And what's he doing with that Ada Spencer, who I see is no longer 'with child'? Dear Sarah, how do you feel about all that?"

Sarah couldn't help but chuckle at the spate of dramatic questions, and told her all about her surprise encounter with Jesse and what had followed.

"Well, I think you've made the right choice," Milly said a few minutes later, just before they walked back to rejoin Nolan and Nick. "Jesse Holt will come to no good end if he doesn't change his ways."

Dinner in the hotel had been wonderful, and since the weather had cooperated to produce a sunny, mild February day, they took Nolan's buggy out to the meadow west of the creek. Nolan couldn't believe he was actually sitting in his buggy with Sarah close beside him and stealing frequent smiling glances at him. If he was dreaming, he didn't want to wake up.

A mule deer doe and twin fawns hopped away as the buggy crossed the bridge. The cottonwoods and live oaks along the creekside were bursting with pale green leaves unfurling from their stems. Birds warbled their songs from the trees or flitted from branch to branch, twigs clutched in their beaks, building their nests.

"Just wait a month, and this meadow will be carpeted

in bluebonnets," Sarah promised him. "And the next month, gold and red flowers, Indian blanket, Mexican hat, primroses—Nolan, you can't believe how beautiful it is!"

"I can't believe how beautiful *you* are, Sarah," he said, cupping her cheek. "And as I said in church, how kind, how brave..."

"Brave? Me? I'm not brave at all," she protested. "Milly would tell you I've been a quiet little mouse all my life. She's been the brave one, the leader."

"I don't think she'd say that anymore, *Nurse* Sarah. In fact, I think you have all the qualities to make an excellent doctor's wife."

When his words hit her, she gaped at him. "Dr. Nolan Walker! Did you just propose to me, on our very first outing together?"

He grinned. "Ayuh," he said, in a deliberately exaggerated "Downeast" accent. "We men of Maine don't waste time. Am I going too fast, sweetheart? I promise you'll get your courtship, never fear, but you and I both know I've been courting you every time we met—as much as you'd let me, anyway—ever since Founder's Day last fall."

She considered his words. "I guess that's true. All right, as long as you don't stint on the courtship—we Texas ladies set great store by courting, I'll have you know—I agree."

"Did you just say *yes*, Miss Sarah, on our very first outing as a courting couple?"

She nodded, blushing a rosy pink that made her even lovelier still.

He couldn't wait any longer, and lowered his lips to hers.

They were still exchanging kisses interspersed with sweet words when they heard horses approaching them from eastward beyond the town.

Letting go of one another, they lifted their heads.

Sarah's first thought chilled her heart—was it another Comanche attack? They were not far from the road—there was no time to hide—they'd both be killed… She sat paralyzed, wondering if there was time for them to run and conceal themselves in the underbrush along Simpson Creek.

Then common sense asserted itself and she relaxed. No, these horsemen didn't seem to be in any hurry, and she could hear the jingling of bits and spurs and the creaking of leather saddles as well as snatches of talk and laughter. Just some ranch hands coming into town for the afternoon…

But the riders who came into view did not look like any cowboys from the outlying ranches. They were bearded and rough, and each had loaded saddlebags with rifles and bedrolls strapped to the cantles. Their hats were worn low over their foreheads. They passed by without seeming to notice the buggy sitting in a grove of trees near the road, and there was something about them that put Sarah in mind of a pack of wolves—or of Jesse.

"Wonder where they're bound for?" Nolan murmured in a low voice. "They look like trouble."

Sarah nodded, keeping her eyes on them.

Snatches of talk drifted back to Sarah as they passed.

"...Said he'd meet us east a' town. Hope he's got some whiskey—saloon's probably closed up tighter'n a drum on account of it bein' Sunday..."

"Reckon he's made up his mind by now..."

"Yeah, well, if he ain't, we ain't hangin' around while he chases some skirt..."

Sarah put a hand out to steady herself against Nolan's arm. "Nolan, I think those men are the Gray Boys—the gang Jesse spoke of being their leader."

He gazed after the cloud of dust they had left behind, then back at her. "Perhaps we'd better wait no longer to tell Prissy's father what we've seen. It's all very well to advertise for a new sheriff, but in the meantime, he's got to have a plan in place to deal with troublemakers."

By tacit agreement, they left the peaceful glade and drove back across the creek into town.

Mayor Gilmore, wakened by Prissy from his Sunday afternoon nap, listened attentively, absently stroking his full beard.

"I don't know that I'm convinced that those men have anything to do with your Jesse Holt, Sarah—"

"Papa, he's not *Sarah's* Jesse Holt anymore!" Prissy cried, her gaze apologetic as it flew from Sarah to Nolan.

The mayor blinked and cleared his throat. "Pardon me, Miss Sarah, I spoke without thinking—meant no offense—but it would probably be prudent to appoint somebody as temporary sheriff, until the right man answers our advertisement, just in case. Trouble is, I don't know who'd be up to the job. His deputy sure isn't. How about you, Dr. Walker?"

Sarah saw Nolan's jaw drop at the question.

Nolan said flatly, "Mayor, I'm a *physician*, not a lawman."

"I know, but you were in the war…I'll warrant you had to be capable with a firearm in the army, even if your weapon was more often a scalpel."

Sarah saw Nolan's jaw tighten, and sensed the turmoil churning inside him from his rigid posture.

"There are several men of the town who were actually *soldiers* in the war," Nolan argued. "Naturally, I'd be willing to assist whoever you select—"

"Yes, there are, but the job calls for judgment and common sense, and the ability to lead, and I'm convinced you have that in good measure, Dr. Walker," the mayor retorted briskly.

"Thank you for the compliment, sir," Nolan said, "but I think I can serve the town better as its doctor."

The phrase "ability to lead" sparked an idea in Sarah. "Mayor Gilmore, what about my brother-in-law, Nicholas Brookfield? He was a captain in the British army, and he certainly led the effort to have the fort built in town last fall."

The old man blinked. "Of course, of course. I think that influenza must have boiled my common sense, not to mention my memory! Do you suppose he'd accept, Miss Sarah?"

"Until a permanent sheriff could be hired, yes, sir. But we won't know till we ask, will we?"

The mayor rubbed his chin whiskers, then said with a flash of his old decisiveness, "I believe we'd better act quickly. Doctor, would you be willing to take Miss Matthews out to the ranch now and ask Brookfield if he'd do it? Of course it'd be subject to town council approval, but I think they'll follow my suggestion if he accepts."

"Of course, Mayor," Nolan said.

"Good. Prissy, would you go 'round to the councilmen's houses now and tell them I'm calling an urgent meeting at ten o'clock tomorrow?"

Sarah sprang up along with Nolan feeling relieved to be doing something to help in the crisis, but she couldn't help wondering if even Nick Brookfield would be enough to stop the trouble that was coming.

Chapter Twenty-Four

By the time they left the ranch that evening, they had not only secured Nick's agreement to serve as the temporary sheriff if the council agreed, but had been given a delicious early supper by Milly.

"Your sister and brother-in-law are delightful people, Sarah," Nolan said as they neared Simpson Creek.

Sarah smiled in the darkness as the horse trotted along. "I can tell they like you, too. And Milly's relieved that I've finally seen the error of my ways. Once she'd met you, she was so upset with me for rejecting you because you're a Yankee." She chuckled. "I wonder what she'd say if she knew you've already proposed, this very afternoon!"

Nolan favored her with a teasing sidelong glance. "Why didn't you tell her?"

Sarah rolled her eyes. "Because then she'd say I gave in too easily! She can't let go of being the big sister who knows best, you kn—"

Her voice trailed off as the saloon came into view, all lit up. From within, the strains of tinny piano music drifted out on the chilly evening air.

"What's going on?" she murmured aloud. "The saloon's never open on Sunday, never. I've always heard George Detwiler would like to, but you know Mrs. Detwiler, his mother—she'd never stand for it." Then she spotted a handful of men striding into it, laughing and talking loudly—and one woman, around whose waist a man's arm was curled.

The buggy drew closer, and Sarah saw the woman turn to hear something the man was saying. Sarah recognized Ada Spencer. The man touching her so familiarly was Jesse Holt—which meant the men pushing open the batwing doors were the Gray Boys.

"Nolan—"

"Unfortunately, there's nothing illegal about a bunch of drifters visiting a saloon, even if it is Sunday," he said, guessing the cause of her apprehension. "And they've committed no crimes, as far as we know. We'd best get you inside out of the cold, sweetheart," he added, seeing her shiver.

That night, she was wakened by gunfire from the direction of the road, and went to her window, which looked out on the street. Pulling aside the curtain, she was in time to see horsemen galloping away. Even through the closed window, she could hear their raucous whooping and hollering and shooting into the air.

Sarah came out the next morning with a load of pies for the hotel just as Nick was mounting his horse at the Gilmores' stable.

"Nick, am I to call you Sheriff Brookfield?" she called, raising a hand in greeting.

"For the time being, yes," he confirmed as he swung his leg over the saddle. His face was grim, absent of the good humor that usually marked it. As he turned to greet her, she saw the five-pointed tin star already pinned to the collar of his coat.

A premonitory trickle of apprehension skittered down her spine. "Has something happened?"

"The ranch was hit by rustlers at sunrise," he told her in his crisp British accent. "They drove off all the cattle in the back pasture, every last head. Micah happened to be out there checking on a cow with a new calf, and they shot him."

She couldn't stifle the sound that escaped her. Micah was the youngest of the Brown brothers who were all cowhands at the ranch.

At her cry of alarm, he held up a hand. "He'll be all right, I think. He's at the doctor's right now, getting the bullet removed from his arm."

What he wasn't mentioning, Sarah knew, was what a devastating effect the loss of the cattle would be to the ranch if they were not recovered. They'd lost almost half their herd last year when the Comanches had raided. Milly and Nick had hoped to build up the herd enough to make a profit when drovers came through next year.

"I—I'll go see him," she said, feeling unfocused, "and see if there's anything I can do to help Nolan."

"You're a good woman, Sarah. I know Micah would like that. Milly's there, but she's rather shaken up, you know, what with waking up to the sound of gunfire, then seeing Micah riding in, his arm all bloody..."

Sarah could well imagine, having awoken to the

sound of gunfire herself. And as stalwart as her sister was, she never could stand the sight of blood, and now she was expecting a child…

"Is Milly all right? Shouldn't you be with her?" She heard a sharp, disapproving edge in her voice, and was sorry, but this was her *sister*. "Perhaps she should stay at the cottage with Prissy and me while you're serving as sheriff."

"I tried to stay with her at the doctor's," Nick protested, "but she knew I was supposed to be at the council meeting here and chivied me out the office door. Besides, your Nolan said he'd check her to make sure all was well with the child. And I *did* already suggest she stay here with you while I'm away from the ranch, but she insists that since there's nothing left to steal, we won't be troubled again."

Milly was probably right. Reassured somewhat by the news that her sister was behaving with her characteristic feisty resolve, Sarah felt her tensed shoulders relax some, though the worry remained.

"Josh and the others have already rounded up a posse to catch the rustlers. I'm riding to join up with them now."

She didn't know if it would prove helpful, but she told Nick about seeing the group of men and Ada going into the saloon last night.

His eyes narrowed. "Your erstwhile friend Ada sounds a right foolish woman," he said. "But thanks for letting me know. Leave word at the jail, if you spot them again."

Stopping only long enough at the cottage to tell Prissy the news and ask her to deliver her pies, Sarah picked up her skirts and hurried down the street to Nolan's office, arriving out of breath and feeling her carefully pinned hair falling down her back.

Milly jumped up from her straight-backed chair in the waiting room and fell into Sarah's arms. "Oh, sister, I'm so glad you're here!"

Elijah, Micah's eldest brother, rose more slowly beside Milly, his face betraying his anxiety.

Milly's shoulders shuddered with sobs. "Your Dr. Walker says Micah'll be all right as long as gangrene doesn't set in…."

Sarah stayed with her sister and Elijah until Milly was calm again, then went through the office door to see if she could be of help.

As she entered, the sharp tang of carbolic stung her nostrils. Nolan looked up sharply from the roll of linen he was winding around the cowhand's arm, but his stare softened as he recognized her.

"I'm glad you've come," Nolan said, his gaze caressing her. "I was afraid it was your sister trying to help again. She means well, but she turned white as this bandage when she attempted to be my assistant a few minutes ago."

"Hello, Miss Sarah," Micah said from the doctor's examining table. Under his dark skin, he looked a little pale himself.

"Hello, Dr. Nolan, Micah." Their formality in front of the cowboy felt odd after what had happened between them at the creek yesterday. "Micah, how are you feeling?" She tried to avoid looking at the small, round metal container beside him in which a bloody, misshapen bullet lay.

"Better now, Miss Sarah," he said in his soft, slurred drawl. "This Dr. Nolan, he's one fine bullet remover. I barely felt it," he said. The pain shining in his eyes, and the beads of sweat shimmering on his brow, however, belied his words.

"Young Micah, you're a very polite liar," Nolan told him. "It's all right to say it hurt like h—that is, it hurt very badly. You bore up well, though."

"Thank ya, Doctor."

Nolan assisted the other man down from the exam table and into the waiting room, where Elijah and Milly waited. Sarah followed.

"You keep that bandage clean and dry, Micah. I'm going to send along enough linen that Mrs. Brookfield can change the dressing every day. Mrs. Brookfield, please have someone notify me at once, day or night, if there's any fever or a great amount of swelling, or any cloudy drainage—*any* of that, understand?"

Milly, Micah and Elijah all nodded solemnly.

"I'll send some morphine pills with you in case Micah's pain gets worse," Nolan told Milly, "though the willow bark tea may well be sufficient."

"Now don't worry about Nick, Milly," Sarah said while Elijah helped his brother into the wagon. "Prissy and I will take his supper down to him at the jail every night."

"And don't you worry about your sister, neither, Miss Sarah," Elijah assured her in return. "I'll guard her and the house like a hawk."

By the next day, word reached town that two other ranches had been struck by the rustlers, as well. At those ranches, the thieves hadn't contented themselves with only the cattle, but had raided the ranch houses, too, and had stolen the ranchers and their wives' valuables, including the heirloom pocket watch of one and the garnet earbobs from his spouse. Sarah couldn't help but wonder if Milly and Nick's valuables had been left alone at Jesse's order because of her, or if the gang had merely grown greedier as they went along.

Nick and the posse returned the second evening without having caught up with the robbers and the stolen cattle, but with the news that yet another ranch had been hit. This time, the rustlers had killed a foreman and gravely wounded one of the cowhands who had attempted to drive them off. He was brought into town to Nolan, but the man had been shot in the chest and died despite Nolan's efforts to save him.

Now that the gang had added murder to their list of crimes, the ranks of the posse swelled and the president of the Simpson Creek Bank announced the formation of a reward account for the apprehension and conviction of any or all of the Gray Boys gang. Sarah heard threats to hang Jesse highest of all since he'd been one of their own, yet was now leading the pack of outlaws who preyed on them.

She felt a pang of grief for the idealistic young Jesse Holt who had gone off to war, promising to marry her and start a family as soon as the war was over, and who had returned as a cold, ruthless criminal. Perhaps it would have been better if he *had* died in battle as a soldier, his honor intact.

As the days went on and reports reached them that the Gray Boys had struck ranches in the neighboring towns, Sarah was the recipient of decidedly odd looks from some townspeople she encountered in the street. She knew the gossips were having a field day telling anyone who would listen about the scene in the hotel restaurant between Jesse and herself, and reminding each other that the two had once been engaged to marry. She wouldn't have been surprised to hear that some of them actually *blamed* her for kindling Jesse Holt's wrath on Simpson Creek by rejecting him.

The outlaw raiding even managed to cast its shadow over Sarah and Nolan's burgeoning romance. The influenza epidemic was over, spring was fast approaching and their love was a growing, thriving thing, yet how could they plan a wedding with carefree hearts when the outlaws' reign of terror over San Saba County continued?

A very discouraged foursome—Sarah, Nolan, Nick and Prissy—had supper at the sheriff's office on the first Saturday in March to toss around ideas of how to capture the Gray Boys.

"Have you questioned Ada?" Sarah asked while she ladled the vegetable soup into bowls and handed them to Prissy to pass out. "Perhaps if she thought she might be arrested as an accomplice, be tried and go to prison if convicted, she'd give up their hideout."

Nick steepled his fingers and eyed the ham Sarah was now slicing. "She might well do so, but the problem is finding her. Have you seen her lately?"

Sarah paused and laid down the knife. "Now that you mention it, no," she admitted.

"Neither has anyone else," Nick said. "'Neither hide nor hair' of her, as they say. She seems to have gone missing, though some of her neighbors have reported seeing her coming and going from her house at odd hours. Just the other night, Nolan, Donovan and I paid a surprise visit in the middle of the night after Donovan spotted a light in one of the back windows and summoned me—"

Sarah looked up, surprised, for Nolan hadn't mentioned it.

"—but the place was deserted when we got there."

"Yes, there was a pile of dirty laundry on the bed," Nolan said. "It looked as if she'd come home to fetch more clothes, and left just as quickly."

"Apparently she's come to enjoy the outlaw life," Nick went on. "The latest reports from the victims of their attacks have mentioned that she's riding along with them and packing pistols just like the others."

Sarah and Prissy stared at one another, horrified. Had it really been less than a year ago when Ada Spencer had been as excited as any of the Simpson Creek Spinsters about meeting a beau through the newspaper advertisements?

Chapter Twenty-Five

"They're overrunning the lines, heading straight at us!" the sentry screamed, his voice a mere thready cry against the din of booming cannon and the crack of rifles and the frantic whinnying of horses and the shouts of men grappling in mortal combat.

A trio of frightened-looking boys—surely they were only boys, even if they wore corporal's insignia on their uniforms—scrambled into the medical tent and huddled in the far corner, trembling. One of them was crying; another yelled "They're after us! We gotta hide till they go past, Doc!"

Nolan wrenched up his head from the bloody operative field beneath his hands. He was in the middle of the amputation of a shattered leg of an unfortunate captain whose limb had received a glancing impact of cannon shot just an hour ago. He didn't have the time to deal with fleeing soldiers using the medical tent as sanctuary—he had time for nothing but the man bleeding and nearly insensible from blood loss and the last of the whiskey.

The Rebel Yell, the unnerving Confederate battle

cry, ululated nearby—*too* nearby—as pounding feet
thudded closer, closer...

"Turn them—you've got to turn them!" he shouted
to the sentries crouched at the tent's entrance.

One of them ran toward Nolan, screaming, "We
can't! They're too many of them! They—" And then
a bullet struck him in the back with such force that he
went down, arms flailing, against the side of a nearby
cot, sending a rifle skidding toward Nolan as he col-
lapsed in a welter of blood.

Wild-eyed men in threadbare, tattered remains
of gray and butternut uniforms charged in, bayonets
fixed.

Nolan lay down his scalpel as carefully as his shaking hands allowed. "Get out! This is a medical tent! By
all the laws of war and decency, you have no right to
be here, interfering while we're trying to care for the
wounded!" Nolan thought the unkempt fellow at the
head of the pack would surely raise his rifle and silence
him with a single shot, but the latter paused only long
enough to spit in contempt.

"We saw them yella belly Yanks runnin' in here,
lookin' for their mamas, prob'ly!" he shouted back.
"You jes' let us have them and we'll let you tend to
your business!"

He couldn't let them shoot at the boys where they
crouched, not only for their sake but also for the sake
of the wounded men lying on pallets and on the bare
ground inside and outside, awaiting their turns for
surgery. Flying bullets were no respecters of canvas
barriers. Grabbing for the rifle the sentry had dropped,
he raised it and shot the man, but too late to prevent

the invader's round from striking one of the huddled corporals. The boy screamed; the rebel fell in a heap in the aisle between the operating tables.

Sentries and Yankees whose wounds were not too disabling ran in now, and used their rifles as clubs and fired their pistols at the rebels. The yells of the combatants rose to a cacophonous din as the air grew thick with smoke and the bitter smell of gunfire.

And still the surviving rebels kept shooting, and many of the previously wounded died like lambs in a slaughterhouse.

A red mist of rage swam in front of Nolan's eyes. Not pausing to reload, he tightened his grip on the fallen rebel's rifle and with a roar of fury, charged the rest of the attackers with the bayonet, skewering one man, then yanking the blade free to go after another.

It took only moments to kill the rest of the invaders, but as Nolan trudged back to the operating table, heart pounding and hands shaking, he saw that death had claimed one more victim. The soldier would not need his leg amputated after all, for he had bled to death while the battle raged around him.

Nolan awoke from the nightmare with a jerk, his entire body bathed in the cold sweat of horror. What battle had that been—Petersburg? Spotsylvania? It didn't matter; by the time the war was nearing its end, they had all blurred together.

Another man might have conceived a deeper hatred for the enemy after this attack; in Nolan it resulted in a more fervent desire to defeat death no matter which color uniform its victims wore.

As a physician, he was still fighting death, he thought

as he lay there feeling his pulse return to normal. Was his dream prophetic? Was he being warned that even though the war was over, violence committed by outlaws such as the Gray Boys still took a toll on lives?

"Let us rise and sing our closing hymn, 'A Mighty Fortress is Our God,'" Reverend Chadwick said with upraised palms, and the congregation stood as one. "And while we are singing it, let us remind ourselves that He is indeed a 'mighty Fortress,' no matter what brand of troubles are besetting us, whether it be Comanches, as it was last fall, or an epidemic, as we have just been through, or the depredations of outlaws, as we are currently experiencing. Let us pray together that God will enable our acting sheriff, Nicholas Brookfield, and his posse, who are at this very moment patrolling the countryside, to apprehend the outlaws who are endangering our peace. The army has been requested to aid us. In the end the Lord will enable us to triumph over all these trials, beloved, never doubt it."

Before opening his mouth to sing with the rest, Nolan added a silent amen to the preacher's prayer. If only he didn't feel so personally helpless in this matter. He, along with Sarah and the other "Spinster Nurses" had been instrumental in turning the tide against the influenza epidemic, but now he could only tend his patients, when they needed him, while other men rode out in pursuit of the gang.

Yes, medicine was his profession—it was up to him to help patients amid the "mortal ills prevailing" that the hymn spoke of, but in the midst of this crisis, it no longer seemed enough. His protestation to the mayor that he could not serve as the sheriff now seemed like a mere excuse to him to stay in his office, safe and secure, while other men risked their lives.

His gaze fell on Sarah as her fingers coaxed the melody of the majestic hymn from the old piano and those around him sang the age-old words of faith. Just to think that this lovely, talented lady loved him gave him a thrill each time he looked at her. He wanted to set a date for their wedding, to plan their future, yet there was no peace while these outlaws, led by one who had once been the center of Sarah's life, preyed on the people of Simpson Creek.

After church, they took a picnic lunch across Simpson Creek, and sure enough, they found the first blue-bonnets peeking up in their striking blue, white-topped glory from the tender new grass in the meadow where he had so recently asked Sarah to be his wife. They reminded him of the bigger lupines he had seen in Maine, but these were more vivid, more *brave* somehow, blooming before the calendar had officially decreed spring.

"Sarah, during church I was thinking—"

Once again they were interrupted by the sounds of approaching horsemen, and both of them went still, only to relax when they recognized the returning posse. But all was not well; Nick cradled in his arms Pat Donovan, the deputy sheriff. Donovan was unconscious, his face pallid, his trousers and the lower part of his coat saturated in blood.

"We ambushed them by Barnett Springs—almost had them, too, but they shot Pat's horse out from under him and then shot Pat in the thigh," Nick called, even as Sarah and Nolan rushed forward. "He's lost a lot of blood…passed out on the way back…"

"Get him to my office," Nolan shouted, gesturing in that direction, as he and Sarah ran for the buggy. His heart sank, for he knew the man was already doomed, but he had to try.

Thank You, Lord, for this dauntless woman. Sarah didn't have to be asked to help him. Once they ran into his office, she just rolled up the sleeves of her Sunday-best dress, threw on the heavy canvas apron he tossed her and began scrubbing her hands and arms with soap before rinsing them in carbolic.

Half an hour later, Sarah stared at Nolan from the other side of his exam table, her eyes wide with wordless grief as Nolan pulled a sheet over the deputy's face.

"He lost too much blood before he got here," Nolan muttered dully, wiping his hands on a towel. He wasn't sure if he spoke aloud or not. "If I'd been with them, maybe I could have saved him…."

"Nolan, you mustn't blame yourself," Sarah said gently, shrugging off her crimson-stained apron and coming around the table to take him in her arms, heedless of the tears that bathed her cheeks. "You did all you could…."

"I have to do more." He hugged her for a moment, then loosed her and pushed open the office door where Nick and the rest of the men waited.

"I couldn't save him," he announced. Some of the men stared at him, others dropped their gazes to their boots. "Nick, I want to take his place, till this is over. Swear me in."

"Nolan, no!" Sarah cried.

"Nolan—Dr. Walker—that's not necessary," Nick began. "The town needs a doctor, and only you can do that."

"I might have saved Donovan if I'd been along," Nolan said. "If I'd been there to staunch the bleeding, apply a tourniquet... No, my mind's made up, Brookfield," he added as Nick opened his mouth again. "You're a rancher serving as a lawman, I'm a doctor and I can help you. I can shoot. My buggy horse is trained to the saddle, too. I'll pack the medical supplies that might be useful in my saddlebags."

He walked Sarah home after that, Donovan's tin star pinned to his coat.

"Nolan, I wish you wouldn't do this." Sarah's voice was choked with unspent tears. "I don't know what I'd do if I lost you...."

"I'll be all right. Don't you see, I have to do this, sweetheart," he said, his arm around her waist as they walked toward the cottage. "Doesn't the Bible say there's a time for war and a time to heal? Right now I have to be willing to fight so I can go back to being a healer, and we can go on with our lives in peace. It's not the first time I've had to put my scalpel down and pick up a gun," he added, and told her about the day he'd done so in the medical tent.

She was wide-eyed when he finished. "Dear me. And yet the man you tried so hard to save, Jeffrey Beaumont, was a rebel."

"I had nightmares for months about the face of the man I had to shoot," he told her, not mentioning the fact that the nightmare had come again last night. "I think that's why I was so determined to save Jeff, to atone for it, even though I'd done what was necessary to save the others."

They had reached the cottage. "You *will* be careful?" she begged, worry creasing her lovely brow.

He nodded, and pulled her into his arms again, kissing her tenderly. "Of course." Then he had another thought. "Perhaps I should teach you to shoot, as well? I'll be away some with the posse—I don't like the idea of leaving you defenseless in case Holt takes a notion of trying to 'persuade' you to come with him again."

She shook her head. "It's not necessary, Nolan. Papa made sure both of us girls learned how to shoot a pistol in case we met up with a rattlesnake or something on the ranch. I have a derringer in the cottage—Milly made sure I brought it, just in case."

"Then promise me you'll keep it handy."

Chapter Twenty-Six

Prissy flushed pink with pleasure as Major McConley, riding at the head of a score of cavalry soldiers, tipped his cap at them as he trotted past. She rewarded him with a flirtatious smile.

"I'm so glad I wore my new bonnet," she said. "The major has such a cute dimple when he smiles, doesn't he? Sarah, do you suppose he's a bachelor?" Her gaze followed the disappearing cavalry detachment. "Perhaps we should issue an invitation to him—and the others in his regiment who are unmarried too, of course—to a Simpson Creek Spinsters' Club event. I might like to be a major's wife, I think."

Sarah thought it would be a long time until they'd be able to plan any more Spinsters' Club parties, but she had to smile at her friend's obvious attempt to distract her from her anxiety about Nolan. Only this morning the bell had tolled at the church—the signal for the posse to assemble there. Nolan had ridden eastward with Nick and the rest to investigate a report that the outlaws had been sighted camping on the banks of the Colorado River.

"Prissy Gilmore, living in a stockade, miles from the nearest stores?" Sarah teased. "I can't imagine it."

"You think I'm just a frivolous flibbertigibbet, don't you? I'll have you know I would make a very good soldier's wife. I'd organize tea parties for the wives, regimental balls… And just imagine the wedding— with his men crossing swords to form an arch over us as we left the church." She sighed dreamily. "But since you'll obviously be married before I will—to your handsome, brave doctor/deputy—perhaps we should ride out to see Milly. She's probably bored to tears with Nick away. I'm sure she'd help you design a wedding dress fit for a princess, then sew it for you."

"I'd love to go see her—I don't like her being out on that ranch without her husband there, even though the hands are sticking close to the house—but you know Nolan advised us not to ride out of town without him along until they've caught Jes—I mean the rustlers." She winced inwardly as she imagined the man she had once loved dying in a hail of bullets, or being marched up a gallows to be hanged.

"Well, we can at least look at the fabrics in the mercantile, and peruse their latest copy of Godey's," Prissy said.

Sarah gave in with a nod. Maybe it would keep herself from fretting about Nolan. She needed another sack of flour and a couple pounds of sugar, anyway, or she wouldn't be able to bake tomorrow.

"My, look at the time," Prissy exclaimed as they left the mercantile, peering at the delicate gold watch pin that had been her mother's. "Four o'clock already.

I had no idea it was getting so late, but didn't we have fun?"

Sarah had to admit poring over fashion designs and bolts of fabrics had been a pleasurable way to pass the afternoon. She'd found an exquisite ivory silk broche and Mrs. Patterson had agreed to put it in the back room for her until she could show it to Milly. And Prissy had gone ahead and bought a dress length of hussar blue cotton which she planned to pay Milly to sew into a party dress for when they invited the bachelors of the Fourth Cavalry to a Spinsters' party, saying, "Won't it look gorgeous against the darker blue of the major's dress uniform?"

Soon it would be time to go up to the big house for supper with Prissy's father, and with any luck Nolan might return to town in time to join her there. She hoped he would bring good news at last.

Crossing the street and entering through the massive gates to the Gilmore grounds, they walked to their cottage. Once inside, Sarah went into the kitchen with the staples she'd bought, while Prissy walked down the hall to her room to put her bonnet back in its hatbox.

Perhaps tomorrow she'd try the new recipe Caroline Wallace had given her for Washington pie. She liked to experiment with new things, and it was probably a wise idea to vary the fare she sold at the hotel and mercantile. It wasn't long before she would be able to get fresh peaches, and—

"Sarah, could you come here please? Quickly?" Prissy called from her room. Her voice sounded strained, unnatural, but Sarah only smiled, for it was the same tone she'd used before when she'd been startled by a mouse scurrying across the room to disappear into a crack in the wall.

"I'll be right there," Sarah called, wanting to finish pouring the five pounds of flour she'd bought into a canister before she went to console Prissy, who was no doubt standing on her bed. Prissy was deathly scared of mice. Maybe it would be a good idea to get a cat, she thought. It might be fun to get a kitten and teach it to chase after a length of yarn—

Sarah heard the door open, and footsteps coming down the short hallway between the two bedrooms.

"Sarah…" Prissy called again, her voice quavery.

Prissy must have managed to get between the door and the mouse.

"I'll get the broom and shoo it outside," Sarah said without turning around, as the now-empty bag of flour sagged in her hand. "You know, we ought to get a cat." She was determined to convey calmness in the face of Prissy's tendency to hysteria around rodents. "Mrs. Detwiler's cat is always having kittens. What would you like, a calico one, or maybe a sweet little black one with white boots—"

"I've always been partial to gray tigers, myself." The voice was female, but it was not Prissy's.

Sarah whirled and looked into the ruthless eyes of Ada Spencer, and then into the bore of the pistol the woman had leveled at her. In front of Ada was Prissy, her blue eyes enormous in a face that was leached of all color, holding her hands in the air, and as Ada pushed her forward, Sarah could see she had the barrel of another pistol poking between her friend's shoulders.

"What are you doing here, Ada?" Sarah's voice

sounded strange in her own ears, as if it belonged to someone else, someone far calmer than she felt, someone whose knees felt more substantial than a half-baked cake. *Dear God, help us!*

"Jesse wants you taken to him, so I've come to accomplish it," she said, as if it should be perfectly obvious and logical. "I'm the only one who can do it. He and his men can hardly storm into town after you—they'd stick out like sore thumbs. That's why they let themselves be seen by some yahoos over on the Colorado River so the sheriff and his men would go riding after them—leaving you here in town alone."

If only I'd put the derringer in the reticule sitting just inches away on the table, as I'd promised Nolan that I would.

Even so, the idea of going anywhere with this madwoman was ridiculous, and ignited her ire. "I'm not going," Sarah told her. "I don't love him anymore."

"You'll go if you want Prissy to live," Ada said, a mad glint in her eyes told Sarah that she would be perfectly willing to pull the trigger of the gun pressed into Prissy's back.

"Sarah…" Prissy shook like a leaf in a gale, and Sarah thought she may faint. If she did, Sarah might be able to use the element of surprise if she acted fast—or it might give Ada an even greater advantage. She would have two pistols to aim at Sarah, and no Prissy to get in the way. *Lord, show me what to do.*

Ada was armed, and not in her right mind. Sarah realized she would have to rein in her temper, and try to reason with a deranged woman.

"Why would you want to do that, Ada? I know you

love Jesse, so I would think you wouldn't want a rival for his affections." If she could distract Ada enough, perhaps she could overpower her before Ada could get a shot off. But she'd be risking both her life and Prissy's.

The woman's laugh was brittle as the sheerest glass. "Oh, you won't be a rival. As if you could be! No, Jesse has other plans for you. And if I do this, Jesse's going to marry me. He said so. He'll buy me a beautiful ring and a fancy dress...." She recited the outlaw's promises in a strange singsong that sent chills down Sarah's back. It was like a child reciting a nursery rhyme.

"'Other plans?'" Sarah echoed. "What other plans?"

"We're taking a little trip with you, going up on the Staked Plains where we'll sell you to the Comanches, along with the cattle the boys've gathered. Some Comanche brave will pay a fine price for you, Miss Yellowhair." She laughed, a laugh that teetered on the edge of maniacal. "Or maybe you'll go to the Comancheros—maybe they could find a use for you. Meanwhile, of course, Jesse's men will...get to know you better." Again, that brittle laugh.

The idea of any of the Gray Boys touching her, then being taken north and sold as a slave to a brutal Indian or the Mexican traders that sold firearms to them paralyzed Sarah, but she couldn't give in to that fear.

For God hath not given us the spirit of fear....

"But why would he do that?" Sarah asked, if motivated by curiosity alone. "He loved me once, but now he has *you*, Ada. He doesn't need me. Why can't he leave me in peace and go off with you?"

"You have to pay, Jesse says." Again, that eerie sing-song tone. "He came back for you, and you broke his heart. I'm mending it, of course, in my own sweet way, but you have to pay. No one gets away with breaking my Jesse's heart." Her grip tightened on the pistol.

"He doesn't have a heart anymore," Sarah said. "He lost it somewhere in the war." She tried another tack. "Why would you want a man like that, Ada? What if he gets tired of you and sells *you* to the Comanches?"

"You stop talking like that!" Ada cried, her voice shrill. The pistol—the one that wasn't pressed into Prissy's back, rose again and pointed at Sarah's chest. "Jesse wouldn't do that. He *loves* me! Now stop wasting time. We have to leave. You two kept me waiting—kept Jesse waiting—too long as it is. I thought you'd never come back here, once the posse left town. We have to go."

Where was Nolan? What time was it? Was it late enough that the posse was even now riding back into town? Was there a chance Nolan would come here, looking for her, and save her from Ada? She dared not look at the clock, but she knew that if she and Prissy didn't show up at the big house for dinner, eventually Mayor Gilmore would send Flora or Antonio to check on them.

Could she stare over Ada's shoulder and convincingly say, "Hello, Nolan, I'm so glad you're here," as if Nolan had returned and sneaked silently into the cottage? Would Ada turn around, and would she be able to overcome the crazed woman before Ada could fire either of the pistols?

It would be taking a chance with Prissy's life. And

she couldn't do that. She couldn't live with the idea that she had gotten Prissy killed.

"If you want your silly friend to live, you better come with me right now," Ada said, waving the pistol aimed at Sarah. "I'll shoot her—it doesn't matter to me."

"But the sound of the shot will make the Gilmore servants come running, Ada," Sarah said reasonably. "You don't want that."

"But she'd still be dead. Maybe you, too."

There was no help for it. She had to walk out of the cottage with Ada, and hope Nolan would intervene before she was in Jesse's clutches.

"All right, Ada, I'll walk out of here with you, and Prissy won't tell anyone, will you, Prissy?"

Clearly mindless with fear, Prissy shook her head.

"But someone will see us," Sarah went on. "It's getting late, and the posse's due back in town any minute now. Even if I leave with you, and Prissy does nothing to stop you, someone will see us walking out of here together. The whole town knows you've been riding with the outlaws, Ada. They're not going to stand by and let you take me anywhere."

"The posse isn't coming back," Ada said. "The boys set up an ambush, and they're probably all dead. Your precious Yankee doctor isn't coming to save you."

Nolan, dead? No, it couldn't be. Surely she'd know it, in her heart, if he'd been killed. But even if the outlaws hadn't succeeded in murdering Nolan, Nick and the others, she couldn't count on them coming back in time to keep Ada from taking her from Simpson Creek, taking her to Jesse.

"All right, then, Ada, what's your plan?" Sarah said, determined not to give in to panic and grief. Even if she left with Ada, Prissy would be left to tell Nolan and the others that Ada had kidnapped her at gunpoint, with the intention of taking her to Jesse and the Gray Boys, to be transported north to the Staked Plains, the Comanche stronghold.

As if she had been able to read minds, Ada killed that hope by raising the pistol she'd held against Prissy's back and striking Prissy viciously over the top of her head—all the while keeping the other pistol trained on Sarah.

Prissy went down without a cry, as limply as the sack of flour Sarah had emptied only a few minutes before. Sarah stared in horror as a red stain spread through Prissy's strawberry-blond hair.

"You've killed her!"

"Shut up. I just knocked out the silly fool, that's all."

"But she's bleeding—"

Ada shrugged. "If she dies, what do I care? She's nothing but a spoiled, pampered daughter of a rich man. She's always had everything she ever wanted—what did I have? Her mother even gave me some of her cast-off clothes, did you know that?"

Sarah shook her head numbly.

"But we're wasting time," Ada snapped. "I'm going to put on her bonnet and coat—and you're not going to do anything or I'll shoot her and make double sure she's dead, understand? No one will look twice at Sarah and Prissy, strolling down the road that runs south of town right between the Gilmore land and the saloon. Jesse's waiting for us just outside of town."

Chapter Twenty-Seven

Ada donned Prissy's coat, keeping the pistol within easy reach.

Sarah's gaze went back and forth from Ada to Prissy's motionless, sprawled body on the floor. If only she would move! After a few moments, Sarah finally detected the slight rise and fall of breathing in Prissy's slender shoulders. So she wasn't dead, Sarah thought, trying to take hope from that slight encouragement. While there was life, there was hope, wasn't there?

But Prissy could be dying, a pessimistic voice within her whispered. There was so much blood seeping from Prissy's scalp and pooling onto the wooden floor, staining it. Beneath Prissy's skull, she could be bleeding to death. Would Nolan arrive in time to save Prissy, at least?

"I'm ready," Ada said, settling Prissy's bonnet over her hair.

Why had she never noticed before how similar Ada's hair was to Prissy's? Prissy's was more vibrantly curly and shiny, but in the fading light, and with Ada's hair mostly covered under the bonnet, no one would notice the difference. The two women were of a similar height. People were so used to seeing Sarah and Prissy together, and they would see what they expected to see.

"Let's go," Ada said. Now that Prissy was no longer a threat to her, she had shoved one of the pistols into the waistband of her skirt. She waved the other one at Sarah. "How convenient that your precious Prissy's arms are longer than mine. It'll make it easy to conceal the pistol—but it'll be aimed at you the whole time, Sarah, never doubt it. If we meet anyone on the way out of town, and you try to tell them anything, I'll shoot you *and* them, I promise you."

"A-All right." Sarah stopped to take one last look at Prissy.

"She won't wake up for hours, if she ever wakes up at all," Ada said with a cruel chuckle. "So don't imagine her telling them where you've gone. Now *move*."

Sarah sighed. *Please save Prissy, Lord. Let her live.* She started for the door, praying with every step.

Maybe Antonio would be lingering outside the stable, as he often did in the late afternoon after feeding the horses, before he went in to help Flora serve supper. He'd see them, realize it was nearly suppertime and remind Prissy that her father hated her to be late to the table. Then Ada would react in an un-Prissy-like way that would betray her true identity. Antonio would get suspicious, approach them, then challenge her. Ada would take fright and flee, despite her threats, for Antonio was tall and as solid as an old live oak.

Or maybe Nolan would arrive, just as they reached the gate. Nolan would never be fooled by Ada, who'd been his patient, after all. He'd recognize her immediately.

But Antonio was not lounging at the barn door, nor did Nolan happen to be entering the grounds.

"You know, Ada, your outlaws would've been smarter to circle around and rob the bank after they lured the posse toward the Colorado," Sarah remarked as they walked out through the gates, her gaze darting all around her for someone—*anyone*—who might be able to help her. But there was no one exiting the hotel or the saloon. "There's a lot of money in the bank and valuables in its safe. That's what I'd have done, if I'd been an outlaw. It sure would have been a larger prize than me. So maybe they aren't so clever, after all."

"Shut your mouth," Ada hissed. "My Jesse's smart as a fox. He's not just any outlaw."

"But maybe he doesn't know how to rob banks," Sarah suggested. "That's all right. Not every outlaw's daring enough to rob a bank." Maybe if she could spark Ada's temper, the other girl would lunge at her and Sarah could wrestle the gun away.

"I said shut up." Ada's voice was definitely a snarl now. "Jesse knows what he wants, that's all. You. Teaching you a lesson is more important to him than robbing banks. He can do that any ol' time, after he's handed you over to some savage.

"This way," Ada said, indicating the road that led south out of town, which didn't make sense if the outlaws were headed north for the Staked Plains. Sarah was about to point this out when she spotted Mrs. Patterson exiting the mercantile. The recent widow was locking the door of the shop, but then she turned around and saw them.

"Good evening, Sarah, Prissy! Where are you headed? Warm for this early in March, isn't it? I suppose that means we'll have a hot summer…Oh, were you headed to the store for something? I could unlock again if that's the case."

Sarah pondered the wisdom of claiming the need for sugar or some other item. Mrs. Patterson would become suspicious if Ada remained where she was standing, but Ada would never dare follow her into the mercantile.

Once again, Ada seemed to have the uncanny ability to read Sarah's mind. Sarah felt the unmistakable nudge of the gun barrel in her side, hid by the long sleeve of Prissy's coat. "Don't try it," Ada said in a low, menacing tone.

"No, no thank you, Mrs. Patterson," Sarah called back. "We…uh…we were headed to Mrs. Detwiler's," she said, pointing down the road which would lead past Mrs. Detwiler's large house. "For supper. She invited us for supper. Wasn't that nice? She knew we'd be bored, especially me, what with Nolan riding with the posse and all…" If she accomplished nothing else, she wanted to imprint on Mrs. Patterson's mind which way they had gone, in case Nolan questioned her about seeing Sarah leaving. Maybe, if Sarah was very lucky, the widow would decide it was strange that Sarah was talkative to the point of babbling, a trait that had never been characteristic of her.

"That *is* nice. Mrs. Detwiler's always been an excellent cook," Mrs. Patterson called back agreeably. "All right, if you don't need anything, I'll just go home and have my supper then. You girls have a good evening."

Sarah felt an ache of regret as the woman waved, then turned and walked away down the side street that ran between the hotel and the mercantile.

Maybe Mrs. Detwiler would be out in her front yard, admiring the tulips coming up in her flower beds, and Sarah could make another attempt to free herself of Ada. Mrs. Detwiler's eagle eye missed nothing, but she would have to be very careful not to endanger the old woman, too.

"A wild-goose chase," Nolan grumbled as they rode westward back toward Simpson Creek in the chilly March air. "They wanted us to catch glimpses of them, but not get close enough to capture them."

"Indeed," Nick agreed, as the two men rode at the head of the posse. Earlier, they'd catch sight of one of the outlaws, who'd gallop off, then disappear—only to be replaced by another of them springing up nearby seemingly out of the blue and running off in a different direction, over and over again. A wild-goose chase, all right—a well-orchestrated one.

"I wonder what that game was about?" Nick mused aloud. "Why not keep out of sight until they struck again, instead of leading us on a merry chase?"

"Unless they were decoying us…." Suddenly Nolan was sure that was exactly what it had been. "Nick, they *wanted* to keep us out here, trying to catch each of them in turn. *They wanted us out of town.*"

"But why? Was part of the gang going to rob the bank? Of course, that must be it. What a fool I've been to be lured by such an obvious trick!" Nick cried. "We've got to get back to Simpson Creek!" He set his spurs to his mount's flanks as Nolan and the others did likewise.

Nolan wasn't convinced the bank had been the target, however. All at once a soul-deep dread had entered his heart, and he was certain within himself that the trickery somehow involved Sarah. *Sarah!* He'd gone haring off with the posse, trying to prove he was just as brave as any other man, *and left Sarah unprotected.*

"Jesse?"

At first, all Sarah saw in the gathering darkness was what appeared to be an extra thick trunk of a live oak tree. Then the long, lean frame of Jesse Holt detached himself from the trunk he'd been leaning against, spitting out the unlit cheroot he'd been chewing.

"Where have you been, woman? You dillydallied so long it's dark now," he grumbled at Ada. "Gettin' mighty cold, too."

Now Sarah could see the shadowy forms of the horses tied to the back of the grove of trees, and heard them stamping and jingling their bits.

"I didn't know this stupid female was going to spend all afternoon in the mercantile with that Prissy Gilmore ninny, did I?" Ada whined, pointing at Sarah. "But I got her here to you. I even had to knock Prissy out with the gun. I think I killed her, but I don't care. I did it for you." Her tone was suddenly servile, and her supplicant posture reminded Sarah of a cringing dog wagging its tail in hopes of not being kicked. *Hmm....* So Ada wasn't quite Jesse's darling as she had boasted—perhaps Sarah could use that to her advantage.

Sarah saw Jesse's eyes narrow and sensed he hadn't liked Ada calling her stupid, or perhaps it was her whiny tone that had set his teeth on edge.

"She didn't hurt you, did she, Sarah?" Jesse asked, coming forward to peer at her.

"No, of course I didn't hurt her!" Ada snapped. "What kind of idiot do you take me for? You said not to, and I didn't. Though I surely wanted to slap her smug face," she muttered.

"She didn't hurt me," Sarah confirmed in the calmest tone she could manage. "But I don't want to go with you." She had little hope that she'd change his mind now after he'd gone this far, but she had to try. "Jesse, we loved each other once, but we've each changed. For the sake of what we had, let me go. I'll walk back into town and tell them you went the opposite direction of whichever way you go. I promise I will."

"Sweetheart, I'm not gonna do that," he said, his tone soothing, his hand rough as he stepped closer and caressed her face. "I'm right pleased you're here, and I'm not about to let you go now."

Sarah hadn't expected him to agree, but she couldn't help backing away from his touch.

"No, you aren't, 'cause you've got big plans for Sarah, isn't that right, Jesse, darling?" cooed Ada. "I've been telling her how you're gonna trade her to some dirty redskin up on the Staked Plains, or maybe some half-breed Mexican Comanchero. I can hardly wait to see that."

"Be quiet, woman, or I'll give *you* to 'em for nothing,"

Jesse snapped. "Me and Miss Sarah, here, are gonna get reacquainted-like, on the way up to the Llano Estacado, aren't we? That long a ride, I reckon there'll be plenty a' time to remember why we were once so sweet on one 'nother," he drawled, keeping a hard grasp on Sarah's chin so she couldn't look away.

His breath smelled of stale whiskey, and now, out of the corner of her eye, she caught sight of an empty bottle propped up against the tree trunk.

"Yes sir, if you're friendly enough, Sarah Matthews, I might forget all about tradin' you and just trade the cattle instead," Jesse continued.

"Jesse Holt, you stop talking that way!" Ada cried. "*I'm* your woman, not her! We're gettin' married after you trade her off, you said so! And I don't share with nobody!"

"Is that a fact?" Jesse inquired, lifting an eyebrow. He sounded as if he didn't mind very much one way or the other, but a prudent person would have detected the cold menace in his gaze as he shifted it from Sarah to Ada.

"Yes, it is. You said you were a one-woman man, and I'm going to take you at your word," Ada said, but her tone had changed to wheedling again.

"I am," Jesse agreed. "Only you ain't the one." As soon as the words left his mouth, he whipped his pistol from his holster and shot Ada.

Chapter Twenty-Eight

"C'mon. The boys'll be waiting for us at the hideout," Jesse said, yanking on Sarah's arm as she stood frozen in horror, staring at the fallen form of Ada Spencer. "We're gonna settle in for the night, snug an' cozy, and then head north at first light."

"You killed her!" Sarah cried, for the second time in an hour, but this time she was very, very sure it was true. She'd seen the bullet strike Ada's chest. "How could you do that, Jesse Holt? Ada *loved* you. She thought you loved her. She said you were going to marry her."

Jesse gave a harsh bark of laughter. "From what I've heard in the short time I've been back to town, ol' Ada believed quite a few things lately—she thought that Englishman was going to marry her, too, didn't she, and that she was with child by your precious Yankee doctor. Some women'll believe anything you tell 'em, 'long as it's somethin' they want to hear. Now get on that horse—we've got some hard ridin' to do, Sarah-girl."

Sarah tried to yank her arm out of his iron grasp.

"But you can't just leave her there, lying in the dirt," she protested. "It isn't right, Jesse!"

He stared down at her and gave her a sardonic smile. "Do you think I'm gonna take the time to bury her? I ain't done much lately you could call *right*, so there's no use startin' now. The critters'll take care of her carcass. Get on the horse now, Sarah Matthews, or I'll shoot you, too."

Just as Nolan had thought, the Simpson Creek bank had been undisturbed. It was closed now for the day, and the bank president assured them that he'd seen nothing of the Gray Boys.

Nolan then gave voice to his fears about Sarah, and the posse had headed for the cottage. Filled with foreboding, Nolan jumped off his horse.

"We'll wait here till you make sure everything's all right," Nick called after him as he pounded on the door of the cottage.

"Sarah! Sarah! Are you in there?"

Had his ears caught some faint sound within, or was he hearing things? He pushed at the door, found it unlocked and ran in, then nearly stumbled on Prissy sitting propped up against the stove, a blood-stained dish towel to her head.

He dropped to his knees. "Prissy! What happened to you? Where's Sarah? Nick! I've found Prissy! She's injured!" he called over his shoulder.

Prissy winced at his shout and favored him with a swollen-eyed gaze. "She hit me over the head. With a gun."

"Sarah hit you with a gun?" Could he be hearing her right?

Prissy shook her head weakly, then moaned at the obvious pain the motion caused. "No. *Ada* hit me. She surprised us here and forced Sarah to go with her at gunpoint."

"Go? Go where?"

"She was taking her to Jesse Holt and the outlaws—said they were going to take her and the stolen cattle up on the Staked Plains and sell her to the Comanches, or the Comancheros."

Her words struck Nolan like a blow, rocking him back on his haunches.

"Why would he do that?" he demanded, as Nick ran in.

Prissy lifted one shoulder and winced again. "Revenge. Nolan, you've got to stop them! Hurry! You can't let them take her!"

By this time, Antonio had heard the commotion and come running into the cottage, as well.

"What has happened? The senorita, she is injured?"

Nolan jumped to his feet, overwhelmed for the moment with conflicting responsibilities. A dangerously insane Ada was taking Sarah to the outlaws, and they intended to sell her to the savages, or renegade Mexicans—but as a doctor, he had a responsibility to tend Prissy, too. A blow from a heavy object like a gun could fracture a skull.

"Nick, you've got to ride after them!" he told the Englishman. "Prissy, do you know if you were knocked unconscious?" He pulled the dish towel gently from Prissy's hands and probed Prissy's scalp with gentle fingers, seeking and finding the swelling beneath, but no disruption of the bone.

"Just d-dazed for a moment, I think… After that, I pretended to be unconscious," she said, and a tear trickled down her pale cheek. "I'm so sorry, Nolan! I was scared out of my wits, but I should have fought her…kept that madwoman from taking Sarah…"

"No, you could have been killed for your pains, my girl," Nick soothed in his sensible British voice, "and then we'd have *no* idea what had happened to her. You did the right thing."

"How bad is your head hurting? Can you see straight? How many fingers am I holding up?" Nolan asked.

Prissy blinked at the barrage of questions. "Three. Yes, I've got a headache, but if Antonio will bring me some ice from the springhouse, I'll be fine. *Go with the posse, Nolan,* don't stay here with me. Go! Every minute, they're getting farther away!"

Nolan nodded. "All right, Prissy, I will. Antonio, can you carry your mistress up to the big house, then get her some ice?"

"*Sí,* senor, I will do this," the other man said, scooping up Prissy as if she weighed nothing. "Flora will stay with her. But it grows dark, and there will only be a half moon tonight. There are lanterns in the stable. Take them."

Nolan locked gazes with Nick. "You know the area better—what way would they go, if they're headed northward? The road between the mayor's house and the saloon is handy—Ada wouldn't have to risk them being seen going through town—but it runs south, not north."

"But only a little way out of town, there's a fork that bends north," Nick told him. "It's the only way north that's close."

"That's likely the way, then. We'd better get those lanterns."

Both men ran out of the cottage. As Nolan headed for the stable, he heard Nick tell the posse what they'd learned.

His brain seethed with rage and fear at the thought of the fate Holt had in mind for Sarah. How could any man contemplate selling a woman—any woman, but especially the one he'd once professed to love—to a savage? And crazy Ada—he should have had her locked in an asylum when he'd had the chance. He'd let compassion blind him, he thought angrily. If he'd done the responsible thing as a physician, realizing she was dangerous and beyond his help, they would not now be riding after the outlaws in the dark, hoping they could find them before they went very far.

How terrified Sarah must be in the hands of the insane woman, much less Jesse Holt and the pack of wolves he ran with! If Holt touched so much as one golden hair on Sarah's head, he promised himself, he'd make the outlaw wish he'd never been born.

If she had lain where she had first fallen, they would never have seen her as they thundered past. But after Jesse had left with Sarah, Ada had crawled with the last of her strength out of the grove of trees, collapsing at last by the side of the road. Even so they might have missed the slight, crumpled form if the wind hadn't picked up as the posse approached and caught the edge of her petticoat, fluttering it in the breeze like a signal flag.

"Look yonder! Somethin'—somebody's layin' by the road!" one of the men in the posse yelled, raising his lantern high and pointing ahead. "I think it's a woman!"

Nolan spotted what the man had seen. His heart rose to his throat and threatened to choke him. Had they killed his Sarah here and left her body for the coyotes to find? He spurred his horse toward the body, vowing retribution against every last one of the Gray Boys gang. He'd make sure Jesse Holt strangled at the end of a rope, if he didn't succeed in shooting him himself.

He jumped off his horse, who shied at the fluttering petticoat, ran to the fallen woman and turned her, his mind going numb at the sight of the dark red stain drenching the front of her coat and bodice.

It's Ada, not Sarah. For a moment he could hardly speak for the relief that flooded through him. Ada was dead. As long as the body he was cradling wasn't Sarah's, there was hope, wasn't there?

And then the woman's eyes flickered, and she took a shuddering breath, opened them, then blinked as she tried to focus on Nolan's face.

"Dr. Walker...f-fancy meeting y-you here," Ada whispered. She tried to smile, but the effort resulted in a grotesquely lopsided grimace instead.

Even in the wavering light of the lantern one of the other men held high above them, Nolan could see the ashy, waxen quality of the woman's face. Her lips were bloodless, her eyes dilated, and a trickle of blood had dried at the side of her chin.

"Ada, where's Sarah? Where have they taken her? Tell me," he pleaded, knowing that he might have only seconds to worm the truth out of her. "I'll do everything I can to save your life, if you'll just tell me."

Ada's slender shoulders heaved with the effort to speak. "E-everything you…can? Isn't…very much… anyone could do, is there? E-easy t' say…"

"Please, Ada," he begged as the woman's eyelids drifted shut. Any second now she would take her last breath, and they'd know nothing more than they had before. *Please, God, give her strength to tell me, and forgive her…*

"Wouldn't have…told you…till that s-snake betrayed me…chose her…instead… He shot me…"

"Holt shot you?" Nick demanded, standing beside Nolan.

Ada shifted her gaze to include the Englishman, tried to nod. "Sh-should-should've known…couldn't trust him. Not any man… Now listen, not much time…"

Nolan had to put his ear almost next to Ada's mouth to hear words that weren't so much whispered as breathed. A minute later, he closed her eyes and laid her body down again.

At Nick's direction, they sent the oldest man in the posse, the mill owner, back to Simpson Creek with Ada's body, while the rest of them rode northward into the night.

Jesse tied her hands together in front, then held a gun on Sarah while she mounted one of the two horses in the grove. This horse was saddled, but bridleless, with a rope around its neck so he could lead it, but she could not direct it. The fact that there were only two horses in the grove told Sarah that Jesse had probably never intended to take Ada with them.

And he'd had to know that if he'd merely left Ada standing there and deserted her, that she'd tell others out of sheer spite where they were headed. So it was likely he'd planned all along to murder poor, foolish Ada. The thought sent icicles shooting through her veins, but she said nothing. What was the point of hearing him deny it, or worse, admit it?

Jesse struck a match against the rock and lit the lantern that had been hanging over his saddle horn, and they headed back onto the road at a lope. They rode steadily in silence until they reached the Colorado River, where Jesse stopped to water the horses. He whistled "Tenting on the Old Campground" as the horses lowered their heads into the water.

"They'll come after you, you know," Sarah said. She didn't know if it was possible, but she had to try to chip away at Jesse's confidence. It was all she could think of. Besides, his answer would tell her whether Ada's assertion that the outlaws had killed the posse was true or not. "Nolan and the rest of the posse won't just let you take me without doing anything about it. You could still let me go, you know, and save your skin."

"Goldilocks, by the time they figure out which way we've gone, it'll be too late."

Then Nolan is alive. Thank You, Lord.

"Who's gonna tell 'em? Ada left Prissy with her head split open, didn't she? She's likely as dead as Ada by now. You tryin' to make me believe there was anyone else there? You're lying."

"There was no one else," Sarah admitted, "but Prissy wasn't dead. I saw her breathing." She prayed it was still true. "They'll find her—in fact, they probably have already because it was nearly suppertime. We're expected at her father's house. And when she comes to, she'll tell them you're headed north, because Ada bragged about the whole plan before she knocked Prissy out."

Jesse's jaw hardened and he spat in irritation. "Why do women have to talk so much? Oh, well, it don't matter, even if she does wake up. We've got a long head start, and once we reach the hideout, they'll never find us."

"And what if Ada didn't die, either?" Sarah needled. "They'll find her, too, and she'll tell the posse exactly where the hideout is, won't she? I'm sure you've taken her there. After what you did to her, she'll be delighted to testify about you and see you hang."

Jesse's hoot of laughter sent a couple of bullfrogs plopping into the water in alarm.

"Oh, crazy Ada's dead all right. You saw where that bullet hit her. She won't be telling anyone anything. I will admit I shouldn't have wasted my time with her, though, if it makes you feel any better. I should've tried harder to sweet talk you into coming with me, Sarah-girl. You could still change your mind and be agreeable about it, you know, and if you're smart, you will."

Sarah's laugh was mirthless. "'If it makes me *feel*

any better'? You can talk till the end of time and I wouldn't change my mind."

He tipped her chin up and stared down at her, and Sarah froze. He could do anything with her right now, anything—even throw her tied up and helpless into the chill waters of the Colorado. She was helpless and alone.

No, you're not alone, Sarah Matthews. The Bible promises God is with me always.

"Yeah, you'd best be reconsiderin' your position before we get up to the Staked Plains. You try spoutin' off to some Comanche buck like that, and he'll decide that yellow hair would look mighty nice decoratin' his teepee. Or he'll let the squaws have you, and I hear that's worse. Either way, I hear captive white women don't live too long among the Comanches, and by the time they die, they're beggin' for someone to put them outa their misery. And if by some miracle you got back to civilization, what decent man would have you?"

His words left Sarah speechless with horror.

Please, Lord, let Nolan save me!

Chapter Twenty-Nine

Sarah awakened from a fitful, miserable doze when the horses halted.

"Took you long enough," the outlaw standing sentry duty grumbled as he opened the gate and let them ride inside.

"Things involving women always take longer than you'd think," Jesse muttered, "'specially when one of 'em's loco."

"Yeah, where *is* crazy Ada?" the other asked, peering at Sarah and beyond her. "You promised she could be mine once you got Goldilocks."

"'You promised,'" Jesse mimicked. "You sound like some little kid. Shut up, Jones. Go find your bedroll and get some shut-eye. We leave at dawn."

"Hope she's worth it," Jones muttered, and stalked away.

"Where are we?" Sarah asked, peering around them in the dim light cast by a campfire, around which lay sleeping men. She made out the dark mass of a barn, with an irregularly shaped corral filled with the cattle lowing, some lying down, some milling slowly around.

She'd lost track of time as they'd followed the snakelike path of the Colorado northwest, finally crossing it at a shallow ford. The water had drenched her skirts nearly to the waist, and now, in the cool March air, she was wretchedly cold.

"Far from home, Sarah-girl," Jesse said with smirk. "This here's the farm of a loyal Confederate colonel, one who hasn't bowed his head to the blasted Blue Bellies, though he pretends to enough to get along. It's far off the main road and other farms that no one pays him any mind. He's been real happy to hide us, re-brand the cattle as we bring them to him, and all he asks is a share of the money when we sell them, to start the new treasury."

"Treasury? Treasury of what?"

"The treasury of the New Confederate States of America," Jesse said proudly, puffing out his chest. "We're gonna help him overthrow the Federals one a' these fine days and he'll be the president of our new republic."

Sarah could only stare at him and fight the urge to laugh hysterically.

The lanterns had run out of fuel and the half moon had gone behind a cloud.

"We've got to stop till first light," Nick said, after Nolan's horse had put a hoof into a gopher hole along the dark road and gone down, throwing him off. Fortunately, the beast hadn't broken its leg, and only Nolan's pride was injured, but now the horse was limping and couldn't be ridden. They'd have to leave him at the first ranch they came to, and return for him later.

Nolan, walking toward the spare mount that had been brought along for Sarah, stopped and turned around. "Not on your life. It won't be dawn for hours yet, and who knows what might be happening to Sarah?"

"Walker, we can't help Sarah if our horses break their legs and have to be shot," Nick pointed out.

"And it'll be tricky finding the right ford in the dark, too," said Amos Wallace, the postmaster. "You risk running into quicksand if you try to cross in the wrong place. Anyway, like as not Holt's stopped, too, Doc."

Wallace was probably correct that Holt and Sarah had stopped, Nolan knew, but what Holt was doing while stopped didn't bear thinking about.

"The horses will be fresher if we rest them now, Nolan," Nick continued. "I promise, soon as it's light, we'll make good time and catch up."

"Holt's horses will be fresh, too," Nolan countered stubbornly. The idea of stopping even for a minute filled him with furious frustration, even though he knew they were right.

"But he won't know we're coming," Nick reminded him. "He'll figure poor Miss Ada died without having the chance to tell us where the hideout is. As far as he knows, we have no idea where he's taken her. If we hadn't known they were headed for the Staked Plains, I'd have figured them to go south, heading for the Rio Grande, to sell those cattle to the Mexicans."

And Sarah.

"I dunno what makes Holt think them Comanches are gonna just tamely trade them rifles or whatever for them cattle," observed another man. "What's t'stop them from scalpin' all them outlaws and takin' the cattle, too?"

And Sarah.

Nolan glared at him, and the fellow realized what he'd unwittingly implied. "Sorry, Doc. Guess I spoke when I shoulda kept my trap shut. Don't you worry, we'll catch them outlaws tomorrow, and get Miss Sarah back safe and sound."

Colonel Robert Throckmorton, late of the Confederate Army, waved a hand in welcome when the posse galloped up the muddy road to his farmhouse the next morning.

"Gentlemen, what can I do for you this fine mornin'?" he called out with bluff heartiness, his lips curving into a genial smile under a heavy silver mustache. "I'd offer you breakfast, but you look like y'all are in too much of a hurry. And surely it's not necessary for all y'all to have your firearms aimed at me. I've offered you no harm."

Nolan studied the man, who looked like the epitome of the defeated but unreconstructed Southern officer. There was something shifty about his gaze, something that hinted to Nolan he'd much prefer shooting them in the back as they left to merely sending them on their way peaceably.

"I'm Sheriff Nicholas Brookfield of Simpson Creek, San Saba County," Nick said. "We need you to tell us which way the Gray Boys are heading."

"'Gray Boys?' I've got no idea who you're talkin' about," the man said.

Nolan cocked his pistol. "Stop your nonsense, or

I'll shoot you where you stand, Throckmorton. We know they've been hiding out here, them and the cattle they've stolen. So you'd better tell us what we need to know right quick."

"First a foreigner, now a Yankee," the man sneered.

"But the rest of us are good Texans who believe in doin' what's right," Amos Wallace said, and cocked his weapon.

Throckmorton visibly flinched at the metallic *click* and turned back to Nick. "Sheriff, honest, I don't rightly know what you're talkin' about," the man protested, palms up. He studiously avoided Nolan's glare. "You see there's no cattle here," he said, pointing at the empty corral and pastures. "I sold my cattle to a drover just last week, as a matter of fact. Got a good price for 'em, too," he said smugly.

Out of the corner of his eye, Nolan saw Amos Wallace loosen a coil of rope that had been tied to his saddle. He calmly began to knot a hangman's noose at the end of it. "I reckon that cottonwood over yonder would serve right well for a hanging, Sheriff."

The florid-face colonel blanched. "Hanging? Me? You can't do that! On what charge?" He turned back to Nick. "You're a foreigner! Are you even familiar with the laws in this country? You can't lynch an innocent man!" he bellowed, his eyes bulging over fat cheeks.

"Oh, can't we? Who's to stop us?" Nick said, looking around him. "I'd think a farmer would have at least a hand or two around, but your place looks fairly deserted. I'd say you sent your men along to help control the herd—and to make sure the Gray Boys don't double-cross you out of your share of the money."

"Throckmorton, the men you've been hiding have a kidnapped woman with them," Nolan said, keeping a rein on his temper with difficulty. "Surely a chivalrous Southern gentleman such as you can't possibly approve of selling her to the savages along with the cattle," Nolan said, giving the man one more chance to redeem himself.

"Of course not!" the colonel said, trying to assume a shocked expression and failing deplorably. "I told you, I've seen no outlaws, and no woman, either. You have to believe me." He pulled at his shirt collar as if it was suddenly too tight.

Nick nodded to Wallace, who trotted his horse over to the cottonwood and threw the noose over it. It bounced obscenely in the breeze.

Throckmorton couldn't take his eyes off of it. He swallowed with difficulty, as if the noose was already tightening around his neck.

"Now, just a minute, gentlemen, surely we can come to some agreement," he said quickly.

"What's it going to be, Throckmorton?" Nick asked. "Are we to hang you or are you going to take us to them?"

"Take you to them?" the man said, his Southern colonel dignity suddenly vanished, his tone now wheedling. "Surely it would be enough to just tell you which road they've taken, Sheriff. They can't be far ahead of you—they left just an hour ago, and they're driving cattle. But please don't make me go—y-you can't imagine how ruthless these men are! Why, they'd shoot me on sight if they saw me riding with you. Please…I'll give you all the information you need…"

"All the more reason for you to go," Nolan growled. "Getting yourself shot is one way you could atone."

"Nolan, Amos, take him into the barn and make him saddle a horse," Nick ordered. "Keep your pistols on him at all times. If he gets up to any mischief, shoot him—but make sure it's only painful, not fatal. We'll need him for directions—I'm told there are at least three roads leading north near here, and we need to take the right one."

Fifteen minutes later, they were galloping up the road again, heading north, with the colonel riding alongside Nick. Behind him, Nolan rode, keeping his pistol aimed at Throckmorton's back.

"So much for your gallant rescuer," Jesse mocked, as both of them watched from the vantage point of an upper window in the old farmhouse as the posse departed. "He an' that Englishman took the bait like a pair a' hungry perch. The colonel will lead them down the wrong road, and meanwhile, you an' I'll be on our way to the rendezvous point with the boys."

Sarah, her hands still tied, a gag in her mouth, watched with a sinking heart until Nolan rode out of sight. She had never felt a despair as complete as the one that swept over her now like icy water, so much colder than the river they'd forded last night. Nolan had come to rescue her, but had ridden off believing she and her captor were with the rest of the gang when she had been only a few yards away from him. If the posse had just searched the house!

As for me, I shall call upon God, and the Lord will

save me. The verse from the Psalms came to her out of nowhere.

All right, Lord, I'm calling. Save me, and please protect Nolan, too.

"We might as well make ourselves comfortable," Jesse said, "since we can't leave for a spell. We need to let them get a few miles on the way before we go."

He laughed at the Sarah's quick step backward. "Don't worry, I didn't mean what you're thinkin'," he said. "I meant we might as well grab ourselves some grub—some a' that ham I spotted hangin' in Throckmorton's smokehouse that he didn't see fit to share. You know, I can't abide selfishness." He stepped forward and untied the gag around Sarah's mouth, letting it fall to the floor.

She swallowed, wishing she could wash away the nasty taste it had left.

"Why don't we mosey out an' get that ham," he said, gesturing with the gun, "and stop by the henhouse and get us some eggs, too. I remember you're a fine cook, Goldilocks. You cook us a good breakfast, one that'll last us till we stop at nightfall."

He untied her hands, and gestured for her to lead the way to the smokehouse. She found the ham hanging inside, just as Jesse had said it would be, and pulled it down. It must have weighed at least ten pounds, but he didn't offer to carry it for her.

"Now the eggs," he said, waving the gun toward the henhouse.

"How am I 'sposed to gather eggs while I'm holding this ham?" she asked.

"Put it down on this," he said, upending a bucket

that was lying on its side near the door to the henhouse. "Carry the eggs in your skirt."

Once her eyes adjusted to the gloom inside, she looked for something she could use against Jesse as a weapon. A pitchfork—anything! She could not tamely get on a horse and ride with him into the Comanche stronghold like a sacrificial lamb. But there was nothing.

Sighing in resignation, she pushed away the hens which tried to peck at her hands, searched until she had collected nearly a dozen eggs, then trudged back outside. Jesse had managed to pick up the ham, while still keeping hold of the pistol with the other.

"C'mon, Sarah-girl, shake a leg, we don't have all day," he snarled. "I'm hungry. You don't think that redskin brave you're gonna belong to is gonna let you dillydally like that, do you?"

She gave him a look, but said nothing. Instead, she went inside, cut slices off the ham and set them frying in a skillet, then cracked one egg after another into another skillet.

"That was mighty fine," he said, a few minutes later, pushing away from the table and shoving the plate over toward her. He'd left her about a fourth of it, not enough to fully satisfy her growling stomach, but it was better than nothing, and probably better than what she would get on the journey. Fare on the trail most likely consisted of tinned beans and coffee.

"You know, it really would be a shame to trade you to the savages," he murmured, watching her eat.

Something in her, something she'd kept buried during the long night of terror, snapped. "You keep saying that, Jesse. Since it *would* be a shame, why don't you stop saying it and take me home?"

He snickered. "Temper, temper, Sarah-girl. You know I can't do that. All I meant was you'd make a great cook for us, if you'd just decide to stop bein' so unfriendly. I'm just sayin' I could get used to cookin' like this—"

"But I doubt they have cooks like Sarah where you're going," said a voice that was familiar and beloved to Sarah.

Sarah jumped, and looked up to see Nolan in the doorway between the kitchen and the front hall. He had a rifle aimed right at Jesse's head.

"Don't move, Holt," said another voice, an English voice, from the steps to the upstairs. A rifle barrel protruded into the kitchen from that direction. Nolan and Nick must have circled back and hidden in the house while she and Jesse were getting the ham and eggs.

Despite the warning, Jesse jumped to his feet, grabbing the pistol he'd laid on the table when he had started to eat.

Instinctively, Sarah threw herself under the table, and gunfire erupted over her head.

It stopped in less than a minute. Jesse's bullet, fired after he'd been struck from both sides, buried itself harmlessly in the ceiling, and he lay dead on the floor. Sarah scrambled to her feet and ran into Nolan's arms amid the haze of gun smoke and floating plaster dust. She promised herself she would never leave those arms again.

"Thank God, thank God," Nolan murmured, in between kisses.

"Take Sarah home," Nick said after a few moments, during which Nolan kissed Sarah thoroughly and assured himself she hadn't been hit by any flying lead. "I'll catch up with the others."

Sarah saw warring impulses in Nolan's eyes—the desire to stay with her and take her home, and the need to offer his help to the posse, to finish the duty he had taken on.

"I could ride with you," she offered gamely, though in truth it was the last thing she wanted to do. "I'll keep to the rear when you catch up with the outlaws, I promise."

Nick shook his head. "We can manage, Sarah. Even if I wanted to take you up on your gallant offer, I have your sister to answer to, you know. Go home, the two of you. The posse's probably already caught up to the rustlers by now. I'm sure I'll meet them coming back, driving the rustlers before them, with the cattle bringing up the rear. We'll see to Holt's body on the way back, as well."

"All right, then," Nolan said. "There was at least another horse in the barn. Sarah, let's go home. You have a friend with a sore head waiting for you there."

"Prissy? She's all right? Oh, thank God!" she said, then turned into Nolan's embrace again. "Home," she murmured. "With you. What a wonderful sound that has."

Epilogue

A week later, Sarah and Nolan sat in the meadow across Simpson Creek from the church, enjoying a picnic lunch among the bluebonnets and Indian paintbrushes that carpeted the ground. Peace had reclaimed Simpson Creek now the rustlers had been captured, due to Colonel Throckmorton's attempt to save his own hide by leading the posse straight to them.

"Where was Prissy off to so quickly after church?" Nolan asked, lounging on his side amid the lush green spring grass and gnawing on a chicken leg. Behind him, mockingbirds called to each other from the cottonwoods. Simpson Creek burbled on its way to joining the San Saba River.

"Oh, she's taken over as chairwoman of the Spinsters' Club, and she's hosting Sunday dinner up at the big house for them. They're planning a big party for bachelors and spinsters in late May, you see, and she thought the ladies should get together and discuss the plans."

"She's perfect for the job," Nolan agreed. "Our Prissy is quite the planner."

Sarah sighed. "I hope she meets someone this time. She had planned to invite Major McConley, you know—she'd been flirting with him outrageously at every opportunity—but then someone told her that he had a wife and four children back east. She was devastated for at least half an hour."

Nolan chuckled. "Never say die, that's Prissy. Don't worry, Sarah, she'll find someone when the time is right."

Sarah sighed. "I'd just like to see her as happy as I am," she admitted. "I know she's happy for us, but she knows she'll have to make a change when I move out and get married. She can hardly stay in that cottage by herself, it'd be too lonely. But she can't quite make up her mind whether she wants to invite one of the other spinsters to live there or move back in the big house with her father."

"That's my Sarah," he said, extending an arm to tickle her nose with a vivid red Indian paintbrush blossom. "Always more concerned for others than herself. It's one of the things I love about you."

She swatted playfully at the flower, capturing it, and tickling him back. That led to kissing, naturally, but after a while she drew back again and studied him.

"I think we should discuss setting a wedding date," Sarah said suddenly.

Nolan laid aside the battered flower. "You do?" he said, clearly pleased. A slow grin spread over his face. "I'm ready to marry you at any moment, you know that, sweetheart. But I thought you wanted to wait a while, to be courted."

Sarah smiled back. "I do. But I think some time in

June would be perfect, and between now and then, my 'Man of Maine' could do quite a bit of courting, don't you think?"

"Oh, Sarah," he said, taking her in his arms again. "I don't plan to ever stop courting you, even when we're married. It's too enjoyable."

* * * * *

Dear Reader,

Thank you so much for choosing *The Doctor Takes a Wife*, the second in the Brides of Simpson Creek miniseries. I hope you enjoyed reading the love story of Sarah Matthews, formerly the meek one of the Matthews' sisters, who learns to stand on her own and become a woman who is a credit to her Lord and her community, and Dr. Nolan Walker, the Yankee doctor who comes to stay and take a permanent place in Sarah's heart. It was a pleasure for me to portray Sarah's emotional growth as she comes to love and trust Nolan, and his spiritual journey back to believing there is a God who cares for and loves His people. I have taken them through various trials, the accusations and plottings of an insane woman, an influenza epidemic and the reign of terror from an outlaw gang. I appreciate you coming along for the ride.

I enjoyed researching the state of medical training in Nolan's era, and came to appreciate the training doctors receive now in comparison to then! Our existence today is different, but we share certain problems with the people of 1800s Texas—disease and crime continue to exist, and we are still fighting them. But I believe the Lord is our "ever present help in times of trouble" if we will just call on Him.

It was a joy to me to visit the site of Simpson Creek, in San Saba County, Texas, and learn from a historical plaque that there *really was a Simpson Creek com-*

munity back in the 1800s. I'll be starting soon on the next story in the Brides of Simpson Creek series.

I enjoy hearing from readers. I can be reached through my website: www.lauriekingery.com.

Laurie Kingery

QUESTIONS FOR DISCUSSION

1. How does Sarah's character, as the meeker, less certain of the Matthews sisters, change during the course of the story?

2. Before the story begins, Sarah loses the man she thought she was going to marry. Have you ever believed someone you loved was lost to you forever, only to have them reappear in your life? How did that work out for you?

3. Sarah believes she can only love a man who was loyal to the Confederacy in the recent Civil War. Have you ever believed you could only love one sort of person, only to fall in love with someone of another very different group?

4. Why is the verse "For God has not given us the spirit of fear, but of power and of love and of a sound mind" (II Timothy 1:7) significant to this story?

5. Why do you think Ada is never healed of her insanity?

6. Years before the story begins, Dr. Nolan Walker loses his wife and child to cholera. Why do you think some healing does not take place despite our prayers?

7. How do you think crime and punishment were different back in the old West, as compared to today?

8. How would you describe Sarah and Nolan's positions in regard to faith at the beginning of the book, compared to the end?

9. How does Nolan's experience in the war compare to that of an army physician today?

10. How do you think online dating services today compared to the mail-order bride concept of the 1800s? Have you ever participated in such a service?

11. Have things occurred in your life that made you believe God didn't care about what happens to people? What evidence have you seen that He does care?

12. Jesse Holt has an expectation that Sarah has been waiting for him, and will go along with his plan for her to live a life on the run with him, but Sarah refuses to do so. Has another person in your life ever had unrealistic plans for you? How did you counter those expectations?

13. Jesse Holt's frustrated desire for Sarah becomes twisted into a desire for vengeance. Have you seen a desire for revenge warp someone's life? How did it impact your life?

14. How does the life of a single woman in small-town America compare with the life of a single woman today?

15. Do you have a loyal friend like Prissy Gilmore? How has she impacted your life? What sort of man would be best for Prissy?

Love Inspired.
HISTORICAL

TITLES AVAILABLE NEXT MONTH

Available February 8, 2011

REQUEST YOUR FREE BOOKS!

2 FREE INSPIRATIONAL NOVELS
PLUS 2
FREE
MYSTERY GIFTS

Love Inspired.

HISTORICAL
INSPIRATIONAL HISTORICAL ROMANCE

YES! Please send me 2 FREE Love Inspired® Historical novels and my 2 FREE mystery gifts (gifts are worth about $10). After receiving them, if I don't wish to receive any more books, I can return the shipping statement marked "cancel". If I don't cancel, I will receive 4 brand-new novels every other month and be billed just $4.24 per book in the U.S. or $4.74 per book in Canada. That's a saving of over 20% off the cover price. It's quite a bargain! Shipping and handling is just 50¢ per book.* I understand that accepting the 2 free books and gifts places me under no obligation to buy anything. I can always return a shipment and cancel at any time. Even if I never buy another book, the two free books and gifts are mine to keep forever.

102/302 IDN E7QD

Name _____
(PLEASE PRINT)

Address _____ Apt. # _____

City _____ State/Prov. _____ Zip/Postal Code _____

Signature (if under 18, a parent or guardian must sign)

Mail to Steeple Hill Reader Service:
IN U.S.A.: P.O. Box 1867, Buffalo, NY 14240-1867
IN CANADA: P.O. Box 609, Fort Erie, Ontario L2A 5X3

Not valid for current subscribers to Love Inspired Historical books.

Want to try two free books from another series?
Call 1-800-873-8635 or visit www.morefreebooks.com.

* Terms and prices subject to change without notice. Prices do not include applicable taxes. Sales tax applicable in N.Y. Canadian residents will be charged applicable provincial taxes and GST. Offer not valid in Quebec. This offer is limited to one order per household. All orders subject to approval. Credit or debit balances in a customer's account(s) may be offset by any other outstanding balance owed by or to the customer. Please allow 4 to 6 weeks for delivery. Offer available while quantities last.

Your Privacy: Steeple Hill Books is committed to protecting your privacy. Our Privacy Policy is available online at www.SteepleHill.com or upon request from the Reader Service. From time to time we make our lists of customers available to reputable third parties who may have a product or service of interest to you. If you would prefer we not share your name and address, please check here. ☐

Help us get it right—We strive for accurate, respectful and relevant communications. To clarify or modify your communication preferences, visit us at www.ReaderService.com/consumerschoice.

Enjoy a sneak peek at Valerie Hansen's adventurous historical-romance novel RESCUING THE HEIRESS, available February, only from Love Inspired Historical

"I think your profession is most honorable."

One more quick glance showed him that Tess was smiling, and it was all he could do to keep from breaking into a face-splitting grin at her praise. There was something impish yet charming about the banker's daughter. Always had been, if he were totally honest with himself.

Someday, Michael vowed silently, he would find a suitable woman with a spirit like Tess's and give her a proper courting. He had no chance with Tess herself, of course. That went without saying. Still, she couldn't be the only appealing lass in San Francisco. Besides, most men waited to wed until they could properly look after a wife and family.

If he'd been a rich man's son instead of the offspring of a lowly sailor, however, perhaps he'd have shown a personal interest in Miss Clark or one of her socialite friends already.

Would he really have? he asked himself. He doubted it. There was a part of Michael that was repelled by the affectations of the wealthy, by the way they lorded it over the likes of him and his widowed mother. He knew Tess couldn't help that she'd been born into a life of luxury, yet he still found her background off-putting.

Which is just as well, he reminded himself. It was bad enough that they were likely to be seen out and about on this particular evening. If the maid Annie Dugan hadn't been along as a chaperone, he knew their time together could, if misinterpreted, lead to his ruination. His career with the fire department depended upon a sterling reputation as well as a

Spartan lifestyle and strong work ethic.

Michael had labored too long and hard to let anything spoil his pending promotion to captain. He set his jaw and grasped the reins of the carriage more tightly. Not even the prettiest, smartest, most persuasive girl in San Francisco was going to get away with doing that.

He sighed, realizing that Miss Tess Clark fit that description to a T.

You won't be able to put down the rest of
Tess and Michael's romantic love story,
available in February 2011,
only from Love Inspired Historical.